Sharon's Song

Published by:
Spirit Light Publishing
Amarillo, TX,
through lulu.com
www.spiritlightbooks.com

Printed in the United States of America

Cover Design, Ash Arceneaux
www.ashleyroland.com

Library of Congress Cataloging-in-Publication Data
is available upon request.

ISBN

978-0-615-26075-4

Sharon's Song

Dennis Bates

Praise for *Sharon's Song*

Sharon's Song is an extraordinary story of how powerful love can overcome the strongholds of painful wounds etched deeply by a culture that focuses on beauty and conquest. Don't be surprised if you find yourself grabbing for a box of Kleenex one moment and cheering for the Chicago Bears the next. This tender story of hope and fear will tug deeply at your heart.

-- Lynn Zuk-Lloyd, author of *Awaken Me! Crying Out for More of the Lord*

~*~

In *Sharon's Song*, Dennis Bates boldly addresses the deep scars left in the wake of date rape and rejection. He's crafted a journey that begins with deep pain and ends in great joy. *Sharon's Song* is a beautiful melody of love and healing.

-- Toni V. Lee, author of *Expectations*

~*~

Sharon's Song is a fascinating adventure in life's untold direction leaping from the first page and twisting through to the powerful ending that left me speechless. This great love story honed from life is guided by prayer, faith and family tenacity. -- M. Farley, Reader

~*~

Dennis Bates creates another moving love story with flawed characters and God's redeeming love which goes deep below the surface of the way we see ourselves, into the way He sees us. It's refreshing to read a sensitive love story from a female's point of view . . . written by a guy. Nice work.

--Peg Phifer, Sips 'n' Cups Blog

DEDICATION

Dedications are tricky. You always forget to acknowledge someone that deserves mention. So let me start with the obvious. I want to dedicate this story to Jane, the love of my life and my wife for the last 39 years, whose love and support have encouraged me to keep going when it would have been easier to stop. I also want to offer this to anyone who has never stopped to see the beauty in themselves or listen to their own song. Each of us is beautiful in our own way and in God's eyes. All of us have a song. I encourage you to listen to yours and see yourself as God sees you.

The young man with the gentle eyes nodded. "It's sure not a good night to be roaming around out there. I can understand why you're worried, but I'm sure he'll be okay. Is there anything I can do to help?"

Sharon studied the unshaven face beneath the hat as she carefully considered her response. He wore layers of flannel like most of the other truckers. The face that peered back at her was fairly decent looking and different from the others she saw there in a way she couldn't describe. His eyes were not only gentle, but also more than a little flirtatious, something she always avoided. She knew she shouldn't get involved with those flirtatious eyes or him, but she extended her hand anyway.

"That's very kind of you. My name is Sharon Winston, and you are..."

"Chris Schmidt," the young man said quickly taking her hand in his and shaking it. "I live close to here, but there's no way I can get my rig home tonight, so I'm stuck here like everybody else. What can I do to help you?" He ducked his head, turning his gaze to the floor.

"Do you pray, Chris?"

Prelude

Terry had to decide. Take the left turn onto old Highway 6, even though he couldn't tell where it was anymore or turn around on the county road and inch his way back to the gas station to wait out the blizzard there.

Heavy, blowing snow had already erased his tracks; it was almost dark; the winds were gusting to 40 miles an hour; and the thermometer had dropped rapidly to zero, so he couldn't just sit there in the intersection all night. At least he hoped he'd stopped in the intersection. He couldn't really tell that anymore either.

The announcer giving the weather report on the radio warned listeners to stay home. Visibility was no more than a quarter mile, temperatures were going to continue to fall, and winds were expected to get stronger. Nearly 14 inches of snow had already fallen, and the storm wasn't finished.

"Stay inside," the announcer advised again. "Most roads are impassable. Interstate 80 is closed due to multiple accidents and blowing snow, and road crews are being taken off the roads for the night. It's even too dangerous for them."

Now he tells me.

Terry shook his head. Ten miles to Grinnell and about eight back to the gas station on equally horrible roads. When a snowplow came off the side road and headed down Highway 6, Terry turned and followed it. The decision was made. The plow would lead him to Grinnell, and he would stay there tonight.

From the phone call he had just received, at least he knew his sister was safe at a truck stop on Interstate 80, so he would meet her tomorrow morning instead of tonight. Now he needed to find a safe place to stay himself.

The flashing lights on the plow started to get further away, so Terry slipped and slid a little, going faster to keep up with it. Even with a four-wheel drive, the roads were like snow-covered ice skating rinks. Plumes of snow thrown off to each side of the plow ahead reflected its flashing lights as the truck cut through the snow. All he had to do was keep the lights in sight and hold his truck on the road for ten more miles, and he could stop.

Glancing down at the dashboard, the speedometer showed 35-miles an hour, but Terry felt as if he were racing as the truck bumped and slid everywhere. He held the snowplow's lights in sight even though they kept getting dimmer and dimmer.

Taking a firm grip on the wheel, he exhaled sharply. Just as he relaxed slightly, a horn blared as lights came rushing up behind him and swerved around him splattering so much snow onto his windshield that he slammed on his brakes because he couldn't see anything.

"What a moron!" Terry shouted as he beat his fist on the horn repeatedly in response, but the car sped off into the distance not even bothering to flick its lights on and off to acknowledge him. Screaming and honking his horn at nothing still made him feel better, even though he had to laugh at himself for doing it.

The lights ahead of him continued to fade and then disappeared entirely as Terry maintained his slow, steady progress down the middle of the old highway. He didn't feel comfortable pushing any harder.

Snow smacked the windshield, and ice started to build up on the wipers making them almost worthless. High beams or low beams, it didn't matter; all they did was light up the wall of snow that came down repeatedly like the final curtain at the end of a play.

The quartering wind caught his blue green pickup truck and practically lifted it off the road surface when he least expected it, and it seemed like it was taking hours to go only tenths of a mile. Then he saw something only yards ahead of him and slammed on his brakes, steering to the right and then the left as he struggled to keep his truck straight when it skidded. He came to a stop only inches from the tail end of the snowplow, which pointed at a forty-five degree angle into the air. The rest of the plow was nose down in the ditch.

The car that had passed him was embedded in the middle of a snowdrift, and a second pickup truck sat crosswise in the road behind it. The sight of the disabled vehicles sent chills down his back that rivaled the chills from the cold as he put his truck into park and jumped out quickly to see if anyone needed help.

Breaking the blowing snow with his arm held in front of his face, Terry checked all three vehicles, and they were all empty. Lights flashed from a few hundred feet away, and Terry watched three figures climb into a second plow.

He screamed, jumped up and down, and waved both arms as high in the air as he could reach, but they didn't hear or see him, and the plow slowly pulled away leaving Terry standing there coated with snow, and feeling totally alone. *Now what?*

The road in front of him was completely blocked, and what he could see of the road behind him was already drifting shut. Terry needed to make a choice again, while there was still time to make one. He could try to turn around and find his way back to the gas station that was now at least eleven miles away, or he could stay inside his truck and hope he had enough gas to keep himself warm all night.

He got back into his truck and called his sister Sharon to tell her where he was, but he didn't tell her about his predicament because he didn't want to worry her. He said simply he was going to be a little while yet and promised he would check back with her as soon as he could.

After sliding his cell phone back into his side pocket, he opened the door to the truck and stepped out, leaning on the door so the wind wouldn't blow it back on him. He tried to look back to see if there was any chance of returning to the gas station, but the ferocity of the wind driven snow numbed his face in only a matter of minutes, and he could barely see the back of his truck, let alone the road behind him.

Carefully he shut the door using all of his strength to keep the wind from ripping the door from his hands; he covered his face, and held the side of the truck bed as he walked to the rear of the truck to get a better look at the road. It didn't look any better from there as he leaned into the wind and walked a few more steps.

Quickly he turned around and headed back to the truck, opening the door with some difficulty before climbing back into it. The wind caught the door slamming it on his left ankle before he could get all the way into the truck cab, and pain shot up Terry's leg as he pushed the door open and pulled his leg inside.

The brief minutes outside drained his energy. It always amazed Terry how quickly a person could lose their strength in cold like this.

Going back was risky, especially since the wind kept blowing harder and harder, rocking the truck back and forth, and obscuring the road with snowdrifts. Staying in the truck all night might be better as long as the engine kept running and didn't freeze up. Even if it ran all night, Terry had to be careful to keep the tail pipe unclogged so the truck didn't fill up with carbon monoxide.

Through the snow, Terry could see a light coming from a window in a small building just off the road. It couldn't be more than a hundred yards. If he could get there, it would be the best place to spend the night, and it might even have a bathroom, which Terry knew he would need before too much longer.

Without thinking anymore about it, Terry shut off the truck, shoved the keys in his side pocket, pushed open the truck door and put his head down to keep the stinging snow from blinding him. He looked up only long enough to make sure the light from the small building was still in front of him. He had no time to waste, so he headed straight for the light. Twenty or thirty feet from the truck he stumbled as the ankle he had caught in the door turned under his weight.

Before he could regain his balance, he stepped into a snowdrift in front of him and sank, first up to his knees and finally up to his waist. The more he struggled, the deeper he sank, and he wasn't completely sure he was even at the bottom of the drift.

Of course! Talk about stupid. There was a ditch along the road that ran between him and the building, and in his hurry to go straight to the building he had walked right into it. There was absolutely no way to tell how deep it was, but he knew one thing. He couldn't move. Not an inch.

The drift started sucking him down like frozen quicksand, and he could hear the chirping of his cell phone in his pocket, but the more he dug to get to it, the more the snow caved in around him. Already the cold had numbed his jaw and his lips, and he wasn't sure he could talk, even if he could somehow reach the phone.

All Terry could think about was that the first day of winter wasn't for another week. Technically, it was still fall. *If I get out of here, I will never go out if it's snowing again, maybe not even on an overcast day in the middle of the summer.* Somehow that thought seemed funny to him, even now.

The lights were just a football field away, but even the shouts he could squeeze out were no match for the howling wind. Besides, he didn't even know if there was anybody inside, but he had to hope somebody would hear him because he wouldn't last very long tonight.

He had made three decisions, all bad. Four if you counted the initial decision to come after his sister in the first place. Then he passed the gas station, followed the plow down a snow covered, seldom used highway, and got out of the truck when he could have stayed inside it.

Not a banner day for decision-making and that was putting it mildly.

Wiggling his toes became more and more difficult. His face burned from the cold stinging snow striking him like hundreds of sharp needles, as the gusts of wind used his exposed cheeks and chin for target practice, and then the icy snow melted, running down his face only to freeze again around his collar. Crazy thoughts mixed with desperate ones.

The lights taunted him from the building with a promise of dryness and warmth. He was 34, single, and just getting his life together. Giving up was not an option. His cell phone chirped again, and he dug his hands into the snow around him frantically trying to reach it so he could tell his sister where he was. He had to let someone know. The last thing he told her was that he was near a sign that said Grinnell was seven miles.

At least Sharon was safe, and he hoped she was praying for him because prayer was about all he had going for him right now. And faith. His sister had that, and right now Terry wished he had a little more of it himself. He had to believe he would get out, somehow. He had to.

~ * ~

The coffee cup warmed her hands as Sharon Winston cradled it between them. Raising the cup to her lips, she stared blankly into the crowded truck stop coffee shop, took another sip, and then set the mug on the table in front of her. The phone in her purse remained silent no matter how many times she looked at it. *What happened? He was supposed to call back. Where is he?*

Her striking blonde hair and fashionable clothes drew admiring glances and appreciative smiles from all the truckers packing the coffee shop while their rigs idled in the parking lot to keep the diesel engines from freezing up, but Sharon barely noticed them. She stood up by the table and bit her lower lip nervously as she ran her hand through her hair.

Concern for her brother obliterated all the quiet whispers and soft whistles, until his voice startled her. She put her hand on her chest and gasped, returning to the truck stop, to the smells of greasy food and bad coffee, and to a pair of gentle brown eyes peering out from under a green baseball cap with a feed elevator logo on the front of it. Eyes that were gentle, concerned and focused on her. For some reason, she welcomed them, and she usually didn't.

"I didn't mean to startle you; I just wondered if something was wrong." He put his coffee mug to his lips and smiled, appearing to be totally relaxed. Never taking his eyes away from her gaze, he took a sip of coffee and waited for her to respond, appearing to be in no hurry, but content to just stand there in front of her.

"I hope not." Sharon fought to keep the fear she felt out of her voice but didn't even fool herself. "My brother is somewhere out in that storm, and I haven't heard from him for some time now. I know he was having trouble getting here to meet me, but I don't know what it was. I'm just a little worried about him."

The young man with the gentle eyes nodded. "It's sure not a good night to be roaming around out there. I can understand why you're worried, but I'm sure he'll be okay. Is there anything I can do to help?"

Sharon studied the unshaven face beneath the hat as she carefully considered her response. He wore layers of flannel like most of the other truckers, but the face that peered back at her was fairly decent looking and different from the others she saw there, and the eyes were not only gentle, but also more than a little flirtatious, something she always avoided. She did not want to get involved with those flirtatious eyes or him she told herself as she extended her hand calmly, not listening to what she had just told herself.

"That's very kind of you. My name is Sharon Winston, and you are…"

"Chris Schmidt," the young man said quickly taking her hand in his and shaking it. "I live close to here, but there's no way I can get my rig home tonight, so I'm stuck here like everybody else. What can I do to help you?" He ducked his head, turning his gaze to the floor.

"Do you pray, Chris?" Sharon could tell by the look on his face as he jerked his gaze back up to hers that he hadn't been expecting that question. He lowered his coffee cup so he could stare into it and rolled it between his hands. Finally, he looked up at her again.

"Not as much as I should, to be honest, but I know how. We used to pray at home all the time." Shifting from one foot to another, Chris seemed uncomfortable, not knowing where to look, what to do with his hands or the cup in them, or what else to say, although it appeared he wanted to say something.

Sharon reached for his hands, touching them lightly until he stopped fidgeting with them, and then she gently took the coffee cup from him and set it on the table to her right, while his eyes followed it.

"Would you sit down and pray with me then? I want to ask God to help my brother."

Chris glanced again at the cup sitting next to Sharon's on the table and didn't hesitate.

"I'd be glad to, but let's get some more help." He clapped hands in the air and shouted, "Hey, everybody, listen up." The noise level in the coffee shop lessened considerably. "This young lady's brother is out there in the storm somewhere, and she's worried about him. She wants to say a prayer for him. Let's gather 'round and help her pray." Chris motioned for the other truckers to join them, and in only moments she and Chris were surrounded. He flashed her a large grin and nodded.

"Go ahead. I know that at least two of these drivers are atheists, but we'll do what we can."

Men and women chuckled softly at Chris and gathered in closer as Sharon relaxed thanks to Chris' sense of humor and the genuine looks on the faces of the strangers gathered around them. The people in the crowd around them bowed their heads after Sharon did, so if two were really atheists, they were hiding their beliefs under their bowed heads.

"Lord, thank You for all these people who have reached out to help a stranger in need. Please honor our prayer, protect Terry, and go find him. It's really my fault he's out there; he was coming to help me. Now he needs Your help. Thanks for going to get him. Amen." Sharon raised her head, opened her eyes and smiled. "Thanks everybody. That meant a lot to me."

Many of those that prayed nodded or shook her hand before drifting back to their tables. Several added brief words of encouragement, and Chris slipped around to his coffee cup, waiting for Sharon to look his way. She knew he was standing there, and part of her wanted him to simply blend back into the crowd, but another part of her wanted to understand the feelings that had caused her to set his cup next to hers.

Chris gave her that opportunity with a simple, almost shy request when she finally looked his way.

"Would you mind if I joined you for a minute to finish my coffee?"

Sharon motioned to the chair next to her before she stopped to think about what she was doing and smiled. "Be my guest."

He banged his knee on his own chair, wincing noticeably and stumbling, as he pulled her chair out from the table and held it for her. Sharon laughed and she approached her chair looking carefully at it and reaching out to hold onto its back.

"Is it safe for me to sit down?" Her smile assured him she was teasing.

"I hope so," Chris responded. "I wouldn't want us to have matching bruises tomorrow. People might talk."

Nodding, Sharon giggled. "Oh that wouldn't be good. Thank you. I hope your knee is okay." She sat down and reached for her coffee cup.

Chris sat down without any further incident and picked up his cup, tipping it back and then forward again, while swirling it without making eye contact with Sharon. Finally, he looked up.

"You pray just like my grandmother used to pray," he said softly.

His open intimacy captured Sharon's attention.

"Is that good or bad?" She leaned forward to get closer to him.

"It's good." Chris grinned like a young boy remembering his childhood. "Her prayers were so simple, but they said everything that needed to be said, and they always made me feel good. Grandma prayed like we were just sitting there having milk and cookies with God. Your prayer was like that, only we're having coffee instead."

The warmth in his comments and in his voice crept quickly across the table between them and made her shiver slightly as only that kind of warmth can. She was about to move her chair even closer and ask Chris to elaborate when a second trucker took the empty chair on the other side of Sharon. He had at least a two-day beard below very tired eyes, and even though she wanted to hear more about Chris' memories, she turned to the newcomer and waited for him to speak.

"Do you know about where your brother was the last time he called you?" The man with tired eyes rested his arms on the table.

"He said he was following a snowplow on old Highway 6, and the last sign said Grinnell was 7 miles," Sharon said. "That was more than an hour and a half ago. He could have pulled in somewhere, but I can't get him on his phone. That's what worries me."

"Really?" The man's eyes brightened slightly. "I know where that is. My little sister works in a grain elevator right by the sign and lives just down the road about a half mile." He took out his cell phone and pressed a preset speed dial number.

"Jo, this is Dave. I'm hunkered down at the truck stop up here on 80, and I'm going to have to wait the storm out. There's a gal here whose brother might be lost out there in your area. I just wondered if you'd seen anybody. The last time she heard from him, he should have been right by the elevator office."

Dave listened to the response from the other end and said simply, "Okay, thanks. Let us know if you see anybody." He put his phone into his shirt pocket and looked across the table at Sharon. "My sister said she hasn't seen anybody, but she will keep her eyes and ears open. She said it does look like there's a light on at the elevator office so maybe he ducked in there to get out of the storm."

Sharon raised her eyes and said simply, "Lord, let that be Terry." She turned back to Dave and reached over to pat his big, callused hand. "Thanks for your help. God bless you."

"Well thanks," Dave said, "but I'm one of the two atheists Chris was talking about. Well, I'm not an atheist exactly. More like a doubter. Don't have anything against God. Just never saw any real proof He exists. I'm trying to help, that's all."

"When God finds Terry safe, will you still be a doubter?" Sharon grinned, almost teasing Dave with her question.

"If your brother turns up…"

"When my brother turns up," Sharon said emphatically, interrupting.

Dave stroked the stubble on his chin with his right hand and smiled. "Okay, when your brother turns up, I'll let you tell me more about God. I'm not promising anything, mind you, except that I'll listen to what you have to say."

"And you'll take your sister to church for a month." Sharon raised her eyebrows and smiled again.

"Deary, if I was unmarried and 20 years younger, I'd make you take me to church. It would be worth it." Dave returned her smile. "If…when…somebody finds your brother, my two brothers, my wife, sis, and I will all go to church for a month, and I'll give you a shot at the whole lot of us. Except for Jo. She doesn't need convertin'. She's gone to church all her life. My wife Marie goes too."

She slapped the table top with both hands and looked almost defiantly across it. "Then find out what time church is, and let your family know you'll be going Sunday. Terry's out there somewhere, and God will find him. I believe that."

Tired eyes or not, Dave grinned and shook his head. "I'm not necessarily looking forward to going, but in this case, I hope you're right." Then he returned her challenge, narrowing his eyes, "But if he comes waltzing in here in the next 30 minutes of his own accord, the deal's off. God has to actually find him out there."

"Okay," Sharon responded tentatively, "but if he comes waltzing in, as you put it, I'm still going to try to get you to church at least once."

"I like your spunk." Dave got up from the table, and nodded. "Let's see what happens." He turned and walked over to the counter to get his coffee mug refilled.

Chris widened his eyes and looked at Sharon. When Dave turned around, Chris let out a big sigh. "I've never seen anybody handle Dave like that. You get big Dave inside a church, and they'll be able to sell tickets to the service."

"Seems like an old softie to me. He can't be all that bad. I don't think he's really an atheist either, no matter what he said. He was willing to help. That's worth something. How about you, Chris? You want in on this?" Sharon tilted her head as she looked at him.

"You mean go to church?" He pushed his green hat back on his head and seemed surprised.

There was something about the way he did that that made her take another look at him. "Yes. You said you used to pray a lot. It's like riding a bicycle. You never forget how."

"If you'll sit with me, I'm there." His eyes got that flirtatious look again. "I'm just an ordinary trucker, who usually gets lost in the crowd, but I wouldn't get lost if somebody as pretty as you sat next to me."

"That's sweet." She felt drawn to those eyes again. "Sure, I'll sit with you." Beneath the green baseball cap with the logo on it, the flannel shirt and the blue quilted vest, she was sure she saw something more than an "ordinary trucker," as he put it.

She always had her guard up to deflect men's advances, which were frequent, and her guard was usually effective, but something about Chris disarmed her and made her take a breath, which she stifled quickly. Still, her words weren't as carefully measured as they usually were.

"I think your good old boy trucker routine might be a little bit of an act. You seem like you might clean up pretty nicely to me. There's more to you than 'aw shucks.'" Something inside her did a flip-flop when she watched him grin as her words snuck out like that.

"I could scrub the daylights out of myself if there was a good reason to." Chris pulled his hat back down over his eyes. "I'll be all scrubbed up good for church since you'll be there."

There was that flip flop again.

CHAPTER 1

Fugue--Jo's Theme

Jo zipped up her silver snowmobile suit, put on her helmet, and pulled heavy gloves over her hands. She fastened several blankets to the snowmobile seat with bungee cords, grabbed a coil of heavy rope, hung it over the handlebars, and climbed onto the seat.

The engine buzzed when she turned the key. After it warmed up slightly, she gave the throttle a twist and started out down the middle of the cold, snow covered highway, blasting through the drifts blowing across it, leaving a white powdery plume behind her.

The light in the office had to mean something, and maybe the missing brother Dave had told her about was stranded there. It didn't hurt to at least check if somebody was stranded out in a storm like this. Dave would have done the same thing if he were here.

The abandoned vehicles became visible right away. Blowing snow already swirled around them, but they were all empty. Jo turned her snowmobile onto the lane to the office. The lane wasn't visible; it was covered with snow, but she could find it in her sleep and often did in the morning on her way to work.

Moving up the lane slowly, Jo looked for any sign of the missing brother. About halfway up the lane she saw something in the ditch. It would have been easy to miss because the object was barely visible and half covered with snow. It was a person! She was sure of it.

The person didn't appear to be moving so time was of the essence. Even as light as she was, the snow wouldn't hold her weight. She took the length of rope from the handlebars and tossed it out to the lifeless figure in the ditch. He didn't see it, or he was too cold to grab for it. After the third toss, she knew she had to try something else.

Jo got down on her stomach to spread her weight out as much as possible and carefully crawled out to the person stranded motionless in the ditch. *It has to be him.* Even wearing a ski mask snow blew up her nose and caked her eyelashes as she slid out to the person and offered him the end of the rope.

He reached for it almost lifelessly but couldn't hold on to it, so she slipped the rope under his arms and tied it around his body before crawling carefully back to the snowmobile, holding the other end of the rope in her right hand.

Once back to the lane, she stood and tugged on the free end of the rope but couldn't budge the helpless person, who was essentially nothing more than dead weight. Tying off the free end of the rope on the back of the snowmobile, she hopped on the seat and started the machine. As soon as the engine buzzed, she tried to pull forward.

"Come on, come on." She willed the snowmobile forward as it groaned under the added weight. It didn't budge. The motor just whined as it wound up to a higher and higher pitch. Jo rocked forward with all her weight, and she could feel the taunt rope behind her holding the machine in place as it buzzed even louder.

"Lord, help me." Jo looked up into the swirling snow and rocked forward one more time. Something broke loose. The rope tightened, and the snowmobile moved, almost imperceptibly at first, but it moved. She rocked harder. Slowly, very, very slowly, more and more of the snow caked body appeared behind her.

"Come on, baby." Jo bent farther over the handlebars to encourage the snowmobile. "Just a little more. Come on." The machine revved and gave one last high speed buzz. It lurched forward. Looking back over her shoulder, she saw hips, then knees, and at last the feet come clear of the drift, and the entire body was finally free.

"Yes! I knew we could do it." She shouted as she slapped the handlebars of the snowmobile with her right hand. "I knew it! Yes, yes, yes!" Almost in tears, she dragged the helpless form behind her slowly and carefully all the way to the front door of the small office. "We did it!" She pumped her fist and looked triumphantly into sky.

"Thank You, Lord!" For a moment the snow seemed to stop.

~ * ~

Terry was just coherent enough to know that something was going on, but too cold and numb to know exactly what it was. He leaned heavily on the silver figure holding him up as it opened the door to the office, and he moved his legs as much as he could even though he couldn't feel them as the silver figure dragged him inside.

Warmth! It surrounded him, and he collapsed onto the floor.

~ * ~

The next morning Terry's face felt a little like he had a bad sunburn, but other than that, he felt deliciously warm. When he opened his eyes, he was lying on a floor he didn't recognize, wrapped tightly in several blankets and two unfamiliar arms. A young woman attached to the arms lay outside the blankets with her body pressed tightly to his.

Even though he was still a bit groggy, she looked like an angel. Strands of soft wavy red hair framed her high cheekbones and dimpled chin. Beautiful long lashes highlighted her tightly closed eyes, and her two chapped lips parted slightly as she breathed slowly.

"Is this heaven?" Terry asked. "Because this has got to be a beautiful angel lying next to me."

"No, it's Iowa, just like the movie," the lips said as their corners turned up into a smile, and two deep turquoise blue eyes opened, looked back at him, and sparkled. "How are you feeling? Are you warm yet? You shivered most of the night."

Actually Terry was quite warm now, but he wasn't sure he should tell the truth because he liked the fact that the redheaded angel was providing at least part of that warmth. She had no blanket covering her, so he started to unwrap the blankets to offer one to her.

"I wouldn't recommend doing that until your clothes are dry," the redhead said, grinning, "but it's your call." Her deep blue turquoise eyes were unlike any eyes Terry had ever seen before. Reluctantly, he looked away from them and saw his clothes hanging on a makeshift clothesline above an oil burning stove that was cranked up and almost glowing. A silver snowmobile suit and a ski mask hung next to them.

Terry vaguely remembered someone in a silver suit pulling him out of the ditch and dragging him into the office. He remembered the blast of heat as he stumbled in the door, and then he remembered very little until waking up a few minutes ago. Surely this slight woman hadn't been able to rescue him by herself. He must weigh 80 or 90 pounds more than she did.

"I had to get you out of your wet clothes, and you were too groggy to do it yourself," Red said. "Sorry."

"So…you…pulled me in here all by yourself and…undressed me? You wrapped me up in these blankets like a mummy all by yourself?"

"I had to. I'm the only one here. Nobody else was stopping by during the blizzard. You were shivering almost uncontrollably and just about unconscious. I was afraid you had hypothermia," the little redhead said matter of factly. "I wouldn't have done it if you hadn't been so wet and cold, or if you could have handled it yourself."

"So, taking off my clothes while I was totally helpless didn't tempt you at all? You weren't the least bit interested?" Terry teased, noticing that her blue eyes and red hair were still less than a foot from his face, and the two arms he woke up in were still holding him tightly. As groggy as he was, he wished he wasn't totally restrained by the blankets.

"I just did what I had to do," the little redhead responded. "It was nothing personal."

Terry couldn't help himself. He closed the short distance between her lips and his and kissed her. He was certain he felt her hug him even tighter and kiss him back before she broke it off.

"Why'd you do that?" she asked with slight anger in her voice, but little if any in her blue eyes.

"I just did what I had to do." Terry grinned. "It was nothing personal."

"Well you shouldn't have. I don't even know you. It's bad enough that we stayed here alone last night."

Terry realized the hollowness of the protest almost immediately. "Then why are you still hugging me if it made you so angry?"

The redhead jumped back quickly and loosened her hold on him. "You…you wouldn't stop shivering even wrapped up in the blankets. You were moaning, and you scared me. I had…to…keep you warm somehow. Holding you like that was the only way you'd stop shivering. I had to."

"Thank you." Terry tried to sound more serious. "I really mean that. I owe you."

"You're welcome, and you don't owe me anything, but you owe your sister one month in church. She said it had something to do with a deal she made with my brother Dave, and she would explain later. Evidently we're all going together."

"My sister!" Suddenly he realized that she must be worried sick about him. "You talked to her?"

"Last night after I got you inside. She called on your cell phone. I told her what I was doing and promised her you'd call first thing this morning." She got up and retrieved a cell phone from the desktop just to the left of the makeshift clothesline. "Here, you'd better call her." The red-headed and red-faced woman handed Terry the phone as he freed his hands from the blankets, and she turned her back to him.

He punched the button that speed dialed his sister. "Hey," he said. "I'm fine, thanks to a beautiful redhead. I love you too. Really, I'm okay. So she didn't tell you that she was young and beautiful, huh? If I hadn't been all tied up in a hundred blankets with my clothes being held hostage, I'd be chasing her around the office right now. I was so out of it last night I didn't even know she was taking my clothes off and holding me all night."

Terry winked when she looked at him. She turned her back on him again when he winked, and Terry thought he saw her smile, and blush just a little, in an incredibly cute way.

"Well, thanks for telling her it was okay," Terry said. "I owe you one too. You wouldn't happen to know her name would you? I'm so embarrassed. A beautiful woman took off my clothes and held me all night, and she hasn't even bothered to tell me what her name is. I feel so cheap. It's Jo? Thanks, that's an interesting name. I'll see you soon."

He closed his cell phone and looked up just in time to duck the clothes that were being thrown at him one piece at a time. "Hey, what did I do?" He spread a huge grin across his face.

"Get dressed. Your sister warned me you might be this way." She turned her back on him again as he retrieved his clothes and put them on.

He knew he was just about over the line, but he couldn't help himself. "Is Jo short for anything?"

She still had her back turned. "Joanne, but the last person that called me that is still limping."

"Now that sounds personal…and painful." Terry pulled on his clothes. "Oh oh, I'm starting to shiver. I think you'd better hug me again and get me warm."

"Not a chance!" Joanne said, shaking her head.

"I knew you wouldn't respect me in the morning. I'm so ashamed. Please don't tell all your friends, at least not the ugly ones." He pretended to wipe a tear from his eye.

Jo whirled around and looked furious. "I don't have any ugly friends. I'm the ugly one." She didn't appear to be kidding.

Terry didn't understand the sudden change in her mood. He was just clowning around, but he was sorry he pushed so far. He had a bad habit of doing that. "I'm sorry. I was just kidding. You can't really believe you're ugly."

"That's what all my friends have told me all my life." Jo shook visibly. "I've been told I was ugly since I can remember. Ugly red hair, dumb eyes, big nose, flat chest."

"Some friends you have." Terry maintained eye contact. "They are so wrong. You are the farthest thing from ugly I've ever seen. You are beautiful, and there's nothing wrong with your hair, your nose, your eyes, or what I can see of your figure for that matter. I love it all."

"You're just saying that because you feel sorry for me and think you have to thank me somehow." She acted as if she hadn't heard a word he said. "Well, you've thanked me, and you're welcome. You don't have to feel sorry for me. I know what I am. Please, just don't embarrass me."

Terry was worried she was going to cry, and that was the last thing he wanted her to do. He pulled his Iowa sweatshirt over his head and stepped toward her. She stiffened defensively crossing her arms, and he stopped abruptly. The sparkle in her eyes was gone, the turquoise turned to gray, clouded by tears. The beautiful lips were drawn thin, and her mouth tight.

"Whoa!" Terry said. "I wouldn't hurt the woman who just saved my life. For that matter I wouldn't hurt anyone on purpose."

"I know." She looked down at the floor.

"Well relax then," Terry said softly.

"I am relaxed." She continued to protect herself with her crossed arms. "Please don't make fun of me."

"That's the last thing I want to do. I'd much rather kiss you and get to hold you this time." He smiled warmly, and for some reason it appeared to make Jo feel better.

She dropped her arms and smiled back at him weakly. "Your sister seemed nice."

"She's great." Terry was relieved to see Jo relax. "Almost as pretty as you are too, and I'm not just saying that. You are very attractive and have the most incredible eyes."

"You probably don't even know what color they are." Jo looked down, scuffing her right toe back and forth over the floor, and then raised her eyes back up to him.

He looked away from her purposely to prove his point. "They are the purest turquoise blue I've ever seen. I've never seen such a gorgeous color. They sparkle like finely polished gemstones when you smile, which you should do more because you also have a great smile. Your mouth turns up on the corners first, and then your lips part and your whole face lights up."

Jo looked at Terry, and he could see out of the corner of his eye that she looked amazed. He continued, completely from memory. "You have classic high cheekbones, beautiful flawless skin that matches the most perfect, incredible red hair I have ever seen, and there is nothing wrong with your figure either, except that you don't show it off enough wearing baggy tops like that."

Terry scared himself. He hadn't realized how much he had noticed about her until she challenged him, and his competitive juices took over. He had noticed almost everything about her, including the wrinkle of her nose when she grinned and the fresh smell of her hair even after she wore a helmet and slept on the floor all night.

"You may be warmer, but your brain is still frozen." Jo turned the corners of her mouth up and smiled again. "Your eyes must have gotten frostbitten too because they aren't working right, that's for sure."

"My eyes are working just fine, and now that you're smiling again, so are yours." Terry carefully stepped a little closer. "Man, they sparkle when you smile like that!"

Joanne half batted her eyes at him. "Oh, you are smooth. You make it sound as if you really mean all that malarkey."

"I do mean it," Terry insisted, "and it's not malarkey, whatever that is."

"Okay, if I'm so pretty, how come nobody ever asks me out on a date?" Jo crossed her arms again, but this time assertively, not defensively.

"I didn't say you were pretty. I said you were beautiful, and I guess you've been saved for me to ask out. I'd ask you out even if the morons around here don't. I'd be proud to be seen anywhere with you because you are not only beautiful, but gorgeous, attractive, breathtaking…"

"And you are so full of it." She put her hand over his mouth. "Stop it. But, even though you are full of it, I would say yes if you asked me, so I'm calling you out, smoothie."

He kissed her hand as she held it on his mouth, and she pulled it back slowly. "How about dinner Saturday night? You pick the place. Make it nice. I want to see you all fixed up. I'll bet you a goodnight kiss that you'll be the most attractive woman there. It doesn't matter where we go. You'd win that bet even if you went the way you are right now."

"Oh please. Give it a rest. I already said I'd go. Just make sure you pick me up by seven. I'll make reservations at the Country Club for seven thirty. I live in the little farmhouse on this side of the road about a half-mile back. It's the only one for miles, so you should be able to find it. Stay out of the ditch though. I understand you can get stuck in them pretty easily."

"So I hear." Terry looked at her curiously.

"And, don't worry if you have second thoughts when your brain thaws out. I'll understand."

Terry tried to figure out what or who had hurt her so badly that she couldn't accept how beautiful she was, both inside and out. Both kinds of beauty showed. Her physical appearance was clear to him. Anyone should be able to see that. But there was also a humble, honest kind of resolve that made those eyes sparkle, and that came from somewhere inside her.

The way she tilted her head and sized him up when she called him smoothie. The fact that she had kept him warm all night at her own discomfort. The fact that she had come after him in a dangerous blizzard and single-handedly pulled him into safety. He was a complete stranger. She didn't know him or owe him anything, but she risked her own life for him. That was stuff from the heart. He couldn't help but feel it.

And yet, an irrational fear shared space in her heart and seemed to hide all that beauty. Maybe that's what all her nearsighted friends and relatives saw instead of what was really there. Maybe that's what she saw too. The shadow, not the substance. She needed to see who and what she really was. He felt a sudden need to show her.

Her turquoise eyes did sparkle. Her red hair danced around a sweet face and even sweeter lips. Her smile lit up the room, but softly, and he wasn't just pouring it on. He meant it! She waved to him over and over in his mind, and he knew nothing about her, yet everything he needed to know.

Uh oh!

~*~

When Jo got back to her farmhouse, she took off her silver helmet and snowmobile suit, hung them on pegs just inside the kitchen door, and laid her gloves on the hot water register to dry. She wanted to find something dazzling and slinky to wear, buy new shoes, new jewelry, new everything. She had to at least try to be the prettiest girl at the Country Club because…she wanted another sweet kiss.

She remembered every word he said, every expression on his face, and every ping inside her…and then she smiled as the full impact of their wager hit her. If she was the prettiest girl at the Country Club, she owed him a goodnight kiss. If she wasn't, he owed her one. She couldn't lose and neither could he. Either way they both got a kiss.

Why that old smoothie!

CHAPTER 2

It wasn't difficult for Terry to find his sister at the truck stop. She was the smiling blonde with at least two dozen truckers sitting around her. Some had coffee cups in their hands, some chomped on sandwiches, and some just sat there looking at Sharon.

They should have all been back out on the road by now. The skies were clear, the wind had died down, the roads were plowed, and traffic was moving normally. Somehow, many of these truckers had missed all that, but they weren't missing Sharon.

She still looked fresh, even though she had spent the night drinking coffee in a crowded truck stop. Her hair was brushed, her lightly applied makeup looked as if she had just come from a mirror, and her eyes showed no hint of weariness. The bright red sweater and her navy slacks looked newly cleaned and pressed, not wrinkled like she had spent the night in them. She looked like she had just come from a photo shoot for a fashion magazine, not an all night vigil at an Iowa truck stop.

Terry watched her joke with the group, listen to their stories, and even flirt with them a little. Every now and then she slipped in something God related, and some of the truckers smiled while others nodded in agreement.

Sharon thrived in large groups like this one. Terry had seen Sharon in this element many times, but he knew that his sister was not always the self-confident extrovert that she appeared to be.

In spite of her ability to draw a crowd in an empty room and her apparent ability to relate to anyone, anywhere, Sharon wasn't as secure as most people thought. Something buried deep inside her haunted her, and she wouldn't even tell him what it was.

Terry could only guess that something or somebody had hurt her badly because while Sharon thrived in large groups of men, she refused to be alone with a man. Or date. Men promised her anything to just take her to the movies, or to a party. They even begged just to have coffee with her. She always said no if it meant being alone with one person.

"He's not the right one," she would say. "Besides, I'm too busy this week. I'm on the road next week. I'm just too tired. But don't worry, big brother, I'll find the right one someday. He's out there somewhere." He was always big brother even though he was barely a year older. Terry didn't mind the nickname. Since their parents died, they were all they had left, and they depended on each other.

He didn't push his sister because she responded in one of two ways: by retreating deeper inside herself, which frightened him or by grinning, looking back at him, and saying, "I'll find the right one when you do," and that thought scared him even more.

Terry enjoyed being single. He dated lots of women and was not looking for any particular woman, especially the right one. Terry didn't want to find her but hadn't counted on her finding him. Last night. He hadn't counted on somebody passing the snowplow and blocking his way either. He thought he was in control of everything.

Most men do, and in this case he was most men.

The more Jo's actions replayed in his mind, the more extraordinary they seemed, and the more he thought about her, the more extraordinary she seemed. He had to take a breath, slow down. She might have been right. His feelings might only be a natural byproduct of gratitude. Maybe. But does gratitude feel like a snowmobile sounds? Does gratitude buzz?

"Terry!" Sharon shouted when she caught sight of him. "Praise the Lord, you're okay." Sharon had developed an Amen corner as she always did in a group like this. When she said, "Praise the Lord," even several of the scruffiest men at the table nodded and said, "Amen."

A big burly trucker came up behind Sharon as she hugged her brother and peered over her shoulder. The trucker tried to sound upset as he looked at Terry. "So, is this the guy that's costing me my beauty sleep the next four Sundays?"

"Yep, he's the one."

Sharon turned to the trucker. "Terry, this is Dave. He's Jo's big brother, the one who called her and told her to be on the lookout for you. Good thing he did, or she might not have heard you when you pounded on her door. He's just too modest to take any credit for his help. Thinks it ruins his bad guy image or something."

"Thanks, Dave." Terry extended his hand to him. "But I didn't pound on anybody's front door. What made you think that?"

Dave rubbed his chin and looked confused. "That's what she told me. She said you came to her front door all covered in snow, and she let you in."

"Modesty must run in the family then because that's not the way it was." Terry shook his head. "Not that I remember all that much."

"What did happen?"

"Your sister saved my life, that's what happened. She came out in that blizzard on her snowmobile and found me half buried by snow in the ditch I stupidly stepped into. I couldn't move, and I had pretty much given up hope." His enthusiasm poured out of him almost as fast as his words did. "She crawled out to me, tied a rope around me, pulled me out of the drift somehow, and dragged me inside the little building where she works. You know how small she is, Dave. I don't know how she did that."

Dave nodded, but he was starting to smile. "Almost sounds like she had help from above, doesn't it?"

"Amen," some of Sharon's choir murmured.

"Knock it off, you guys." Dave looked around behind him. "It was just a figure of speech."

"Interesting choice, though." Sharon winked at him.

"Amen," came the chorus again.

"Will you guys quit it?" Dave growled, looking over his shoulder again.

"Anyway," Terry continued, "I passed out. I don't remember a thing after that. Somehow she managed to get me out of my wet clothes, and she swears she kept her eyes closed. Honest, Dave."

"That's what she told your sister. That part I knew about." Dave shrugged. "No big deal under the circumstances, I guess."

Terry was relieved to hear him say that. "She wrapped me up in blankets and rolled me over next to the oil burner and cranked up the heat. I was almost afraid it would explode when I saw how red hot it was this morning. Your sister is a heroine as far as I'm concerned,

Dave. A real, live heroine."

In spite of the fact that Jo's big brother appeared to understand the circumstances, Terry decided that discretion dictated that he leave out some of the details, like the hugging and the kiss, for example. This was one time Terry definitely didn't want to say too much.

"I'll be." Dave took off his hat and scratched the top of his head. "She was probably afraid I'd be mad that she went out in the storm. I always knew the girl had a big heart. I guess she has a lot of guts too."

"That's for sure," Terry said. "She has lots of guts and a big beautiful heart, just like the rest of her." *Whoops.*

"Did you just call her beautiful?" Dave looked amused.

Terry was thankful for that look too. "Well, yeah. I guess I did. No offense, Dave."

"None taken. It's just that all her life people have called her plain, and some have called her worse than that. Mom used to call her plain too."

"Why?" Terry raised his voice. "Your sister is gorgeous! She has incredible turquoise blue eyes that sparkle when she smiles, and she has a great smile, skin like a porcelain doll, an adorable dimple in her chin, the most exciting red hair I have ever seen and…" *What are you doing, dummy? This is her brother!*

"And you kind of liked all of that, huh. You kind of liked her?" Dave was clearly amused at Terry's expense, and he looked like he was trying to stifle the big grin on his face. "It's okay if you do, in fact, it's great if you do as long as your intentions are honorable, and you treat her like a lady. She's never got much attention before. It would do her good."

"My intentions are honorable." Terry nodded, happy that Dave was taking this so well. "I asked her out to dinner Saturday night. I really have to see her again."

"Good. I hope she said yes. I like you." Dave stuck out his hand to Terry, and Terry took it. They shook hands like old friends. "Sometimes she can get a little strong willed, if you know what I mean."

"She said yes," Terry said. "And I do know what you mean. I got a little glimpse of that, but I just attributed it to her red hair."

Dave laughed. "Got to take the bad with the good. If I knew you better, I'd give you a bad time. Seems to me like Jo got to you a little. Any of you other guys think so?" He looked over his shoulder and winked. Laughs mixed with a smattering of "Amen's" came from the group, and Dave smiled and shook his head.

"I think you know me pretty well." Terry put his hands in his pockets and looked a little sheepishly at the floor. "I guess your sister did get to me a little."

"Sounds like it was more than a little to me." Sharon jumped in to join the fun. "No woman has ever gotten to my big brother before. I've got to meet this redhead. She must be something."

Terry felt like he was making a final argument in a big case. "She is." Then he realized how crazy he must sound. "Although I don't know how she could be Dave's sister. She's a lot better looking than he is."

Dave led the laughter. Apparently, he could take it almost as well as he could dish it out. "Who isn't? I can see why Jo liked you." Dave slapped Terry on the back. "You're okay."

"Who said she liked me?" Terry grinned. "She just took pity on some dummy who can't tell the ditch from the road." He turned to his sister and asked, "You still need a ride home?"

"Afraid so. The mechanic in the garage said I need new wipers and a new alternator, but he won't be able to get to my car for a couple of days. I'm going to have to leave it here and come back for it later when it's finished, I guess."

"I can fix it." Chris stepped up in front of the group. "I'll bring it to church Sunday."

"That would be fantastic!" Sharon looked at Chris and appeared to be a little uncomfortable all of a sudden. She looked at the ceiling, down at floor, and then at Chris. "Keep track of everything, and I'll pay you then, if that's okay."

"Don't worry about that," he said, "we'll work something out."

"I'll bet, uh huh." Invisible voices from the group teased him. "Sure you will."

"Hey!" Chris whirled around. "I didn't mean it like that. Sharon's a lady, you jerks." He grinned, but nobody pushed him any farther.

In fact, several of the men even mumbled, "Sorry, Sharon."

"I know you're just teasing. Thanks, Chris." She gazed directly at him. He flashed a smile back. "See you Sunday."

Chris looked embarrassed and a little red faced. He only nodded.

"Thanks for taking care of my sister, guys." Terry waved to the group gathered at Sharon's table. "In case you didn't notice, she's kind of good looking herself."

"Amen." The group shouted louder than any "Amen" before.

Dave laughed. "Now, that one I agree with. I guess I'll see you both Sunday too. Great to meet the two of you."

"Nice to meet you too, but I'm sitting by Jo Sunday, so make sure you leave room." Terry smiled and turned to his sister.

"How the mighty have fallen." Sharon teased him with the twinkle in her eyes and the sister in her voice. They waved to the group and left the coffee shop. Terry and Sharon walked out to his truck and climbed in. Sharon fastened her seat belt and looked over at her brother, grinning, but didn't say a word.

"What?" Terry asked, even though he was pretty sure he knew what she was grinning about.

"What?" Sharon mimicked back. "You know what. She really did get to you, didn't she?"

Terry didn't even try to deny it. "Wait until you meet her. She is the most incredible woman I have ever met, next to you, of course."

"Save it, big brother. I want to hear about the redhead, and I want details. This has got to be good."

"It was unbelievable!" Terry drove as he talked. "She really did crawl out to me and tie a rope around me and do all those things I said in there. In fact, I have the bruises under my arms from the rope to prove it. I couldn't help her or move. I was just too cold. My memory fades in and out after that.

"I'm not sure if I imagined things, if they were a dream, or if they really happened. It's all a big blur. I remember Jo apologizing as she took my wet clothes off and trying to look away as she wrapped me up in the blankets. I kept saying, 'It's okay, it's okay.'"

"I'll bet you did. Good thing for her you were half frozen." Sharon poked him in the arm. "Go on."

"I just couldn't stop shivering. I have never been that cold before, and I hope I never am again. She rolled me over right next to the oil stove. I remember thinking it was glowing. I'm not sure it really was, but it was hot, that's for sure.

"Anyway, I remember her taking a blanket she had around her and wrapping it around me instead. Then she wrapped her arms around me and used her body heat to keep me warm. I must have kept shivering because she just kept pulling me closer and holding me tighter.

"All night long I was sure that I was either dead or dying because every time I shivered, this angel whispered to me that I would be okay, and she kept holding me and stroking my forehead."

"Oh, this girl's good."

"What? I was freezing to death out there. I was."

"Um huh." His sister shook her head. "Go on."

"When I woke up this morning, that angel had her arms still wrapped around me, and her beautiful face was only inches from mine, sleeping peacefully with the greatest looking lips and long eyelashes."

"Did she have her clothes on?"

"Of course she had her clothes on, what kind of question is that?" Terry looked over at his sister incredulously as he continued driving.

"Just a reality check. It must have been real because if you had been dreaming, knowing you, she wouldn't have had her clothes on."

"She is not that kind of girl."

Sharon couldn't keep a straight face. "I'm sure. Just giving you a bad time. Then what happened?"

"I kissed her."

Sharon lost it. "'She's not that kind of girl, and then I kissed her.' That's beautiful. How Hollywood!" His sister wiped tears from her eyes laughing.

"It was just a sweet kiss. I was wrapped up in those blankets like a mummy. It couldn't have been any more than that. Give me a break here."

"Did she sweet kiss you back?"

"Well yeah, sort of. Come to think of it, I did have to tell her that she was still hugging me, even after she broke it off."

"Perfect!" Sharon laughed again. "Still shivering, were you? I'm surprised you said anything."

"Hey. A beautiful redhead who just saved my life is hugging me and you think I wanted her to stop? No way. I'm sorry I told her though for lots of reasons. Things got a little strange after that for a few minutes. I'm still not sure what happened."

"What did you do?"

"I didn't *do* anything. We were just kidding around, and I said something about not telling her friends, or something, and then I said something clever about the ugly ones. I don't remember what I said exactly, but she freaked and told me she didn't have any ugly friends. She said she was the ugly one.

"She said she'd always been told she was plain or ugly or worse, and I couldn't believe it. That woman is gorgeous! She was great just the way she was. I can't imagine what she would look like if she fixed herself up. Anyway, it made me mad that somebody had hurt her like that, and I just wanted to smack someone. I guess women don't react that way."

"Nope. They mostly internalize and smack themselves."

Sharon's comment bothered Terry. It sounded a little too personal. She was about as perfect as anyone Terry knew. What would she have to internalize about?

"So, then what happened?" Sharon asked.

"I told her I thought she was beautiful and attractive. She changed it to pretty. I said she was that too, and she said she didn't believe me. She said if she was so pretty why didn't anyone ever ask her to go out on a date. I said I would go out with her."

Sharon winced.

"What?"

"You made her feel like you were asking her out because you pitied her, that's what. Men!"

Terry shook his head. "That's not why I asked her at all. It wasn't like that."

"Well that's how it sounded to her, and I would have probably felt the same way," Sharon countered. "So, why did you ask her out?"

"Because…hello…I think she is gorgeous, and I wanted to see her again. Men aren't that complicated and devious." Terry looked at his sister again and frowned.

"I'll agree with the complicated part, but not the devious part." Terry couldn't tell whether she was serious or teasing. "So, the only reason you asked her out is because you think she is pretty?"

"Are you listening?" Terry tugged on his ear to emphasize his question. He was starting to get just a little annoyed. "I said I wanted to see her again, and I said she was gorgeous, attractive, and beautiful, not just pretty. You're the second woman in less than 24 hours who has tried to change my words to pretty. What's up with that?"

"Pretty is a great, non threatening word." Sharon's eyes took on a glassy stare. "Every little girl wants to be pretty. It makes them think of pink frilly dresses, red balloons, lemonade, sunshine, and birthday parties.

"Words like gorgeous, attractive, and beautiful carry more weight, more baggage. They make us feel like…"

"A woman?" Terry asked. "Is that so terrible?"

"It can be!" Sharon looked at her brother with what seemed to be a mixture of anger and fear. "But I can't expect you to understand that!" Sharon stopped and took a deep breath, and patted his arm. "I'm sorry I said that. I didn't mean it. You're a great brother…"

"Even if I'm a man," Terry added.

"Even if you're a man." Sharon tried to smile. "I guess I can't understand what it's like to be a decent man either. It just seems so much easier for men."

"I'm not going anywhere near that." Terry shook his head. "Maybe sometime, but not now. Just ask yourself this, would a woman be stupid enough to get out of a perfectly good truck in the middle of a blizzard because she was mad somebody just passed her and made her stop?

"Would a woman think she was so tough that she could easily make it to a nearby building where there was a light shining, and end up in a ditch, waist deep in snow, slowly freezing to death, and all of a sudden wonder why she was trying to get to that building in the first place?"

"Probably not. So why were you trying to do that?"

"Because I have no idea, that's why. I just reacted. Men do stuff like that. They think it's cool, and then they go brag to their buddies, and they all think it's cool too. I haven't got a clue why I did it, but if I hadn't, I would never have met Jo, so I guess it all worked out okay."

"Let's get back to Jo," Sharon said. "You can tell me how stupid men are later, when I have more time to enjoy it."

Terry laughed. He was glad his sister's sense of humor was back.

"You told Jo that you would take her out because you thought she was...beautiful. Is that word okay?

"Beautiful is fine, and give it a rest, please," Terry said. "I also wanted to see her again..."

"And?"

"And, I wanted to kiss her again, this time with my arms around her."

"Ah ha! Just as I thought." Sharon laughed a little derisively.

"What's wrong with that?"

"It's all you men think about, that's what, and that's only for starters."

"You're not going to cut me any slack are you?"

"Should I? Are you any different from other men just because we have the same last name and had the same parents? I know your history, big brother. You aren't exactly a saint."

Again, Terry wasn't sure if Sharon was just giving him a hard time, or if she was serious.

"Okay, I admit it. I'm no saint." Terry shrugged. "I have gone out with my share of women, and I have kissed more than my share of them, which, by the way, is all I'm going to admit to. You seem to have your opinion already, anyway. But, I'm telling you, this was different. When I kissed her, I wanted to be good. Remember when Jack Nicholson said to Helen Hunt, 'You make me want to be a better person.' That's how Jo made me feel. I can't explain it."

"I think I can," Sharon softened her voice. "And I think it's wonderful. I think it called *l...o...v...e*, and I think you have it bad, bro. Does Jo have any idea?"

"I don't think so," Terry said, "and that makes me sad, frustrated, and..."

"Angry?"

Terry thought about that a minute. "Yeah, I guess a little."

"Well, don't take it out on her. She didn't do anything."

"What do I do? I can't just go up to her and say, 'Hey, remember me? I took one look at you, and I'm pretty sure I've fallen madly in love with you, even though we've known each other only a few hours and I've only been conscious about one of them. I think you might be the one, and I'm pretty sure I want to marry you and spend the rest of my life with you. Have I told you what my last name is, where I live, what I do for a living, or any of that kind of stuff, because I probably should? Oh, and by the way, do you want to have children because I'd sure like you to be the mother of mine?'"

Sharon started to lose it again. She laughed heartily as Terry looked at her helplessly.

"I don't know," she said through giggles, "it might just be me, but maybe you should save at least part of that for the second date." When Terry didn't laugh, her gaze grew serious. "Do you really mean all that?"

"What good would it be to try to hide it? Yeah, I'm pretty sure I do. How pathetic is that?"

"Not pathetic at all, but no woman wants a man who is 'pretty sure.' Women want a man who is absolutely sure, as in totally sure. Are you pretty sure or are you totally sure?"

Terry grinned. "I'm pretty sure that I'm totally sure."

"Terry!"

"Okay. Seriously, I've never been this sure about anything in my life, and I mean that. I just feel stupid about it. I can't just come right out and say those kinds of things, even on our second date."

"Why not? What a refreshing change that would be."

"Well, for one thing, I don't know whether she feels anything for me, let alone that much anything. Second, shouldn't there be just a little romance first, a little courtship? Third, guys just don't do that."

"You're telling me." There was no trace of a smile on her face. "I agree a little romance is nice, a little courtship would be great. No woman wants to be forced into something they're not ready for. No woman wants to be forced into anything."

"I hope you're not speaking from personal experience, sis." The faraway look in her eyes and the feeling that she appeared to be retreating at that moment worried him. "If somebody has hurt you, I'll make them hurt twice as bad. Let me know."

Sharon touched his arm and looked at him with tears in her eyes. "You're a great brother and my best friend, but it isn't always that simple. You can't just go around beating up everybody that hurts you, especially if they're stronger than you. The Bible says we need to forgive those that hurt us, even if it's almost impossible to do."

She took a deep breath and almost said to herself, "They crucified our Lord, you know, and He didn't curse them or beat them up. He forgave them, even though they killed Him."

"Does everything come back to that for you?"

"It does now," Sharon said. "I guess it always should have. Remember that guy that killed those little Amish schoolgirls in Pennsylvania? What did the Amish community do, go over and beat up his family? No, they went over and forgave his family. Can you imagine that? What a wonderful testimony. We can all learn from their example."

"I don't think I could do that." Terry shook his head.

"Somehow we have to. It's really the only way a lot of life makes any sense. It's the only way we change things. We have to be as strong and as loving as those Amish people were because when we are, other people can see God's stamp on our hearts, and they can see God in us."

"So does the way I feel about Jo come down to that too?"

A gentle, almost wistful smile took over Sharon's face. "Absolutely."

Terry thought back to the night before. He just didn't see the connection. "I couldn't see anything when Jo pulled me out of the snowdrift last night at seven-fifteen. I just remember thinking I wish I had my sister's faith right now, and I sure hope she's praying for me. The next thing I know, this person in a silver suit is rescuing me. This morning it turns out that person had red hair and great eyes."

Sharon looked at him and seemed startled. "Wait a minute. What time did you say it was last night?"

"I think it was about seven-fifteen. At least that's the last time I remember from my watch. Why?"

"Because I did pray for you a few minutes before that. A lot of the people in the coffee shop did too. We prayed that God would go find you. That's why Dave has to go to church. He said he had never seen any proof that God exists. I told him I'd give him proof. The proof would be that God would find you."

"And?"

"Don't you get it? Jo found you right after that. She's the proof. She was God's instrument. She went out there because God sent her out there to find you. Not only did she save you, but that one single act is going to save a lot of other lives too, starting with her brother's. I'm sure of it. You are right to love her. She's proof that God exists."

"Okay, slow down a little, Sharon. You're getting a little deep for me here. I feel strongly about Jo, but how is she proof of anything, other than I'm a sucker for redheads?"

Sharon's eyes flashed with excitement. "God knew that, just like He knew you'd be a sucker for the blue eyes, but the reason she got to you, whether you want to believe it or not, is you saw a beautiful woman, who everybody else has always called plain, by the way. And you saw God's mark in her. You saw God in her."

"Huh?"

"Come on, Terry. Don't be such a clueless man. Let's try this one more time, and this time, follow the bouncing ball. I'll try to make it simple enough for a man to understand." Sharon smiled, but her words were almost frenzied. "Musical instruments are proof that somebody made them. For example, Stradivarius violins are proof that a man named Stradivarius existed. As Emeril would ask, are you with me so far?"

"I hate it when he does that. Yeah, I'm with you so far."

"Good. I hate it too, by the way. Anyway, think of Jo as the instrument. You saw beauty stamped inside her and displayed all over the outside of her. God knew how slow you can be so he made it really obvious." She grinned as she teased.

"You saw the beauty, and since it is His beauty, you saw Him. That proves He exists. You saw His name stamped inside, outside and all over her. Just so there was no question about it, He sent her as an answer to my prayer, the prayer you asked God for. I move for a directed verdict, counselor. Any objections?"

"No m'am." He shook his head. "A little convoluted, but I'm not going to argue. I got the decision I wanted. Now let me ask you, using your own analogy, when is somebody going to see the mark inside and all over you? Cause it's really visible. Even your clueless brother can see it."

"Someday, I hope." Sharon whispered, and then she spoke with strength. "But for the moment, at least, this is about you and Jo. Take your time. Don't rush. You can tell her you have strong feelings for her, even that you love her, but it would be way better if you showed her you loved her. Show her you see God's stamp inside her. Treat her like she has it. That's so much better than, 'gee, I think, I might, aw shucks, uh huh.'"

"Come on, I'm not that bad. What if I just grab her, pull her to me and kiss her passionately like a pirate? It works in the movies."

"No, don't!" Sharon said emphatically. "Just... don't. Trust me on this one. It could backfire, especially if she's like you describe. That approach isn't a good one. Woo her. Take your time. Cool your red-hot jets and show her you love her. In the long run, that will work a lot better."

"And how does a clueless man with red-hot jets do that?"

"Ask God to help you. It was His idea in the first place and it's His messenger you're dealing with. He'll help you come up with something."

Terry was listening intently to his sister. "Would you ask Him for me? You're so much better at this."

"Spoken like a man. No, I won't and I can't. You have to do it. But I'll pray with you if you want."

Terry pulled his truck to a stop at Sharon's apartment. He put the gearshift into park, turned off the key and took a deep breath. "Okay, I'll take that. Let's do it right now before I chicken out." He bowed his head, and Sharon did the same. She reached over and held his hand as he prayed.

"Lord, I'm sure You've been listening. I need Your help. I've fallen in love with one of Your angels. Show me how to treat her right. Show me how to let her know that I love her and help me move at just the right speed. She's been hurt enough in the past. Don't let me add to it.

"And one more thing. Thank You for my sister. She is a real Stradivarius, Lord. Please send her Your best musician, someone that can do a Stradivarius justice and see Your mark on her heart. She deserves it. Amen." He squeezed her hand and let it go. When he opened his eyes, his sister was crying.

"Why did you do that? I'm no Stradivarius believe me. I'm not even close."

"What is it with you women?" Terry asked, trying to cheer her up. "A guy can never win. If we upset you, you cry. If we compliment you, you cry. Learn how to take a compliment, please. Believe me; if you'd just start by doing that, you would make our clueless male lives a lot easier."

"That's not our job," Sharon said, trying to smile through her tears. "We aren't supposed to make your lives easier."

"I give up!"

"Sorry, that's not an option either. I love you. Thanks." She kissed him on the forehead. "See you Sunday. I can't wait to meet your redhead. Have a great time Saturday, but treat her right."

~*~

Sharon got out of the truck and waved one last time at her brother. She prayed as she walked slowly to her apartment. *Lord, if You have my violin player ready, with Your help, I think I want to try again. Just don't make him believe I'm a Stradivarius. You and I both know that I'm not.*

CHAPTER 3

Jo Lowry, what have you done now? You can't go out with somebody like Terry. You can't even get the local losers to take you anywhere. He is gorgeous, to use one of his words. What were you thinking?

She looked at herself in the mirror again. Maybe there was some potential. Maybe, just maybe, she could make herself presentable and not embarrass herself and Terry. Some great new clothes and the right makeup could help her pull this off, except for one thing.

There was no way to hide her hair. Why did it have to be so…so red? The only person she had ever known with red hair was her father. The color of her hair had always been the first thing others had made fun of. Even her mother had made fun of it. She said it made her complexion look washed out and clashed with her hideous blue eyes.

The grade school kids called her big red, or carrot top, or Bozo the Clown and made her cry. Two high school girls stretched big red into The Big Red Ugly, and the name stuck, but Jo refused to cry anymore by the time she got to high school.

Why did Terry like her hair? Why did he insist on calling her beautiful and all those other names that made her tingle? She held onto him tightly all night long. He kissed her, and she kissed him back. Why? And why oh why had she liked it so much?

The only other boy that ever kissed her was Bobby Krone, and that was in the seventh grade. It happened so fast then she didn't have time to think about it, and it was over just as quickly. He never kissed her again, and Jo always wondered if she'd done it wrong. She hadn't really minded the fact that he kissed her. Was she supposed to?

But when Terry kissed her, she didn't stop to think about how to do it. When his lips touched hers, she just responded, and that seemed to work a lot better. After all, she'd been waiting since seventh grade, and Terry kissed a lot better than Bobby did. But now what? What happened after this? Would this kiss go the same place Bobby's had? Nowhere.

A knock on Jo's bedroom door startled her.

"Jo, it's Dave. Can I come in for a minute?"

What is he doing here? She turned away from the mirror quickly and said, "Sure, come on in. I'm decent." The door opened slightly, and Dave stuck his head in, grinning like the proverbial Cheshire cat.

"Come on in," she said.

"So, I understand you're a hero, and you have a date Saturday." He sounded almost as if he was teasing, and he seemed happy. He was the only family member that acted like they cared about her after their father died, but even he had accepted their mother's pronouncement that she was plain looking. But then, everyone had.

Her father had been the one who stuck up for her, but he died in a strange accident when she was 12. She still didn't know much about what happened because nobody wanted to talk about it. Her father stepped through an open trap door in the hayloft and fell to his death below, landing awkwardly on a disassembled tractor.

The door had never been used and shouldn't have been open, let alone covered with loose hay, but that one day it was. That day when she was supposed to go to the hayloft and bring back some empty burlap bags stored there, but her father offered to go get them himself, and died.

Their mother blamed her for everything that went wrong after that. Dave was the only person who tried to soften their mother's wild ranting and accusations, and he often told Jo to go hide when their mother started screaming at her.

Then he lied about knowing where she was. He tried, but he couldn't protect her like her father had. And even Dave thought she was plain looking. He said so, without really looking at her, with pity in his voice when he talked to her.

"How did you know that I had a date?" Jo studied her brother's face because his question didn't have the usual pity in its tone.

"Cause I met the guy and his sister at the truck stop. She's a real looker. Drop dead gorgeous blonde, but a real genuine person, and down to earth as they come. He seemed like a nice enough fellow too. Terry, isn't that his name?"

"Yes." Jo liked her brother, but she had still learned not to share too much with anybody, including him. Her words, thoughts, and feelings always seemed to get twisted around somehow, and it was just better if she didn't share them anymore than she had to.

"He couldn't stop talking about you." Dave almost seemed excited. "He said lots of things about you, including that you saved his life. How come you didn't tell me what really happened?"

"It was no big deal." Jo shrugged. She didn't care about being a hero; she wanted to hear more about the "lots of things" Terry had said. "Besides, I thought you'd be mad that I went out in the storm."

"Well, young Mr. Terry thought it was a big deal, and so did a lot of guys at the truck stop. They couldn't believe you did that. It made me proud of you, Jo. I didn't know you had it in you."

"There are lots of things you don't know that I have in me," Jo half mumbled.

"So I hear. What did you do to that guy, anyway?"

"I didn't do anything," Jo said quickly and almost too forcefully. Had Terry told everybody about the kiss? That's all she needed. Poor pathetic Jo falls in love with some guy she didn't know just because he gave her a simple little kiss. They probably already had a good laugh about that. Hopefully, Terry hadn't told them she had undressed him. She sure didn't need that passed around. How would she live that down?

"Well you must have made a pretty big impression doing nothing because it sure sounded to me like he was just a little smitten with you." Dave was teasing now. "All he could talk about was how beautiful you are, how blue your eyes are, how gorgeous your hair is. Even when I told him folks around here have always called you plain, he…"

"You told him people thought I was plain?" The old hurts, the ones she never let anyone see anymore, throbbed inside her. Even her own brother thought she was plain. Why did he have to remind her, when she had such a good feeling from last night?

"I guess I did, Jo, I'm sorry."

She turned back to the mirror. Just what she needed from her own brother. "I don't know why you'd be any different from all the rest of them. I just thought you were, that's all. Guess not."

Dave looked down at his feet, and he shook his head. "I am sorry, Jo," he said softly, "I really am. I don't know why you've always been called that. You're my sister. I should be on your side. Mom always said you were a plain girl. I guess I never really looked at you any other way. I should have. Mom was wrong about a lot of things. Obviously, Terry doesn't agree with her about you."

"He's just taking me on a pity date, that's all. I'll probably mess it up just like I mess everything else up. I probably shouldn't even go." She wanted to believe that it wasn't a pity date and that he really did want to go out with her, but it was still hard for her to accept that. Her arms fell to her sides, and she couldn't look at herself in the mirror. Her reflection emphasized the word "plain," and her reflection hurt.

Dave took a short tentative step and touched her shoulder so she would turn and look at her. "I definitely think you should go, if my opinion means anything."

"You do? Why?"

"First of all, because you need to get out and meet people. You need to have some fun. Second, there was something about the way he looked when he talked about you. He insisted that you were beautiful and that you had a beautiful heart. I think he means it, really means it." Dave turned her completely around so he could look Jo straight in the eyes.

"I think you got to him, Jo. I think that young man sees something in you that the rest of us insensitive loud mouths have missed, and I think he may be right. Give it a shot at least. Why pass it up? What have you got to lose?"

Her heart pounded like a tympani. "You really think he wants to go?"

"I think he's looking forward to it." Dave's smile showed assurance and love all at once. "I'm positive you'll disappoint him if you back out."

Jo wanted to believe her brother was right, and she certainly didn't want to disappoint Terry although a guy like him could get dates anywhere. But Dave had never encouraged her as much as he was now, so what was that all about?

"So his sister is attractive, huh?" Jo tried to buy time while she sorted out her jumbled thoughts.

"On a scale of one to ten, I'd say she's about an eleven. She's a real looker, and she's no dummy either. That's the other thing I needed to tell you if you didn't already know. I kind of owe her a month of going to church thanks to you. She was pretty upset when she couldn't reach her brother last night. I tried to encourage her, so I said if somebody found her brother, I would go to church for a month. Got to take Marie and our brothers too. Save us a seat will you, towards the back?"

Jo laughed before she could stop herself. "My three brothers are going to church? That'll make the papers."

"Well I'm glad you think it's funny, 'cause I sure don't, but a deal is a deal, so we'll be there. Marie's going to love it watching me squirm. Anyway, that's Sunday. You have Saturday to think about first. Do you have something real nice to wear?"

"I thought I'd just wear a skirt and sweater. I don't really have anything else. My extensive social life doesn't require more than a new pair of jeans and a few sweatshirts now and then."

It was interesting that Dave brought that up. She had been wondering what she was going to wear too. In fact, she was thinking about going shopping, but she had no idea what to look for or where to look for it.

"Why don't you go buy something real nice to wear?" He took out his billfold, removed a credit card, and offered it to her. "I'll buy."

"I don't need you to do that. I can buy my own clothes."

"I'm sure you can," Dave responded, "but let your big brother buy you something nice, just this once. Get the whole works, shoes, earrings, your hair done, everything. Get all dolled up, and enjoy yourself. You deserve it. You're a local hero all of a sudden. Can't have a hero going to the Club in a skirt and sweater."

"Actually I'd be a heroine, not a hero, but that's okay." Jo smiled at her brother's gesture.

"You're right, sorry." Dave smiled back. "So look like one and show the locals what the real Joanne Lowry looks like."

"You sure?"

"Positive. Use my card. Just remember it has a ten thousand dollar limit. You can't go over that."

"I think I can stay under that." Jo took the credit card. "But it might take quite a bit to make this plain girl look half way good."

Dave frowned and shook his head. "Quit calling yourself that. The more I hear it, the dumber it sounds."

Jo looked at her brother. "Thanks for everything. I'll do the best I can."

"You're welcome. Remember; sit in the back. I'll see you Sunday." He shivered a little after he said that but smiled and left.

Jo turned back to the mirror and looked at herself as she heard her brother's truck pull out of the short lane to her house. She squinted and got up close to the mirror. Maybe with God's help and Dave's credit card she had a shot at slightly pretty. *That would be okay, Lord. Just keep me from messing it up. Thanks.*

~*~

Jo pushed the clothes around in her closet and realized that there might be some reason why people called her plain. She had one dress from her sophomore year in high school, two sweaters, two skirts, one pair of nice slacks and three blouses. Two of them were white, with button down collars. That was pretty much it.

The rest of the closet was filled with shirts from the grain elevator, khaki pants for work, and an assortment of baseball caps. When you never go anywhere, you don't need much more.

The only time Joanne ever had her hair fixed at a beauty parlor was when her brother took her to the senior prom. He paid for that too, now that Jo thought about it. Her mother said it was a waste of money. She wasn't allowed to get anything new so she borrowed an old dress from a classmate who felt sorry for her.

To say the least, Jo didn't know where to start when she thought about going to the Country Club, and she was starting to feel a wave of total panic when the phone rang. That frightened her. Was it Terry calling to cancel? She told him to if he had second thoughts.

She never got phone calls, so it had to be him. She was one of the few people she knew who didn't sign up for the "no call" list. She actually looked forward to phone calls from telemarketers because they were the only calls she got. *Please Lord; make it a telemarketer, not Terry.*

"Is this the residence of Joanne Lowry?" a voice at the other end asked, and immediately Joanne figured it was a telemarketer because nobody called her Joanne except Dave.

"Yes," she said simply.

"Hi, my name is Sharon Winston. My brother is Terry. Are you the woman who pulled him out of the ditch last night?"

"Yes, that was me." Jo smiled at the thought of talking to Terry's beautiful sister. "How's he doing?"

"He's doing great, thanks to you. I called to thank you for everything you did. From what Terry told me, you saved his life."

"He's exaggerating," Jo said quietly. "I really didn't do that much. I was just glad to help, but thank you for taking the time to call me. That is very nice of you. For what it's worth you made quite an impression on Dave and the other guys at the truck stop yourself."

"Well, thank you. It's nice of you to say that, but I was safe and warm. You were the one out in the blizzard. You're not giving yourself enough credit for what you did. That took courage, and you were a real answer to prayer; don't sell that short."

"It's interesting you put it that way," Jo said, "because I felt I had to go out there. It's kind of hard to explain."

"I don't think it's hard to explain at all," Sharon said. "We prayed for God to send someone out there at seven o'clock. You went out right after that and found my brother. God sent you. You should believe that."

"Well, I certainly believe in God," Jo said. "I just didn't think He would pick a nobody like me."

"He picks who He picks. I'm convinced He picked you this time. Anyway, if there is anything I can ever do to repay your kindness, feel free to ask."

Jo thought about what Sharon had just said, and before she could stop herself, she responded, "Well, maybe there is something you could do to help me out, but don't feel like you have to because you really don't owe me a thing. This phone call is all the thanks I need."

"What do you need," Sharon said. "I'm all yours."

"Well, Terry asked me to go out to dinner Saturday night, and I really, truly don't have anything decent to wear," Jo said tentatively. "I don't go very many places, like any, and I am just a little freaked out right now. Could you tell me where you shop? Everybody around here is talking about how pretty you are. I thought you might be able to tell me where to look for some nice clothes."

There was a slight hesitation on Sharon's end of the line, and Jo wished she hadn't asked. It was a little presumptuous on her part. Sharon was just being nice, and Jo was about to say, "Never mind," when Sharon spoke again.

"Would you like to get your hair done too? Terry said you have beautiful red hair."

"Could you give me a recommendation for that too?" *And could you tell me what else he said about me?*

"I have a better idea. Tomorrow's Friday. Can you get off work?"

"Probably," Jo answered. "I never use my vacation days."

"Why don't we go shopping at the mall in Iowa City? If we don't find anything there, I know a few other great little shops we can go to. I'll make a hair appointment for you too if you want, and we can make a whole day of it, lunch and all."

Jo could hardly believe Sharon's suggestion. "Really? Are you sure? I'd love to do that, but I don't want to be a bother." It was more than she could have hoped for. She never did things like that because she didn't know anybody to do them with. Sharon's invitation was exciting, and she would get to meet the blonde bombshell her brother had described.

"Are you kidding me? Shopping is never a bother," Sharon said. "You are talking to a power shopper, and I'm dying to meet you. Terry hasn't quit talking about you."

"Tell me everything he's said, and I'll come get you, as long as you don't mind riding in a second hand pickup truck." Jo couldn't hide the flutter in her voice. "It would be just between us girls, of course."

"Perfect," Sharon said. "I'll give you details. He's my big brother, but we women have to stick together. Let's get an early start. Can you pick me up by nine?"

"No problem. Now you are an answer to my prayers."

Sharon gave Jo directions. She lived in a medium size town not too far from Jo. They talked briefly about what she might want to wear.

After a few more brief comments, Jo hung up. *Speaking of answers to prayers, so is your brother.*

~*~

Jo knocked nervously on the door marked number eight the next morning. She wore her nicest sweater and her only pair of decent pants, but suddenly she felt totally inadequate. An eleven lived on the other side of door marked number eight.

The door opened, and Jo knew immediately her brother had not exaggerated. Sharon's blonde hair and hazel green eyes were stunning, and the simple sweater and pants outfit she was wearing looked like it was made for her exclusively. How could it have fit so perfectly? Even Sharon's tennis shoes looked good on her. Jo wished she had worn hers. They would have been a lot more comfortable than what she had on.

"Hi," Sharon held her hand out to greet her. "You have got to be Jo. Come on in while I get my coat."

"Thanks." Jo shook her hand and stepped through the door. "Now I know why my brother thinks you're so pretty."

"Well thank you, and now I know why my brother thinks you're so beautiful." She looked Jo over from top to bottom. "Shopping with you is going to be fun. You will look great in anything. The first thing we're going to do is find the size that makes the most out of that beautiful shape of yours."

"You don't have to say that," Jo said, feeling very uncomfortable all of a sudden. "Are my clothes too tight?"

"Too tight?" Sharon laughed as she slipped her coat on. "On the contrary. In my opinion, they're at least a size and a half too large."

Joanne could feel the heat on her cheeks. "I'm sorry."

"No need to apologize. You are going to be a joy to shop with. I can't wait. I can see why my brother is…" Sharon stopped and put her hand to her mouth.

"Is?" Jo raised her eyes a little. After all, this was one of the reasons she came.

"We'll get to that," Sharon said. "Let's put it this way for right now. He is very interested. Let's find something that will keep him that way."

"That's why I'm here." Sharon's statement that her brother was "very interested" made Jo feel strange and warm. She knew there was more from what Sharon had said but "very interested" would hold her for now. "And, I'm looking forward to this. I don't go shopping for much besides sweatshirts and jeans."

"No sweatshirts and jeans today. Today, we're on a mission. Terry was right about your eyes. They are the deepest turquoise blue I've ever seen, and they sparkle, especially when you smile. There has to be something out there to compliment the color of those eyes."

"So, do you think they'll be able to do anything with this hair?" Jo pulled her fingers through her hair as they left the parking lot. She already felt comfortable with Terry's sister, even as beautiful as she was. Sharon made her feel like they had been best friends all their lives.

"I hope they don't do too much to it." Sharon fluffed it with her right hand. "It has a beautiful shine to it and a natural bounce. If they know what they're doing, they'll trim it, shape it a little, and leave it alone. You don't see that many natural redheads around here."

"Or blondes, either."

"Who said this is natural?" Sharon winked. Jo couldn't help but laugh, and Sharon laughed too.

In the first shop, Jo tried on more dresses than she had tried on in her entire life. Sharon insisted. Jo would have bought one of the first dresses she tried on, but Sharon shook her head.

"They don't do you justice. Let's keep looking."

Jo thought they were beautiful dresses and couldn't imagine why Sharon didn't think they would work on her. She had never worn anything nearly as nice as any one of the dresses in the first shop. But, they moved on to the next.

"Remember these two." Sharon held two blue dresses out with one hand. "We can come back to them if we have to, but they're still not right."

They were even more spectacular than the dresses in the first shop. Jo couldn't believe they wouldn't work.

"Take these for another day. They look fabulous on you." Sharon handed a light blue strapless dress and a high-necked burnt orange dress to Jo at the third shop. "But we still have to find one for tomorrow."

Jo took the outfits Sharon recommended and put them and two more on her own credit card. She had never done that before, and it was exciting. A couple of pairs of shoes got added too. She would put only one dress on her brother's credit card. She didn't mind putting the rest on own card. This was too much fun to be conservative.

"That's it!" Sharon said at the fifth or sixth shop. Jo had lost count. "What do you think, Jo?"

"I love it!" Jo turned from side to side looking at herself in the mirror. "But I'm not sure I'd have the nerve to wear it." She wondered if that was really her standing there. The dark royal blue color brought out the deeper turquoise shades of her eyes and accented the redness of her hair, making it look almost silky.

The carefree cut of the neckline was significantly more carefree than Jo had ever considered wearing, and it plunged just enough to be alluring. The spaghetti straps and low back revealed her lightly freckled shoulders, making them look soft. The dress itself fit her perfectly, just like Sharon's clothes fit her.

"This dress was made for you. There's always at least one." Sharon beamed as she walked around her looking up and down at every detail.

She nodded approvingly from every angle. "Ask God to give you the nerve to be as beautiful as He made you because this dress does that. Do you have anything white and lacy to wear over your shoulders? You'll need something besides a coat this time of year."

"Not really," Jo said softly. "I've never been the white and lacy type."

"I don't know who told you that." Sharon frowned. "You are definitely the white and lacy type. A little something draped over those soft shoulders, you let it drop slightly every now and then, innocently of course, and you'll have every man with eyes looking at you in this." Sharon exaggerated the moves as she danced around Jo with a make believe shawl.

"I'm really only interested in one pair," Jo said, forgetting herself for a moment.

"Don't worry." Sharon patted Jo's arm reassuringly. "I had my brother in mind when I saw this. Trust me; he won't be able to take his eyes off you all night. I know him pretty well."

Jo felt herself getting bolder. "Are you sure?"

"Positive. Terry will flip when he sees you in this."

"I'm taking it then." Jo raised her head resolutely. "Flipping is exactly what I'm after. Lord, please give me the nerve to wear it," she added less resolutely, looking up with her eyes.

The sales clerk brought two different white lacy shawls for Jo to try on. She put one on her shoulders and then the other.

The clerk checked the price tags. "I think they're both great, but I like the first one best, and of course, it's the most expensive."

"Brother's treat." Sharon smiled at the sales clerk and then looked at Jo for confirmation. "Isn't that what you told me, Jo? Do you like it?"

Jo put the first shawl on and turned around so she could watch herself in the mirror. "It's beautiful. I love it."

"I think that means she'll take it." Sharon handed the shawl to the sales clerk. "And the dress, of course. What else do we need here?"

The clerk folded the shawl and laid it on the counter.

"Well actually, this is kind of embarrassing, but I guess it shows how unused to this I am…" Jo hesitated, feeling the flush in her face. "What do I wear under this dress? I got a feeling a T-shirt won't work."

"You wear as little as you can get away with." Sharon spoke more softly. "That definitely rules out T-shirts. With your gorgeous figure, I'd say you could get away with very little. Less is more in your case, but it's totally up to you. I'll help once you decide."

"Make that a double dose of nerve, Lord." Jo looked up again. "Okay, you're the fashion expert. Are you really serious about my shape, because I've always been called things that aren't very nice."

"Sounds to me like the people you hang around with aren't very nice," Sharon said almost casually. "There's more to beauty than big pompoms if you know what I mean." Sharon winked. "You have a body that I would put somewhere between model and super model. You should be proud of it.

"The key is to feel confident. It changes everything. I wasn't exaggerating when I said you'd look good in anything. You caught Terry's eye in baggy sweat pants. This should catch all of him if you want that." Sharon giggled.

"I guess I could always throw him back if I don't want him after I catch him." *Not likely I would though.* "You're right. I had on old clothes the other night. Thank you," Jo said shyly. "I should hang out with you more often. You make me feel good for a change."

"Any time, Jo. I could use a friend like you. Besides you're fun to shop with. Now you have two Winstons who care about you."

"Who's the other one?" Jo asked.

"Who do you think? There are only two of us." Sharon touched Jo on the arm and tilted her head. "The other one is the person you're going to wear that incredible dress for tomorrow night."

"Terry? Oh come on; he's way too gorgeous…" Jo put her hand over her mouth. "I mean…"

"It's okay." Sharon leaned forward and whispered. "This is just between us girls, but honestly, I don't know which one of you is the more clueless. I've seen the look in his eyes when he talks about you, and believe me, he cares about you. He cares a lot.

"I've never seen him look like that before, and he hasn't even seen you in this incredible blue dress yet. I love my brother more than anything, but this is a girl thing. Make him earn a woman like you, and just for the fun of it, make him suffer a little too. In a lot of ways, you are way too good for him." Sharon laughed, and Jo smiled.

Making him suffer is not really what I had in mind. I really shouldn't go where I'm thinking though.

Sharon was barely visible under all the shopping bags and packages on the way home, but she insisted that she "loved every minute of it." She was even more beautiful than Jo had imagined she would be, but otherwise nothing like Jo had expected. There was no haughtiness or conceit in her, only genuineness and kindness.

In addition to the shopping bags, which would require at least three separate trips to get them all into the house, Jo had a new hairdo and a manicure. The shop owner had insisted that it was complimentary for all new customers, so Jo accepted it. She had never had her nails done before. It made her feel incredibly feminine.

She liked the way her subtly highlighted red hair framed her face. It was shorter, but fuller looking and the soft, wavy curls bounced when she moved her head even slightly. Sleeping would be a challenge. But even sitting up didn't erase the image Sharon's words had created in her head. What did Terry's eyes look like when he talked about her? Did they look anything like the pinging she felt inside her right now?

CHAPTER 4

Jo looked into the mirror one last time. Her makeup was lightly applied to accent the porcelain quality in her skin, and her hair framed her face with a natural bounce when she moved. She had slept sitting up all night to keep it that way. With Sharon's help she was slightly pretty, and that's all she could hope for, and what she had asked God for.

The dress was another thing. It was slightly fabulous, and even she couldn't deny it, although the scarcity of foundation garments made it cling slightly. Sharon assured her it clung just like it was supposed to, and Jo had to trust Sharon on this one because she always thought clinging was a bad thing.

With a little practice, Jo mastered throwing her shawl over her shoulder with a flourish, pulling in slightly, and then letting it slide innocently off her shoulder, just like Sharon showed her. However, most of the time it caused the strap on her dress to slide over her shoulder with it.

"It's supposed to," Sharon said. "Wait, look down, blush, slide the strap and then the shawl back up very slowly. Smile. Everyone will notice, especially Terry. Don't worry. Your dress won't fall off."

Jo was new to all of this, but she had to admit, it was kind of fun. After all, she wanted Terry to notice her. Not too much, but not too little. It was a fine balance, but it would be a shame to have spent all this time and money and not get noticed at least a little.

She heard the door to the house open and she turned around, thinking it would be Terry. It was only Dave but he looked at her and whistled. His mouth dropped, then the sides curved up in an amazed smile, and his eyes opened to the size of salad plates.

"What did you do with my sister? You know…the little redhead in baggy clothes. The one they used to call plain?"

"Okay, what's the punch line?" Jo asked.

"There isn't one. Are you my sister?"

"Knock it off, Dave. What do you think? Be honest." Jo turned around slowly and dropped her shawl for practice.

"You look amazing; I mean it. The hair, the shawl. Letting it slide off your shoulder is a nice touch, by the way."

"You knew?"

"Marie used to do that. Doesn't matter. It's still a nice touch." He couldn't stop looking at her. "The dress is spectacular, and where did you get that…that…?"

"What?" She looked at her dress nervously trying to see if it had a spot on it or something.

"That figure. Sorry, I can't think of anyway else to put it. Jo, you are a gorgeous woman. You've grown up, and it looks so good on you." Dave looked down at his feet. When he looked up again, he quickly wiped a tear away from his cheek.

"A lot of people have been pretty big horse's backsides to you, and I should have stepped in for you like Dad used to do. I'm sorry I let you down," Dave said. "But you are going to have the last laugh because while those folks were looking the other way, you grew up, and you grew up beautiful. I won't let you down again. I promise."

She felt the ache of all those years pounding in her stomach. Even the beautiful dress and the perfect shawl couldn't erase it completely. "I'm not going to pretend it didn't hurt. Sometimes it really hurt. But I promised I'd never let them see me cry again, and I'm not going to cry now either. It would ruin my makeup, and I don't have time to put it on again." She forced a smile.

Dave was having trouble, searching for words, so she put her hand lightly on his shoulder.

"Thanks, Dave, you're getting more like Dad every day." Jo hugged her brother and gave him a light kiss on the cheek. "You're turning out to be a pretty good big brother. I'm glad you stopped by."

"I wouldn't have missed it. Have a great time tonight, and go easy on Terry. He's not going to know what hit him when he takes one look at you." Dave grinned.

Jo walked him to the door. "See you in church Sunday, and I'll get there early so I can get your back row seat for you."

"You had to remind me, didn't you?" Dave winced. "Talk about ruining the moment."

"On the contrary, I think God made this moment just for us, and it's pretty special." She reached up and touched his cheek fondly. "Besides your little blonde heart throb will be there."

Dave smiled. "You're going to like her."

"Already love her to death. We spent the whole day shopping together yesterday. She's the one who picked out this dress and helped give me the nerve to wear it." Jo dropped her hand.

Dave looked admiringly at his sister again. "Well as pretty as she is, she wouldn't look as good in this dress as you do. It was made just for you."

Her brother's comment stunned her. There was no way she could be compared to Sharon, even if she did look slightly pretty in the dress. Dave was exaggerating, but it was awfully nice of him, anyway.

"You'd better get out of here, or you're going to make me cry." Jo motioned toward the door as she pulled it open. "That was an awfully sweet thing to say, even if it isn't true."

"It is true," Dave said. "You know me. I'm honest to a fault. That's why the Good Lord made me so big and ornery. He knew I'd have to be able to defend myself when I shot my big mouth off all the time."

"Do you realize you just said the Good Lord made you? I didn't think you believed in the Good Lord. You haven't even been to church yet and you've already given God the credit for the way you are. Keep it up. We're looking for new Deacons." Finally, she got to tease him.

"Just a figure of speech. It doesn't mean a thing," Dave grumbled as he turned to leave. "I'm getting out of here before you try to get me to sing *Amazing Grace* or something."

"I would never do that," Jo said. "I've heard you sing."

"Good point." Dave smiled. "It's too bad Dad can't see you now. He would be awfully proud of you. I know I am." Jo's brother turned and walked out the door, whistling as he walked. Joanne shook her head. Whether he knew it or not, Dave was whistling

Amazing Grace.

Dad would have been proud. I wonder what Mom would have been? She tried not to think about it. Her brother's compliments made her head spin and made her feel good. A few minutes after Dave left, Terry arrived. Dave had made her head spin, but Terry's reaction made her downright dizzy, and that was before he said a word.

Terry's hands fidgeted at his sides, and he just stared at her for a moment. Finally he said with some difficulty, "You have to be the most beautiful woman I have ever seen, and I have a pretty beautiful sister."

That was twice in the past few minutes somebody compared her to Sharon, and Joanne felt a little guilty. Sharon was the most perfect woman Jo had ever seen. There was no way she deserved to be compared to her, and besides, Sharon was her friend.

"Thanks," Jo said almost inaudibly. "Your sister picked out the dress and the rest of the outfit."

"She told me you got together." Terry clasped his hands in front of himself. "She also told me I would be dazzled. That wasn't nearly strong enough. You're an absolute heart breaker tonight."

There's only one heart I want, and breaking it is the last thing I want to do with it. Jo shivered a little as she thought that, and her shawl slipped off her shoulder taking the strap of her dress with it. She took a breath, blushed and looked down, but before she could do anything else, Terry gently slid the strap back up and put the shawl back into place, holding his hand on her shoulder for just an instant while he looked at her.

"Thanks," Joanne whispered.

"My pleasure," Terry said, looking into her eyes.

Joanne smiled. She took Terry's arm and carried her coat as they walked to his truck. She had hoped to avoid wearing her coat because she wanted to show off the dress, but it was just too cold. "I'm going to need my coat."

Terry held it as she put it on and then helped her step up into the cab.

She had hopped up into pickup trucks most of her life, but if Terry was going to help her, she sure wasn't going to turn his help down. Being a woman had its advantages as long as you were with a gentleman. Besides, the step up was a little higher in heels and a dress—especially one like this.

Terry ran around the front of the vehicle and hopped into his side of the truck, rubbing his hands together from the cold. He glanced over at her and smiled, but suddenly seemed far more nervous than she remembered him being the first time they met.

"I wasn't sure you'd remember me without ice cycles hanging from my nose." Terry pulled out of the short drive by Jo's house. "I even wore clothes so you didn't have to roll me up in blankets again. You're going to have to tell me where I'm going, by the way. I have no idea."

"Turn right at the next corner," Jo said. "I hope you didn't tell anybody about that. It's a little embarrassing."

"Just my sister." Terry turned right where Jo had indicated. "But you already told her. In fact, I think you asked her if it was okay. She hasn't stopped giving me a hard time about that."

"Like how?"

"Mostly little digs here and there." Terry kept his eyes straight ahead. "She did say she wondered why someone like you would go out with me after you'd seen the real me."

Jo almost responded that what she noticed didn't seem that bad to her, but she caught herself. She'd made every effort not to look as she peeled his wet shirt off, but it was impossible to avoid feeling the tight muscles in his arms and shoulders.

"I kept my eyes closed," she said simply. "Left up here at the intersection."

"That explains it then." Terry turned left. "I'll make sure I tell her how you endured it. If you don't mind, however, try to keep your eyes open tonight. I don't want to miss how blue they are."

It was a line. Jo knew it, but it was a pretty good one, and if she could drop her shawl, she guessed he was entitled to a line or two. Fair was fair.

"Can I at least close them when you kiss me goodnight?" Jo asked. *What was I thinking there?*

Terry just smiled as he turned to look at her. "I hope so. That'll mean I get a goodnight kiss."

Stop while you're ahead, girl, or at least only a little behind. "One more right turn up there and we're there." Jo took one last deep breath.

"I know you warned me about calling you Joanne." Terry pulled into the parking lot next to the Country Club. "But somehow Jo doesn't seem appropriate for a woman who looks like you do tonight. Joanne is a beautiful name. Do I have your permission to call you Joanne tonight?"

Where did all the air go all of a sudden? "That would be fine, and thank you for the nice compliment again. You'd better quit, or you're going to spoil me."

Her father had always called her Joanne. She was named after his mother. When he called her Joanne, it made her feel special. She had always liked the way he said it. Her mother didn't say her name the same way and had insisted on calling her Jo. She hadn't objected, as if it would have mattered.

In a way it allowed her to keep her special relationship with her father just between the two of them. It helped her keep his memory alive long after he was gone. Terry said Joanne just like her father had, and somehow she felt that was her father's way of telling her he approved.

"You've seen through me already." Terry opened her door and helped her down from the truck. "It's my plan to spoil you as long as you'll let me, Joanne."

"That has a nice sound to it," Joanne said, trying to keep her words light and cheery.

"I'm glad you like the way I say it. I'm just glad your name isn't Priscilla. That's a lot harder to pronounce."

Terry exaggerated the pronunciation of Priscilla, and Joanne laughed. She didn't tell him that it wasn't the way he pronounced her name that she was talking about. It was the "as long as you'll let me" part she liked. She wondered if forever would be long enough.

Terry and Dave were both right. Everybody looked at her as she walked in on Terry's arm, and even Joanne could tell they weren't thinking, "What is she doing here?" The looks were more like, "Who is that?" Some smiled, others nodded, and a few even waved.

"Hey, Stephen, how are you doing?" Terry stopped. "Joanne, this is Stephen Sokol. He's a client of mine." Terry pulled Joanne to the table to introduce her. He didn't need to. Stephen had been a year ahead of Joanne in school and also one of the many schoolmates who had called her all the nasty names that still hurt.

He stood and acknowledged Terry's comment, but he didn't take his eyes off of her. The woman sitting at the table with Stephen was not amused, but that didn't seem to faze Stephen.

"Do I know you from somewhere?" His obvious ogling was intensified by the patent smarminess in his voice. She was on Terry's arm, and he was with another woman, but that didn't stop him from hitting on her! And the worst thing was, Stephen thought he was so smooth.

"You were a year ahead of me in high school." She would leave it there, if he would.

"I couldn't have been. I would have remembered someone as gorgeous as you." He didn't even try to hide his intentions as he touched her arm lightly. Jo felt Terry's arm tense up as she held it.

Game on! She patted Terry's arm lightly to let him know she could handle this, and he seemed to get the message. Stephen laid his hand on Joanne's arm more suggestively, stroking it and trying to look her directly in the eyes. Even a week ago she would never have been able to deal with that, but tonight it was different.

"I'm Joanne Lowry. You used to call me carrot top, among other things."

"Wow." His obvious gaze traveled up and down her body as he continued to stroke her arm. "You certainly have changed. We should get together and talk about old times one of these days."

That did it. "Maybe we should." She let her shawl and her strap slide off her shoulder. His eyes followed them. By the numbers, she hesitated, blushed, reached down slowly and slid it back up even slower. His eyes followed her hand as it pulled up her shawl, slowly, and when Joanne leaned toward him only slightly. Stephen almost choked.

Joanne patted the hand that was rubbing her arm even harder now and licked her lips. "It could be fun. I have changed." She smiled as Stephen tugged nervously on his collar. "I've changed a lot. It's too bad you didn't know that.

"I'm pretty tied up these days though." She looked at Terry and gave him an adoring look through half closed eyes, and he kept a straight face as she pulled her arm back from Stephen slowly allowing his hand to drag across it one last time. "Good seeing you again. You too…?" She turned to the woman at the table. "I'm sorry. I didn't catch your name."

"Claire," she said, about as coldly as the glass of ice water sitting in front of her.

"Nice to meet you, Claire." Joanne patted Stephen's cheek lightly. "Stevie and I go way back."

"I'll bet," Claire responded. Sharon was right. Even with her oversized pompoms, Claire didn't look all that attractive at the moment and not the least bit intimidating staring daggers from beneath her poorly bleached blonde hair.

"Shall we go, dear? Our table is ready." Terry pulled Joanne close to his side.

"Sure." Jo executed a risky coupe de grace. She pulled in her shoulders slightly and let both sides of her shawl drop from her shoulders with both straps following down almost to her elbows. The collective sigh from all the men in the room was almost audible. Stephen steadied himself on the table. Terry responded on cue. He gently reached over to her with both hands and slipped the straps back up to her shoulders.

He lightly kissed her right shoulder as he slid her shawl back to her shoulders and looked tenderly into her eyes. The sighs from the women in the room were audible.

"Thanks, love," Joanne cooed softly. "I'm going to have to be more careful. I don't have that much on under this dress."

Stephen's knees gave way, and he almost fell. Three salad forks, two knives and several water glasses hit the floor, and the waiters scurried in all directions to retrieve various items dropped all over the room.

Terry smiled, put his hand gently in the small of her back, and led her to their table. "I'm trying not to think about what you just said." He tried to keep his voice down. "You sure you've never done this before?"

"Never, and I'm totally embarrassed." She sat down with all eyes in the room following her to her chair. "Was it as much fun for you as it was for me?" She felt the corners of her mouth come close to touching her ears as she grinned.

"I think maybe more." He shook his head. "Do the words 'I told you so,' have a familiar ring? The club just lost a lot of glassware because of you." They both laughed until Joanne felt tears in her eyes. "If you're going to do that all night, I'd better call 911. Several of those older guys were close to cardiac arrest."

"Stop it." Joanne reached across the table and slapped Terry's arm. "You're making it worse." They had almost quit laughing when they looked back and saw that Stephen was still standing looking at her. Finally, Little Miss Oversized Pompoms pulled him unceremoniously into his chair with a thud.

"That was perfect." Terry opened his menu. "Stevie, as you called him, is such a jerk. I take it he's always been that way."

"Horse's backside. That's the term my brother Dave uses. A little crude, but somehow I think it fits Stevie. I'm going to have to pray for him tonight…right after I ask God to forgive me for enjoying that so much. By the way…love...thanks for rescuing me. I'm not sure the double strap move was such a great idea. I was a little worried for a second."

"My pleasure. You almost had me convinced for a second when you said you didn't have much on under your dress."

Joanne didn't respond. She just smiled at Terry coyly and opened her menu. "I wonder what the specials are tonight." She ducked behind the menu. Sharon had taught her well. This was the suffering part.

"The filet mignon looks good." She spoke from behind the menu. "I like mine rare. How about you, Terry?" She peeked from behind her menu across the table, and Terry was still staring at her. She flashed a quick grin. Finally he grinned back at her and looked at his own menu.

"I'm not going to let you and Sharon hang out together anymore." He looked up from his menu. "You learn too quickly."

"What?" Joanne batted her eyelashes twice.

"Stop it, Joanne." He grinned. "This is our first date, you know."

"Does that mean there will be a second?" She tried to sound light and airy as she let her shoulder strap slip again. She looked down at it and then looked across the table at Terry. "You going to get that, or am I going to have to call Stevie?"

"Have you always been this naughty?" He reached over and slid her strap back to her shoulder, brushing the back of his hand lightly over her arm, sending chills down Joanne's back.

"Well, it started the other night when I found this guy buried in the snow. Strange place to find a good looking guy."

"So this guy you found was good looking, huh?" Terry asked, as he surveyed his menu.

Joanne shrugged. "Not bad. I'd go out with him if he asked."

"He'd be a fool not to go, then." Terry played along. "You are an incredible woman."

Joanne caught herself. Now she did feel a little embarrassed. "Thank you. I'm sorry. I'll try to be good now. I got a little carried away there."

"You deserve it." Terry laid his menu down for a moment. "You had it coming. Don't worry about it. I loved it."

"You're pretty incredible yourself." Jo studied the look in his eyes. "Let's just be normal for the rest of the night though, okay?"

"I'll try, but somehow I have a feeling normal is never going to mean quite the same thing to me from now on." He picked up his menu again and studied it.

The only thing wrong with the rest of the evening was that it went too quickly. They were gone hours, and it seemed like minutes. When Terry walked her to the door and said quietly that this was where she could close her eyes, she didn't realize what he was really saying, until she felt his soft warm lips brush up against hers. It was only her third kiss since seventh grade. She jumped backward and took a deep breath.

Terry seemed to be confused. "I'm sorry. I thought you wanted me to."

Joanne's head was spinning. She couldn't think clearly with her lips tingling the way they were, and old insecurities grabbed her. The night had been wonderful. *Don't mess it up*, she kept telling herself. *You always mess everything up just like Mom said.* She didn't want to this time, but she was disoriented all of a sudden.

"Is something wrong?" Terry asked. "I thought we had a great time. Didn't you?"

"It was fine." Joanne's words weren't coming out right. "Thank you. You don't have to be so nice anymore. You've paid your debt. You're free of me." There was sheer panic in her words.

Terry took a small step backward and looked at Joanne. "Now I'm really confused. This is one of the best times I've ever had. I thought we were getting along great." He touched her cheek and brushed a bouncy red curl back behind her ear. She raised her eyes and looked at him, trying to keep her jumbled thoughts from coming out until they went back together. Why did his touch feel so incredible?

"I don't want to be free of you." He smiled and held her face as he looked at her with the softest look Joanne could ever remember seeing. "I have to see you again, Joanne, and it has nothing to do with anything I owe you or you owe me. I like being with you. I like it a lot. I can't let things end like this."

"You barely even know me." Joanne crossed her arms defensively like she did the night in the grain elevator office. "You just like this incredible dress." She knew that didn't make much sense, but she couldn't make sense right now, even to herself. She was turning somersaults inside, and the fact that she liked the feeling so much petrified her.

"The dress is incredible." Terry smiled so gently it would have been easy for her to get lost in it. "But it wouldn't be nearly as incredible on anybody else." He seemed to back away ever so slightly. "The way I see it, we're stuck with each other for at least the next four weeks. How about giving me a chance to get to know you better over those four weeks? What do you say? Four weeks?"

"What happens after that?" Joanne asked, biting her lip to keep it from quivering. Was her aching from wanting him or just from how nice he was being? It seemed so embarrassingly obvious. She had fallen for him already and didn't want to get her hopes up only to have him tire of her and walk away. It would be easier if he left now.

"After the four weeks you'll have to decide what you want." He held her cheek softly in his hand. "I'm sure I know what I want, but it will be up to you. How about it? Will you give me four weeks?"

He was awfully cute, his hand was incredibly warm on her cheek, and she rubbed her cheek over his hand as he smiled and held his hand there softly, so very, very softly. Four weeks was 28 days more than she had to look forward to a few hours ago. *What am I doing? Of course, I'll give him four weeks, more if he wants them, lots more if he keeps touching me like that.* Just like that she was back in control of herself again.

"I suppose," She let her strap slip one last time. "Oh dear. Could you get that for me? And, could I have a 'do over' on that eye closed thing? I wasn't ready."

"I suppose." Terry said it the same way she had. He reached over and brushed her strap up onto her shoulder with his hand and held it there on her shoulder as she closed her eyes. He brushed his lips against hers again and kissed her, and she kissed him back without analyzing it.

He backed away and looked at her, and she knew she would never be able to get this moment and the way he held her in his arms out of her mind. "See how much better I kiss when my arms are free?"

"Let it go, will you?" Joanne whispered.

"I don't think so."

"I was counting on that." She leaned forward to kiss him again and both straps slid off her shoulders, quite by accident for the first time all evening. Terry started to reach for them. "Forget them. Just hold me, kiss me like that once more, and keep your eyes closed."

"What are you wearing under that dress?" he asked, almost in a whisper.

"Just keep them closed tight, real tight," she whispered back, and they kissed again.

CHAPTER 5

Joanne didn't know whether to be thrilled or frightened as she closed her door behind her. She needed Sharon's advice. In the clingy blue dress she had captivated the Country Club crowd and Terry with her beauty and coquettish innocence, but the needy dark shadows from her unhappy past still made her doubt herself and wonder what would go wrong next.

Dinner with Terry exceeded Joanne's wildest expectations. Terry had treated her with respect even when she was "naughty" as he put it. She was really only being that way for his benefit; in fact, everything was for his benefit, even Stephen. And Terry treated her with warmth and gentleness and allowed her to feel special, pretty, and even beautiful.

The way he looked directly into her eyes when he talked to her and tenderly put his hand in the small of her back made her shiver. She could still feel the heart-stopping tickle on her skin as he slid her strap back to her shoulder, even when he knew what she was doing.

She would never forget the way he looked past her insecure outburst, waited for her to regain her composure, and earnestly begged for her to give him four weeks. And, of course, most of all, she would always remember the way he kissed her goodnight.

He kissed her like she was someone beautiful to be cherished and remembered, not just something ordinary to be used up and forgotten. There was sweet passion in his kiss, but also respect, warmth, and gentleness. Love.

And it was love on a higher level, a level that not only felt good but also allowed her to dream and have hope. A love that cried out to be shared with somebody special. Somebody like Terry. She knew now, her brother was right.

She had become a woman, and there was no turning back. She didn't want to. When she was a child, she thought like a child, she spoke like a child, and she felt like a child. Now that she saw face to face what it was like to be a woman, she had to put her incomplete childish ways behind her, know, and be known as a woman. She had to love because love never fails. She didn't think Paul would mind her borrowing those words because they were about maturity, and they fit here too.

The door closed behind her, and she heard Terry's truck drive away. It was a lonely sound. It was a sad sound. Joanne didn't want the evening to be over. Where did she, as a woman, go from here?

For the last few hours Terry showed her she was beautiful, and she had looked, acted, and felt beautiful. There was a wholeness and completeness to the way she felt now that was so much better than the incomplete feelings she had before God led her to Terry in the snowdrift.

She didn't want those incomplete feelings anymore. Before she even took off her coat and removed her shawl, she sat down at the kitchen table and bowed her head.

Lord, thank You for tonight. Thank You for Sharon and thank You for Terry. Thank You for having both of them show me that I can be beautiful. You promised in Philippians that Your peace would guard my heart and mind if I bring everything to You in prayer with thanksgiving. Well, here I am. Guard me. I know You will because You promised. Give Terry a special blessing for me. Amen.

~*~

Terry felt special warmth as he drove home. It was similar to the warmth he felt as he shivered on the grain elevator floor, but more intense and focused. That warmth saved his life, calmed him, relaxed him, and assured him he would be all right.

The warmth he felt as he drove home made him feel better than all right. It made him feel more content than he had ever felt before.

What was happening to him? Was the trauma of the night in the blizzard finally catching up to him? Was he coming apart? Or was the warmth he felt coming from the silent touch of a guardian angel sent specially for him, and did that special angel have red hair and blue eyes?

~*~

Darin, Dan, and Dave sat in the second to last row of the church the next morning, along with Dave's wife, Marie, and Joanne. They wore their Sunday best, and Joanne had on one of the new sweater and skirt outfits she bought during her recent shopping spree.

Sharon sat in the pew ahead of them and beamed when she saw the whole family sitting there together. Terry tried to look casual as he wedged himself in next to Joanne, but he didn't really fool anybody. Even Dan noticed the way they looked at each other, and Dan didn't ever notice anything.

Terry looked at her and absent-mindedly brushed a wayward strand of Joanne's hair from her cheek. She blushed almost red enough to match her hair. Then they realized the other family members in the pew were watching them intently.

Sharon rolled her eyes in mock disgust, grinned at both of them, and nudged Chris, who was sitting next to her, pointing toward Joanne and Terry. Chris smiled and waved. Marie smiled wistfully as if she remembered what it had been like back in the day. Dave tilted his head curiously and winked at his sister. Darin just stared into space.

Joanne smiled back at Sharon and waved back to Chris, who had been her friend for a long time. She couldn't wait to tell Sharon how perfect last night had been, and how well her helpful hints had worked. It was easy to understand why men noticed Sharon and couldn't take their eyes from her when she came into the room. They even stared at her in church when Chris was sitting with her.

Joanne once dreamed of having that kind of mindless attention from men when she walked into a room. Just once, it would have been nice to be noticed. Last night that had happened. Now, being noticed by lots of adoring men didn't seem to be all that important. She just wanted to be noticed by one man, and he was sitting next to her.

Okay, so it also felt kind of nice to watch Sandy and Jennifer turn doe-eyed in the pew across the aisle when Terry walked into church. They almost drooled openly when they saw him, and they didn't make any attempt to hide their flirtatious grins when he glanced at them and smiled courteously. Sandy even waved at him.

Joanne's resentful feelings for her two former classmates weren't right; she knew that, but they were the two who gave her the "The Big Red Ugly" nickname. They also got all the other kids to call her that. The two had dates to everything, were considered hot stuff in high school, and were still legends in their own minds, if nowhere else.

It didn't seem to matter to anyone that Sandy had already been divorced twice and that Jennifer only put up with her wayward husband because he had family money and allowed her to be wayward too. They always had that same smirk on their faces when they looked at her...until right now.

When Terry snuggled next to her again, smiled adorably, and brushed her hair from her cheek once more, their smirks disappeared and their jaws dropped. Any discomfort, blushing, or embarrassment Joanne felt from Terry's tender touches was worth it. She wanted to kiss him, but right now for totally unromantic reasons, and those reasons still had their mouths wide open across the aisle.

Joanne smiled sweetly at Sandy and Jennifer as she put her arm through Terry's arm and pulled herself closer to him, scrunching her shoulders for full effect. He reciprocated, smiled at her again, and patted her arm gently as he held his gaze on her.

She returned his warm smile and adoring gaze with equal warmth and then returned her eyes to Jennifer and Sandy. Their mouths were finally closed, but Joanne was almost positive that they started to stick their tongues out at her, but stopped before they did. *Perfect!* She scrunched her shoulders again.

Joanne's dating life had been nonexistent in both high school and the local community college. Not only had she never had any goodnight kisses, she had never had a boyfriend of any duration in the past.

It had probably been as much her fault as it was anyone else's, but having someone draped over her arm in church was a welcome change. Having someone as handsome as Terry draped over her arm and sitting so close to her was fantastic!

If only her father could be there this morning to see how happy she was for once in her life. He would have been pleased. She used to sit in his lap when she was little, and he told her she was his princess. He told her she could do anything if she wanted to but that the most important things were to love the Lord and be happy with whatever He provided. She couldn't lose if she did that, he said.

Right now the Lord had provided Terry, and she was more than happy with what He had provided. She was ecstatic. She looked at Terry sitting next to her again. He continued to hold her arm, smiled back at her, and made her feel warm and content.

These were the feelings that a woman felt. Getting even with Sandy and Jennifer weren't. They were the partial childish thoughts and feelings she needed to put behind her. So were the angry thoughts about her mother and all the others who had hurt her in the past. They were destructive, but they couldn't all be dealt with overnight. Joanne knew that because she still struggled with them.

~*~

The church service was a typical small town service. There were announcements, three hymns, a time for sharing, a twenty-minute sermon about something relatively innocuous, and an offering at the end. The service lacked real excitement, but it was comfortable. The additions of Terry, Sharon, Chris, and Joanne's brothers brought the average age of the congregation below 65 for the first time in months.

At the fellowship time after the service, Sharon had her usual entourage of admirers in relative short order, but, surprisingly, so did Joanne's family members and Terry. The church regulars seemed to be genuinely friendly as they welcomed Terry and Sharon and teased Joanne's brothers about scaring the church mice away by showing up.

Sandy and Jennifer swallowed up Terry quickly after the service and shamelessly monopolized his time. They giggled at almost everything he said, whether it was funny or not. They touched him continually like they were old friends, on the shoulder, on the arm and on the back. Sandy draped her arm over his shoulder on several occasions, and Jennifer just threw her chest out proudly in his general direction.

Joanne stepped back as always until Terry looked her way as if he were begging to be rescued. Joanne responded, stepped in, and smiled at her two former classmates, making it clear she was reclaiming him.

"Hi, Jennifer. Hello, Sandy," she said as politely as she could.

"Hey, big red," they said, almost in unison, barely looking her way as they spoke. "Where did you find this incredible hunk?"

"Somebody lost him in a snowdrift, actually," Jo responded casually. "I found him there, pulled him out, and cleaned him up a little."

She wanted to tell them that she had also undressed him, held him all night, kissed him good morning, and make it sound much more salacious than it really had been, but she didn't, however interesting it might have been to see the looks on their faces if she had.

"What an incredible find," Sandy said, trying to sound charming and flirtatious at the same time.

"Yes he is." Joanne agreed before she could stop herself. It was time to have a little fun. After handling Stephen at the club last night, these two would be even easier. "You know, I'm glad we ran into you two today. I need to apologize for disliking you both all the way back to high school. It wasn't the right thing to do. If you could forgive me, I'd like to start over and be friends."

Joanne held out her hand to Sandy. Neither Sandy nor Jennifer responded immediately. Instead they shifted from one foot to the other and looked at each other uncomfortably, unsure about how to respond. They mumbled something unintelligible and said, "Well…"

"Oh please." Joanne held her hand out insistently. "I forgive you for all the mean things you said about me. Maybe I was just overly sensitive. I'm sure you didn't really mean to hurt my feelings. I especially forgive you for naming me The Big Red…"

"Okay, friends." Jennifer grabbed Joanne's hand and shook it.

"Me too," Sandy said a little more reluctantly as she grabbed both their hands and made it a three way handshake.

"Great!" Joanne said. "I don't know about you guys, but I feel better already." She smiled and turned to Terry, putting her arm through his again. "I'm hungry you incredible hulk…or was that hunk? Where we going for lunch?"

"Anywhere you want," Terry said, shaking his head as he looked at the calm satisfaction in her eyes. "You're the boss." He turned to Sandy and Jennifer and added, "Nice to meet you, ladies. I'm sure that Joanne and I will be seeing a lot of you two in the future. Maybe we can all go out sometime.

"In the meantime, I have to take this incredible redhead to lunch." Terry smiled at Jennifer and Sandy, pulled Joanne a little closer to himself, and walked away while Jennifer and Sandy still stood frozen in place.

"Thanks for the rescue," he said quietly to Joanne. "Remind me not to cross you. I take it they aren't exactly your best friends."

"Not even close," Joanne said, "but I meant the apology and the part about forgiving them. I wasn't going to add that, but it seemed they needed a little encouragement."

"Indeed." Terry laughed.

"I had all those ugly feelings in my heart, and they were cluttering up things and taking up space I'd rather use for a lot better things. It was time to unload them. I might even consider being their friend, but I doubt that it will ever happen."

"So, what was the Big Red thing?"

Joanne turned her eyes down and let a big breath escape from her lips. "They used to call me The Big Red Ugly. They got all their friends to call me that too, and for all I know, they still call me that. I had never been able to say that out loud before because it hurt my feelings so badly." Joanne looked over at Terry. "Now that I have, it doesn't bother me nearly as much, and I wonder what took me so long."

"And you still want to be their friend?"

"To be totally honest, no, but I would be if they really wanted me to be because we're supposed to love our enemies, remember? And those two would be near the top of that list for me. When I saw them fawning all over you, my first reaction was to scratch their eyes out, so I prayed about it. The Lord showed me a better way, and it felt kind of good, actually."

"I could see that." He opened her door and helped Joanne get into his truck. She allowed him to open it again, of course, but one of these days she would forget, and the game would be over.

"Is Sharon coming?" Joanne asked. "I am dying to talk to her."

"She drove herself, but, if you want, I can ask her if she wants to join us. Where we going, by the way? You asked me, remember?"

"I'm sorry." Joanne stiffened in the passenger seat. Of course, how could she be so stupid? "I thought you would want to go to lunch after what you said last night, but you don't have to go. You probably have better things to do than go to lunch with The Big Red Ugly. I'll bet Jennifer and Sandy would love to go to lunch with you."

Terry slammed her truck door shut and stomped around to the back of his truck. He banged on the tailgate with his fist as he passed it, then stopped and took several deep breaths, walked slower to his truck door, and opened it deliberately. Joanne knew he was furious, but she could see he was working hard to control himself.

"We need to clear a few things up." Terry looked at her. "I lost my temper. I'm sorry. I am confused, frustrated, and a little hurt, but that's no excuse. Please don't ever call yourself that horrible name again or anything like it. You are not ugly, and you are definitely not big."

Joanne trembled. The bitter taste of the past was back. "Why did everybody always call me that then? You don't understand what it was like. My own mother told me I was pathetic and plain." She tried to smash the feelings inside her, but they overpowered her. "I was just supposed to take it. I wasn't allowed to have any feelings about it because I deserved to be called that."

"You didn't deserve it then, and you sure don't now," Terry said, shaking his head. "It wasn't right for anybody to call you that, especially not your mother. Did she really use those words?"

"Yes, and sometimes worse." Joanne still shook. If only he knew how much worse, and if he had been able to see the hate in her eyes when she said them. "You don't believe me either."

"Of course I believe you, but you have to quit thinking of yourself that way. Your mother was wrong. What she said was hateful!"

Joanne was on the verge of tears. She ached and she couldn't tell if the pain was coming from the ugliness of the past or the words of someone she cared for from the present. Someone named Terry.

"Please don't yell at me."

"I'm not yelling. I'm just excited and my voice gets this way when I get excited. Yelling is much louder than this for me."

His words felt like yelling and they felt angry as they brought back ugliness she thought she had controlled. "Yes, you are. You're yelling. Everybody yells at me. I don't deserve to be yelled at all the time."

Terry turned to Joanne, fighting to keep control of everything, especially his voice. "Why does this happen? One minute everything is fine, and the next minute it's all confused like this. I have no interest in doing anything with the two wicked stepsisters in there, and it was unfair for you to even suggest it. They are definitely not my type."

Joanne couldn't hold back the tears anymore, and they rolled down her cheeks. Her confused pain had won again, and it hurt even more this time because she wanted so desperately to feel good. "I'm sorry. Do you see how I always mess everything up? I was so happy about everything, but I couldn't leave things alone. I had to mess things up just like my mother always said I did."

His eyes reflected tenderness as he touched her shoulder gently. "You didn't mess everything up. Forget all that rubbish your mother told you, and believe in yourself. You are one special and beautiful woman. Why don't you see it?"

Joanne took a tissue from her purse and wiped her eyes. "Because everybody always rejects me, that's why." She could feel herself standing all alone. Her classmates, and even her own family pointing at her and laughing before they just disappeared, and it was the quiet after they disappeared that was almost the worst.

"Who rejects you?"

"Everyone does. My family, kids in school, people in church. I guess it must be me." Joanne said her words with air sucked in instead of pushed out.

"Did your father reject you?" Terry asked.

Joanne sniffed and looked at Terry. "No. He was my father. It would have been hard for him to reject me, but who knows how he'd be today. He's been gone for a long time."

"Apparently your mother didn't have any trouble treating you poorly, and she was your parent too."

"They were different." Joanne's words still came from her pain and felt that way. "My dad wasn't mean like my mother was. He could say dumb things, but he wasn't cold and mean. My mother was just cruel."

Terry let out a long, slow breath. "How about your brother Dave? Didn't he buy you that blue dress?"

"Yeah. I guess he did. Sometimes he can be awfully sweet, but he used to call me plain too, just like all the others." Her voice cracked.

"What about Jesus? Did He reject you?" Terry asked.

"He doesn't reject anybody." She looked down at the tissue in her hand.

"Maybe not, but the way I see it, there are at least four people who haven't rejected you, and there are probably more, so not everybody has rejected you."

Joanne was confused and took a deep breath as she thought about what he had said. "Who's the fourth one?"

Terry looked at her so intensely that it almost frightened her. "You really don't know?"

"No, I don't. I guess I'm just being stupid. I don't get four." She was starting to get slightly angry herself because of all his questions, but her anger made her feel slightly better this time.

Terry shrugged. "Well, hello. How about me? I want to be around you, and we have a deal for at least a month. Remember?"

"I'm sorry. I had a great time last night, but I'm still having trouble believing that you really want to be around me." Joanne shook her head and looked away from Terry.

"Well, I do," he said quietly.

"Why?" Something inside her snapped as she turned back to him.

"To be totally honest, I have a few theories, but I really don't have a reason. Since I met you a few days ago, I've made you angry, more than I've made you happy. I've made you cry more than once. I keep trying to tell you that I think you're beautiful, and you argue with me, and…"

"And what?" Joanne asked, almost demanding an answer.

"This sounds stupid. I don't think I want to say it right now."

"Say it!" Joanne said, again more like a demand than a request.

"And in spite of everything," Terry hesitated. "In spite of everything, I think I may be falling in love with you. Happy? You got me to say it."

Joanne frowned in disbelief. "You may have said it, but I don't believe it. What are your other theories?"

"Actually, that's the only one I have. There's nothing else that explains how I feel." Terry leaned over to Joanne and kissed her on the cheek. "I told you it sounded stupid."

Joanne shivered. These were new words to her and new feelings went with them, feelings she wanted to embrace, but wasn't prepared for. "Nobody's ever said that to me before. It makes me feel confused and frightened."

"How about good?" Terry asked seriously. "Does it make you feel just a little bit good?"

A grin spread across her face. "Well, yeah. I guess that too, but I need to work some of my own stuff out before I'm ready to know exactly what I feel."

"I can wait." He touched her chin gently with his hand and held her gaze in his. "But let's work that 'stuff' out together. Okay?"

The wishes in her mind were turning into horses, and the beggars were riding. "Why would you be willing to do that? You saw how Sandy and Jennifer fell all over you. I'm sure that isn't the first time women have reacted to you that way. You could have just about anyone. Why would you want me?"

Terry took a deep breath. "I don't want this to sound conceited, but frankly, I've tried just about anyone. It always left me wanting a new anyone, and, you're right, they're out there. I told one of my buddies just the day before I met you that I wasn't ready for any kind of a serious relationship."

Terry took another deep breath. "Well, I didn't find anyone. Someone found me. Someone named Joanne. And in a very cold instant, a blink of an eye, everything got warm and it changed." Terry snapped his fingers.

"You're telling me!" Joanne laughed. "I've never even had a boyfriend before. Now you're sitting here telling me you think you might be falling in love with me. If I read this in a book, I wouldn't know whether to sigh or gag."

"Please don't gag." Terry brushed her hair back behind her ear again.

Joanne leaned her cheek into his hand as he did. "I wish you'd quit doing that. I like it too much."

"Really?" Terry brushed her hair back with both hands. "I hope you'll decide you like it well enough that you want me to stick around and do it some more."

"I think you're smart enough to know the answer to that already." Joanne shivered. Her new feelings were starting to grow on her. "Stop it. You're making me crazy. Don't do it for anymore than an hour or so more. Please. Okay, maybe an hour and a half."

They both looked at each other and laughed.

"You've got me all confused." Joanne pulled back slightly. "Whenever I get this way, I mess things up. My mother was right about that. I can still see her shaking her finger at me and telling me I would never amount to anything because I always messed things up."

Sandy and Jennifer walked by the truck behind Terry. They puckered their lips at Joanne and made cross-eyed faces. Instinctively, Joanne pulled Terry to her and kissed him for their benefit. Terry reciprocated. Joanne pulled back, but he held her firmly and finished.

"Hey, you started it," he said playfully.

Joanne was embarrassed. "I'm sorry. I shouldn't have done that."

He looked into her eyes and frowned. "Really, why not? I saw them and you definitely got their attention. I know you got mine."

Joanne raised her arms and let them drop into her lap limply. "Do you see what I mean? I always mess things up." She took two deep breaths and let one out slowly. "We're in the church parking lot, and I do something like that just to show off. I'm totally humiliated now. Why don't you just take me home?"

"Are you serious?" Terry's voice got agitated again. "Why would I want to do that just because you knocked my socks off with a kiss? Do you want to be unhappy all the time?"

Why would he say that? It hurt. "Of course not!"

"Well stop it then," Terry fired back. "I've never told anyone I was falling in love with them…well…and really meant it, anyway."

Joanne glared at him. "So I'm not the first one?"

"I just said you were, didn't I?"

Joanne couldn't believe she wasn't cowering as she would normally have been, but she was burning inside all of a sudden.

"No. You said you told others and didn't mean it."

"When I told others, I was just telling them what I knew they wanted to hear, so I could…" Terry stopped. He softened his voice slightly. "Let's put it this way. I haven't always been a real nice guy in the past. Let's leave it at that."

"I don't want to leave it." Now she felt pain, humiliation and anger boiling over inside her. She almost made herself totally vulnerable, and he took advantage of it. "How do I know you're not just being the same way now? How do I know you aren't just telling me you're falling in love with me so you can get me to fall for you and do things like you did with all the others?"

"I guess you're just going to have to trust me, Joanne." Terry raised his voice another notch. "I guess I'll just have to prove it to you. I've got a month coming, unless you're going to back out on that, like you seem to do with everything else. I am going to keep coming back, and I'm not going to try to get you to do anything. You don't even have to kiss me. I'll still be here."

Tears started to roll down her cheeks again. What did that mean? "Don't you want to kiss me? Don't you want to do things with me? What's the matter? Aren't I pretty enough?"

"Oh come on. You're not giving me a chance here." Terry spoke through tightened lips. "You're twisting everything I say. I can't win."

In spite of her tears, Joanne asked angrily, "Is that what this is all about? Winning?"

"Stop it! Please, stop it!" Terry shouted.

Joanne's entire body shook as she watched Terry pound the sides of his head with his hands. She'd felt this kind of anger before, and it scared her. "Just take me home. Let's just forget everything. I'm not hungry anymore, anyway. I don't deserve to be yelled at." Inside her, cold took over.

With a shake of his head, Terry backed the truck out of the parking spot, squealing the tires. He gripped the steering wheel so hard, Joanne thought he might break it. At the turn, he cranked it hard to the left.

"I'll be glad to take you home. I don't have to put up with this either!"

His words hurt her more than any fist could have. He looked

straight ahead, refusing to even look at her, slammed the gearshift into drive and headed for the parking lot exit.

"Fine. Do that." She screamed with no control as her anger boiled over. "I knew it. You're just like everybody else."

CHAPTER 6

Terry stopped the truck abruptly about half way out of the parking lot and looked over at Joanne. Tears streamed from those gorgeous eyes he had fallen so hard for, black splotches of mascara streaked her cheeks, and her lips trembled as she bit them.

Even her red hair was messed up, and Terry had never seen it that way even after she took off her snowmobile helmet. But in spite of her disheveled appearance, in spite of her icy words, and in spite of her unfair accusations, Terry knew more than ever that, yes, he did have to put up with it.

He couldn't help it. He wasn't falling in love with her. He had already fallen in love with her. In fact, even though his chest was still heaving from anger, he realized he was angry because he loved her desperately, and he couldn't stand to see her this way.

He was in for a bumpy ride with Joanne, but it was a ride he had to take. He would never be able to smooth out the road entirely, but hopefully, he could beef up his shock absorbers, fill in a few potholes here and there along the way, and try with all his might not to create too many new ones.

Taking a deep breath, Terry calmly pulled his truck back into the parking place and turned off the motor.

"I want you to take me home," Joanne insisted, crossing her arms defiantly.

"I will in just a minute, if you really want me to." Terry looked directly at her. "But just let me say a couple of things first."

"What?" Joanne asked sharply.

"I'm sorry," Terry said. "I'm sorry I yelled, I'm sorry I got angry, I'm sorry for my past, and I'm really, really sorry for upsetting you. That is the very last thing I wanted to do. Sometimes I can stay calm, but sometimes my bad temper wins out. I'm sorry."

"It wasn't your fault; it was mine." Joanne sobbed again, sucking in a big gulp of air. "It's always my fault."

"Truthfully, I think you do have some responsibility here." Terry nodded. "But I let things get out of hand, not you. I'm the one who yelled. Look, I can't change anything about my past, and you can't change anything about yours. It just doesn't work that way. All we can do is move on from here and try to do the best we can. We need to start by telling each other the truth. I am not falling in love with you, Joanne…"

"I knew it." She turned from him and looked out her window. "Just take me home." She bit her lip and squeezed her eyes shut again.

"Please let me finish." Terry told himself to stay calm even though he was still frustrated that she constantly interrupted. "I am not falling in love with you. I *am* in love with you. You can ask Sharon. I told her, and she's the one who said I should let you know how I really feel. I love you, Joanne. You are all I've been able to think about since you pulled my sorry carcass out of the snowdrift only two days ago. I don't know how or why this happened so quickly, but actually, I don't care."

~*~

Joanne's face softened. She wiped her face with a tissue and looked down at herself and then back up at Terry. She tried to speak, but she couldn't. She wanted his words to be true so much she ached.

"Last week I didn't even know who you were, and now I can't imagine ever doing anything without you. It's so nuts it has to be true. And for the record, when the time is right, I look forward to getting you to do 'things' with me as you put it." He rubbed his fingers lightly over her cheek and gently tucked a wayward strand of hair behind her ear.

She wanted to pull away from his touch, but the chills it gave her made it impossible. In fact, they made her want him to touch her even more. "I wish I could believe that," she said, trying to keep from sniffing as she talked. "I wish I could trust you because…I want to. It's just that all my life I've always been disappointed."

"I'll try to keep from disappointing you." Terry brushed her cheek again and she couldn't do anything but close her eyes and lean her cheek into his hand. "I can't promise that I'll always succeed," he said softly as he continued to immobilize both her and her anger with the strokes on her cheek, "but I promise to try hard, very hard. We may have to have a lot of 'do overs' though." He smiled, and it was such a quiet smile as she opened her eyes that she wanted him closer, much closer.

Reaching up to hold his hand on her cheek, she sighed deeply and returned his smile. "Does that mean you want me to kiss you?"

"That would be nice," he said with both his words and his touch, "but I want to make sure you trust me first. I don't want you to kiss me just so you can get me to fall for you and do things. I'm not that way anymore, not since I met you."

"Stop," Joanne said softly as her eyes brightened and sparkled. "I'm sorry I said that." She leaned over and kissed Terry sweetly on the lips. "I wish I didn't look so bad. I'm starting to get hungry again."

"That's a good sign," Terry said, touching his lips lightly to hers in response. "You look fine to me, but if you have a can of tomato soup at your place, that would be fine with me."

"With grilled cheese sandwiches?"

"Perfect!"

"I like ketchup on mine," Joanne said.

Terry reached over and held Joanne's chin in his right hand. He smiled as softly and gently as he could. "So do I. Would you do me a big favor?" He ran the back of her hand lightly over her cheek again, and then ran his fingers through her hair to straighten it.

"Whew," Joanne said, taking a deep breath and blinking her eyes, "I'll try."

"Would you start believing in yourself? You're so hard on yourself. And while you're at it, please trust me. I really do love you. You can trust that. If you don't feel the same way, let me know so I don't make a complete fool out of myself. A guy has his pride, you know?"

"Wouldn't help your image to get dumped by The Big Red..." She stopped when Terry gave her a huge frown. "Sorry. I just don't want to get my hopes up, that's all."

"Blessed is he, or in this case, she, whose hope is in the Lord his God, the Maker of heaven and earth," Terry said without thinking, "and I have no idea where that came from."

"It comes from a Psalm," Joanne said, smiling. "I didn't know you quoted scripture. Do you do that with all your girls?"

"Only the one I'm trying to get to trust me. In the new spirit of honesty, however, you're not the only one with issues. I'm not always convinced my faith is as strong as it should be."

"What will it take to convince you?"

"I don't know for sure. What will it take to convince you that you're beautiful, and I love you?"

"It's not the same." Joanne turned her eyes from Terry and looked out the window again.

"Why not?"

"Because I can see my appearance in the mirror and know what I am. I see Jesus when I look into my heart."

"Maybe you should try looking at yourself in your heart instead of some mirror," Terry said. "Seems to me your vision is a lot better there than it is when you look into the mirror."

"You're being silly, and you know it," Joanne said.

"Why?"

"Because I can't see myself in my heart,"

"Then how can you see Jesus there?" He started the truck again and put into reverse, much more gently this time. "You have a television? There's a Bears game on this afternoon."

"Yes, I have a great television. The Bears play the Packers at 3:30. I was planning to watch the game. I guess it would be okay if you watched it with me."

"You like football?"

"I love football, especially if it's the Bears."

"Have you ever been to Soldier's Field to watch a Bears game?" He couldn't believe he'd finally found a woman besides his sister who liked football, let alone the Bears.

"No."

"Would you like to go?" Terry asked casually.

Joanne turned quickly and looked at him. "Can you get tickets?"

"I already have tickets." He smirked slightly. "Vikings, last game of the season. Sharon and I are going on a bus with a group of people. I have two extra tickets. One of them is yours if you want it."

"Are you kidding? You have tickets to the Viking game?"

"Yes, I have tickets, and no, I'm not kidding. So…"

Joanne couldn't believe what he said. "Of course I'll go…if you're sure I won't ruin something you and you sister had planned to do together."

"Trust me. Sharon will love it."

"I trust you." Joanne looked at him and tried not to let everything inside her overflow.

"Really? That's a start." Terry grinned without looking directly at her but still noticing a twinkle in her eye.

"So…I said I trust you. Do you trust Jesus?"

Terry had to smile. Joanne was so totally unpredictable. Maybe it was her unpredictability that made her so fascinating to Terry, along with her hair and eyes, of course. One minute she was an insecure, almost totally irrational bucket of tears, and the next minute she was cleverly manipulating him. On top of that she was a Bears' fan!

"Tell you what. When you can honestly tell me you see yourself as a beautiful woman, you ask me that question again."

"Don't make light of it, Terry. I didn't mean to be flippant about what I was saying. I shouldn't have said it that way."

"I'm not making light of anything." Terry looked at her. "If the Lord can make you recognize how beautiful you are, then I'll recognize Him in front of the entire church congregation on a Sunday morning."

"The Bible warns us not to put God to the test," Joanne said, shaking her head.

"I'm not putting God to the test. I'm putting you to the test. You show me your faith, and I'll show you mine. I believe it was James who said, 'faith without works is dead,' wasn't it?"

"Yes, it was James, but I'm not sure that's exactly what he meant."

"I think it's exactly what he meant." Terry grinned. "To put it in simple words, 'talk, talk, talk. Let me see something.' To be honest with you, I get up in front of groups all the time, but it still scares the stuffing out of me. So I won't do it unless I mean it. It will scare me to death."

She laid her hand lightly on his arm to get his attention, and gazed at him with eyes still red from her tears. "Terry?"

He stopped the truck before pulling out of the parking lot and noticed her eyes. "Yes?"

Biting her lip nervously she blinked slowly, "Could you do me a favor now?"

He smiled softly. "Sure. Anything."

Joanne moved her shoulder like she did the night she wore the blue dress and looked down at her arm. "Could you get that strap for me…and could you touch my face like you just did once more? And let's have another do over."

~*~

Terry's comments bothered Joanne. He was right to a point. How could she hold the beauty of Jesus in her heart when it was so cluttered with ugliness and pain? Which of the two occupied more space, Jesus or her pain? Beauty and ugliness couldn't occupy the same space. Maybe the crowded quarters had something to do with her inability to see what she really looked like.

She thought about those things as she took the cheese from her refrigerator and sliced it for their sandwiches. Terry buttered both sides of four slices of bread and watched the soup as it heated on the stove. It was genuine gourmet soup straight from a gourmet can.

Joanne put the sliced cheese on the bread and put the sandwiches into the skillet. They sizzled immediately. She tried to concentrate on browning the sandwiches as she stood next to Terry. He silently stirred the soup on the adjoining burner. She liked the basic feeling of standing there together making a simple meal. Sometimes it is the simple things that are the most meaningful and romantic.

Terry insisted he thought she was beautiful and told her straight out that he loved her. She hadn't even told him that she loved him, and it is supposed to be men who have trouble making their feelings known.

For some reason she couldn't bring herself to say "I love you" back to him even though she knew she did and wanted to tell him. It took trust, and it made her completely vulnerable, completely defenseless, and completely exposed putting everything she felt out in the open.

Terry casually slipped his arm around her waist and squeezed her as he continued to stir the soup with one hand. Whether she wanted to or not, Joanne let her guard down slightly. She closed her eyes and let herself trust, feel and enjoy the simple romance in his touch, moving closer to him as he squeezed her waist more firmly.

"Did anyone ever tell you how beautiful you are when you're cooking?" Terry looked at her and smiled.

"Nobody's ever told me I was beautiful period." Joanne didn't look at him, concentrating on the sandwiches in the skillet. She was afraid she would melt faster than the cheese on the sandwiches if she looked anywhere else.

"But me, you mean," Terry said.

Joanne blushed and looked up at him. "But you," she said softly.

"Then obviously, nobody's ever seen you cook before." Terry pulled Joanne even closer.

"Hey, I'm trying to cook here." Joanne grinned and pulled away but not enough to really move from him.

"So am I." Terry pulled her back to him again.

Joanne giggled, but she stayed right next to him. "Stop it."

"I can't. You make me crazy."

"I think you had a pretty good start on that before you ever met me." Joanne turned and looked him directly in the eyes with her face only inches from his.

She studied his eyes and every inch of his face. He was cute, handsome even, and all that, but the fact that he was standing there next to her having fun making grilled cheese sandwiches and canned soup with her…that made him irresistible.

"All right then, let's do this your way. I'm tired of playing games." She rose up on her toes and kissed him. "There, is that better?"

"Much. But don't burn the sandwiches."

"See if I do that again, buster." Joanne laughed.

Terry kissed her back on the end of her nose. "It's okay, I like mine burnt. I was only thinking of you."

"Prove it." She slid the sandwiches on a plate by the stove and turned back to face him, putting her arms around his neck. "I said prove it, or am I being too subtle?"

~*~

Fortunately the soup didn't get burned.

They ate their simple lunch, cleared the table, and sat down next to each other on the sofa in front of the television. Joanne kicked off her shoes as she usually did and pulled her feet up underneath her, which tilted her slightly toward Terry. He slipped his arm around her shoulder as she turned on the television with the remote control, and he pulled her closer.

"It just occurred to me that I have no idea what you do for a living," Joanne said as she continued to get comfortable.

"Do I really have to tell you?" Terry turned and looked at her.

"Well, yes. Is it something awful?"

"Some people think so," Terry said, smiling.

"What?"

"I'm an attorney, strictly small town stuff if that helps any."

She winced and pulled back to look at him. "You're an attorney?"

"Does that mean I don't get to watch the Bears game? I'm sure the Bears have lots of fans who are attorneys."

"Oh brother! You're an attorney, and I don't even have a four-year degree. Talk about a mismatch. Couldn't you have been a shoe salesman or something, you know, ordinary? Good looking, an attorney…why are you wasting your time watching football with me?"

"Easy. You're a Bears fan, and you have a great TV. So you think I'm good looking, huh? That's the first time you've said that. Thanks." He kissed her playfully on the cheek.

Joanne poked him in the arm. "Cut it out, Terry. You know you're great looking…or good looking…or whatever I said."

"Even assuming I do know, and for the record it was good looking, I don't mind hearing it. Guys have feelings too, you know. I was beginning to think you were just in this for cheap thrills…you know, to get me to do things."

"You aren't ever going to let that go are you?" Joanne realized that for once she hadn't overreacted when she was teased. In fact, she decided she could play too. She leaned closer to him, touched his face softly with her hand, and moved her lips to within inches of his. "But as long as you brought it up, just exactly what kind of 'things' are we talking about? Give me a few examples."

He took a deep breath. "How 'bout them Bears!" Terry took the remote from her hand and turned up the volume.

~*~

Joanne had rattled him, but not as much as she did when she smiled after seeing his reaction, put her head on his shoulder, snuggled closer to him, and put her hand gently on his chest.

"The Bears' defense is incredible today." Joanne looked up at him during the last part of the first half. "I don't think I've seen them any better this year. The quarterback isn't getting any time to throw." She put her head on his shoulder again.

Terry tried to focus on the football game. He was a rabid fan. Joanne said something about Chicago having the best middle linebacker in the game today. He knew that. And then she talked about the Green Bay quarterback again. He only remembered those two things because Joanne had lifted her hand from his chest to make her points. When she laid it down again, everything got blurry. Man, was her hand warm!

Lots of women had gotten this close or closer to Terry in the past. Certainly at least one of them had put her hand on his chest like this, laid her head on his shoulder, and snuggled. Why was he so warm and confused this time? In the past, he would have responded much differently, but now, with Joanne, he wanted to do the right thing. He didn't want to act the way the old Terry had. Well, he did, but he didn't.

Before he knew it, the game was over, and Joanne sat up on the couch as she looked at him. "When were you planning on telling me you were a hotshot attorney?"

"Never." He felt completely drained from the warm hand on his chest and the game he hadn't watched. "I'm not a hotshot attorney. I'm strictly a small town guy who tries to get by doing small claims cases, court appointed criminal assignments, wills, and all that boring stuff. Every now and then I get an interesting case or two, but believe me, it's not all that glamorous."

A frown covered her face. "Right. It's not nearly as glamorous as being a part-time bookkeeper, full time gopher, and Gal Friday for an exotic grain elevator in the middle of nowhere Iowa, earning slightly more than minimum wage for way too many hours. I don't know how you put up with it."

"Good support staff is really hard to find. I'm sure you're very valuable to the elevator. I couldn't get along without my support staff. That's for sure."

Joanne stiffened, but she didn't seem to be angry or defensive as she had been earlier. "Support staff. How PC! Any of them men? I'll bet they're just all a bunch of dedicated gals. Do any of them make even half of what you make?"

If they had been playing football instead of watching it, there would have been a flag for unnecessary roughness. He sensed her challenge and responded. "Why do I always feel a little like I'm on trial when I'm with you? Can't we just be good little boys and girls, fall in love, get married, have babies, and live happily ever after?"

She didn't back down. "How many babies you planning to have Mr. Male Hotshot Attorney? I didn't know men had those. Quit changing the subject, and just answer my question, counselor."

Now he had to come clean. "Okay. None of the support staff are men. They're all women. For the record, one of the attorneys is a woman too. None of the support staff makes half as much as I do. None makes half as much as our female attorney either—although several are fairly close."

"Aha! Just as I thought." Joanne crossed her arms, but defiantly unlike before.

It was time for rebuttal. "But, none of them have nearly as much invested in education, in office equipment, in rent, in malpractice insurance, books, annual Bar dues, or any of that either. None of them has their name on a bank note for more than a half million dollars, and none of them has to try to convince some judge he ought to rule in your favor even though he's playing golf with your opposing counsel in half an hour at their Country Club."

He ended with one final point. "And, for the record, again, attorneys like me probably make a whole lot less than most people think. I do taxes for truck drivers and farmers who cheat for more than I make."

Joanne kept her arms folded, but her frown turned to a smile. "You're pretty good. Anyone ever tell you how cute you are when you're all puffed up and angry like that? I guess I can love you even if you are a hotshot attorney."

"You can love me, huh?" He hadn't missed what she said even though she tried to hide it in the middle of a lot of other words.

Her eyes turned to the floor, but her big, shy grin was still visible. "I guess."

"Not good enough. You're equivocating." He wanted more from Joanne after all that.

She tried to suppress her grin and looked up. "I'm what?"

"You know what. You're playing me now, quite well, I might add. You'd make a good attorney."

Joanne shook her head. "Don't want to be an attorney. I don't have a big enough ego."

"You could develop that," Terry said, keeping a straight face. "Most of us do."

She thought a minute and then dismissed his statement with a wave of her hand. "Nah, don't want to."

"Good. I have better things in mind."

Joanne toyed with her hair. "Oh really? Care to tell me what, counselor?"

He stroked the back of his hand over her cheek. "Close your eyes. I'll do better than tell you."

Joanne closed her eyes and moved closer to Terry. He brushed her cheek with the back of his hand again and tucked her hair behind her ear. "On second thought, you got any ice cream?"

"Ter-ry!" She giggled and opened her eyes.

He put his arms around her neck and pulled Joanne toward him. She ducked out of his grasp, got up and looked at him. "Butter Pecan, okay?" She ran toward the kitchen, and he jumped up and ran after her.

She stopped at the entrance to the kitchen just as he caught her. She turned and looked at him fiercely. "I love you, Mr. Hotshot Attorney. I'm saying it plainly so there's no doubt in your mind, even though it scares me to death. Did you hear me? I love you. So don't you dare disappoint me or let me down."

He hugged her tightly and almost cried, something he had never done. She finally said it, and it felt so good to him. Joanne hugged him back, and they just stood there that way for several minutes.

"Let the record reflect that Mr. Hotshot said okay, he promised," Joanne said softly.

"So noted," Terry responded hoarsely.

~*~

Terry's mind was mush as he drove home that night. It had been quite a day, full of incredible highs and lows. He took pride in keeping calm in court when he was under pressure and in having an almost photographic memory. He still remembered a lot of the arguments he made in court, almost word for word. So why couldn't he remember the final score of the Bear's game that ended just a few hours ago?

He might not remember the score of the game, but he would never forget the day, at least the last half of it. Warmth, lightly resting on his chest. Moistness, flashing sparkly blue turquoise, fragile, uneven tempered, trusting and holding on in red curly softness, begging not to be betrayed. The Rubicon was yesterday. There was no turning back.

Today was buttery cheese toasted and tomato soup ordinary. It was a perfect day, topped with the delicious, long lingering taste of butter pecan. It was too small and ordinary for the world to notice, but too grand and important for God to have it any other way. Terry was beginning to understand, and just the small piece of knowledge he got today overwhelmed him.

God and His plans were too large, too complex, and too everything for Terry to comprehend. All he could do is sit back and enjoy the ride, trusting that it would take him where he needed to go. God would drive while he and Joanne cuddled in the back seat.

"I love you, Mr. Hotshot Attorney. I'm saying it plainly so there's no doubt in your mind even though it scares me to death. Did you hear me? I love you. So don't you dare disappoint me or let me down."

Joanne's words echoed over and over like something hollered over the rim of the Grand Canyon. "I love you," and with those words, "I trust you" although she never said them. It had been a difficult thing for her to say as insecure as she was. It made her vulnerable, but she took the chance anyway.

Beautiful women had told Terry that they wanted him, desired him, needed him, and even that they loved him, but they always spoke through sultry eyes with well-calculated words that purred. Joanne's eyes were not sultry, and her words did not purr. Her eyes and her words were better. They were honest and sincere. Love meant love to her. Nothing more and nothing less. Terry knew that now.

~*~

Joanne brushed her hair and watched it float softly over her shoulders in the mirror. She was happy, excited, frightened and confused, all at the same time. Those feelings had to be put in their proper places so they could be addressed. Joanne didn't know exactly how to do that. *How, Lord? How do I sort it out? Show me.* She continued brushing her hair. Her happiness mixed with fear that her joy couldn't last, and excitement wrapped around the confusion of what to do next.

She had to take her snowmobile out into the blizzard that night and find Terry. Everyone had assumed that God sent her out so she could rescue him. That was true as far as it went, but from the very beginning Joanne had also wondered if God had another purpose in mind, an even grander purpose.

Terry argued that she was beautiful. He was persistent, persuasive, and couldn't explain his stubborn advocacy even to himself, but it was the clear advocacy of an attorney who had been trained well and had refined his skills to never give up. That's who she had been led to.

And then there was Sharon. Joanne would never have met her if she hadn't gone out into the blizzard after Terry. She would never have gone shopping, bought the little blue dress, or learned how to wear it, and would never have made a friend like Sharon.

Her new friend knew where to buy the clothes and get the makeup to maximize Joanne's physical beauty, and she also reminded Joanne where to get the nerve to draw out the beauty of her soul. Both kinds of beauty had been given freedom to grow because of Sharon.

Had God used Joanne to save Terry, or was He using Terry and Sharon to save her? Not for eternity. She already had that. But for bigger and betters purposes, right here, right now?

How big are You, God? I can't even imagine. How big are Your plans? Remember, it's just little old me You're dealing with down here.

For the first time in her life, contentment was within reach, and she was starting to understand. Sometimes you have to realize how small you are, before you can realize how big, big can really be. Starting out as a mustard seed has its advantages because it leaves so much room to grow.

Joanne was that mustard seed. Now it was time to grow.

CHAPTER 7

Joanne's mother and father had identical wills that left her the small farmhouse where she and her brothers had been raised. The 260-acre farm and nearly everything else had gone to her three brothers. Her father had insisted that she receive the house, and her mother had begrudgingly agreed, but not before saying that she guessed an old maid would have to have somewhere to live.

Barely 12 years old when her mother made that comment, her mother seemed totally unconcerned that Joanne was sitting in front of her when she made it, and since then Joanne heard that comment every day in her head. The comment made her father furious, but he died in the freak accident a few months later before he could undo the hurt that it caused.

Not only did Joanne lose the father she adored, with the hair that matched hers, but also she lost the only person who stuck up for her. Dave had been the nicest of her three brothers, but they were all bullied by their mother, and Joanne was collectively ignored on her good days and blamed for everything that went wrong on most of the others.

Images of her mother still made her shudder, especially when she remembered her mother's brown spotted, loose skinned hands swinging wildly in the air when she yelled, threatening to crash down on her at any moment. She could still see the malevolent smile on her mother's face as she lay dying and heard the words "useless old maid," as her mother reminded her one last time the farmhouse was now hers.

Those ugly, painful memories and the small farmhouse where most of them were created were her mother's only legacy to her. It was a legacy she would have gladly turned down until aromas of grilled cheese sandwiches and canned tomato soup combined with Bears football to replace ugliness and pain with hope and happiness.

Those same aromas filled the house already this morning, and it was only three forty-five. Grilled cheese sandwiches and tomato soup had become a Sunday tradition for Joanne and Terry, and today was Sunday, but not just any Sunday. It was the Sunday Joanne had looked forward to since Terry invited her to go to the Bears-Viking game. The bus left at six, and she needed about an hour to get there, so the lunch for the game had to be made now.

Excitement kept Joanne from being tired as she made extra grilled cheese sandwiches and wrapped them. So did thoughts of Terry as she imagined he was standing there next to her stirring the soup as he usually did. He was making an extra large pan of soup so they could share it.

Terry's presence was so palpable that Joanne could hear him stirring the soup and see him grinning. He was about to say something funny and put his arm around her as he stirred. Unconsciously, she moved closer to where he always stood and pretended to be bothered by his arm around her waist as she always did. Her protests were part of the tradition, almost like an old fashioned rite of courtship, and they made Joanne smile just thinking about them.

She packed the sandwiches and soup into a large grocery sack when they were finally done and carried the sack out to her truck. The stars sparkled their brightest in the clear, cold black winter sky, and the snow reflected their light. The sun would not appear for hours, and even then it wouldn't bring a lot of warmth with it. No doubt the winter winds were rehearsing already over Lake Michigan, preparing to blow in over Soldier's Field and make certain that temperatures remained cold.

Dressed in multiple layers, Joanne brought two heavy blankets to help keep warm at the game. The barnyard thermometer read eleven degrees, and there was little promise that it would rise significantly even when the sun finally did, but Joanne didn't mind. She was going to watch her favorite football team and wrap Terry in blankets once again, but this time she was going to wrap herself inside them with him.

As she drove through the darkness to meet the bus where she

would meet Terry, she thought about her brothers and Marie sitting in the back row of the church. The four Sundays Dave had promised Sharon had come and gone, but he still had everybody there every Sunday. Other truckers and neighbors had started coming too, largely because Dave was there, and he promised Sharon he would keep coming if she and Terry did.

Sharon told Joanne she didn't mind because she had grown very fond of the small, but growing local congregation, and she had also grown very comfortable sitting next to Chris. Even though Terry, his sister and she were going to miss church today to attend the football game, Dave had promised he would have "the rest of the brood" there.

People were already starting to board the bus when Joanne pulled into the school parking lot where they were supposed to meet. Some of the people had grocery sacks like she did; some had large thermos jugs; and a few had small coolers. Terry, Sharon, and Chris stood next to the bus waiting for her.

Chris was there too. How interesting. Sharon insisted that she and Chris were just good friends when Joanne teased her about him, but even this early in the morning, they looked a lot like a couple to Joanne.

By the time she parked the truck, Terry was there to meet her. He gave her a big hug and a quick kiss on the cheek and took the grocery bag from the front seat as Joanne blushed and closed the door to the truck. She took his arm, and he gave her another quick kiss on the cheek.

"Terry, there are people watching," she said softly.

"What? I can't hug the woman I love and give her a couple of little kisses on the cheek?"

"Not so loud," she said again with a grin that really said she didn't mind. "You'll embarrass me."

"You ain't seen nothing yet, babe."

"What's that supposed to mean?" She hoped he was just being his slightly goofy self because he knew how easily she got embarrassed, and she was hoping to have a great day with no major incidents.

"Nothing," Terry said quickly. "You know me; I'm always clowning around. Come on. We've got seats saved inside, and the rest of our stuff is already on the bus."

"Nice to see Sharon's buddy here." Joanne pointed at Chris. "He was one of the few guys that was ever decent to me when we were growing up. He couldn't seem to take his eyes off Cindy Coffman, though. Asked her to marry him, in fact, and she did, but she ran off with some guy from Grinnell the first year they were married and broke his heart. He's pretty much kept to himself since then…until he met your sister."

Terry turned his head to Joanne. "There's nothing between them, is there? Sharon says they're just good friends."

Intuition told Joanne that might be an understatement. "Yeah, that's what she told me too. We'll see."

"So, did you and Chris ever go out?" Terry tried to sound casual.

"No," Joanne responded. "We've always been good friends, nothing more. What's the matter, are you jealous?"

"I'm jealous of anyone who comes within ten feet of you, especially now that the word's out about how great you look in little blue dresses with spaghetti straps."

"So the word's out, is it?" Joanne couldn't admit to herself how good those words felt. "You're in rare form today. You're blowing smoke full blast already. So, was Chris planning to come all along?"

"No, we had a spare ticket, and Sharon just happened to mention Chris was a huge Bears fan, so I asked him if he wanted to come along. You'd have thought I offered him the winning lottery ticket." They walked a little faster toward the bus. "He practically hugged me; he was so excited, even when I told him he'd probably have to sit with Sharon."

"I'm sure that really bothered him. So, Sharon just happened to mention it, huh? Interesting." Joanne tapped her smiling lips with her fingertips as she glanced at Chris and Sharon again.

"Yeah, she did, but what's so interesting about that?"

"Men are so clueless." Joanne raised her eyes. "Are you really that dense?"

"Hey, who you calling dense? My sister calls me clueless too, but she's never called me dense."

"She's your sister. She's just being nice," Joanne tapped her lips with her fingertips again. "You really don't see it? I'm sure Chris is a big Bears fan, but if you can't tell from the look in his eyes that he's a huge fan of more than the Bears, you aren't looking."

"Huh?" Terry looked ahead to watch Sharon and Chris. "The look in his eyes doesn't look any different from the look in my sister's…" Terry stopped.

"Hello. Exactly. How exciting!" Joanne could hardly contain herself.

"I think you might be jumping the gun here a little. Sharon had a really bad experience in college. I don't know exactly what happened, but I know she's never dated since then. It's almost like she's afraid to." Terry shook his head.

"Maybe that's why we hit it off so well," Joanne said. "Beautiful Sharon and plain Joanne, drawn together by serious dating issues from the past. Although in my case, it's more like serious non-dating issues."

"I thought I asked you not to call yourself plain." Terry stopped and looked at her with a frown.

"Counselor, I believe the record will reflect that you asked me not to call myself ugly or any euphemism for that. You didn't say anything about plain. Have the transcript read back if you like." She batted her eyelashes in a triumphant, flirtatious flutter. "You'll just have to learn how to be more specific."

"I'll remember that." Terry elbowed her playfully on the arm and ran ahead of her.

Joanne ran after him and danced around him in circles, chattering like a schoolgirl as he kept walking toward the bus. "I hope your sister likes classical music because Chris loves it, and if they're an item, she's going to hear lots of it."

Terry stopped and looked at her in seeming disbelief. "She loves classical music, but a truck driver that likes classical music? Now that's interesting and a little rare, don't you think?"

Joanne stuck her face under his nose to look up into his eyes as he stood there. "He loves to cook too, and there are a lot of other things about Chris that don't fit the trucker stereotype." She started circling around him again. "He really is a great guy, and I think they make a cute couple."

"Well, that's great, but I'm still working on making us a cute couple." Terry started walking toward the bus again.

"Keep working on it. I'm starting to like it, but Sharon says you haven't suffered enough yet. I think she might be right about that."

Joanne batted her eyelashes again, giggled and turned to run to the bus. She looked over her shoulder to make sure Terry was right behind her. He grabbed the grocery bag tighter and ran after her.

Climbing the steps to the bus two at a time, Joanne slid into one of the vacant seats in front of Sharon and Chris while Terry found a place for the grocery sack on the rack above the seats and plopped down in the seat beside Joanne.

"Take a look, oh clueless one." Joanne leaned closer to Terry and nodded at Chris and Sharon behind them as his sister scrunched closer to Chris and chatted freely with him as if they were old friends.

Terry turned around and pretended to count the number of people on the bus. When his count got to Sharon's seat, her eyes locked onto his, and he tried to sound casual as he asked, "You two okay back here?"

Raising her eyebrows at her brother, Sharon responded quickly. "Sure, why wouldn't we be?"

"Just making sure." He continued his count and muttered to nobody in particular, "Looks like we're all here."

"Well?" Joanne poked him playfully in the arm as he sat back down next to her.

All Terry could do was grin. "You were right. Interesting."

~*~

Shortly after the bus crossed the Mississippi River on the interstate near Davenport, the dawn started painting the sky with almost florescent pinks, yellows and oranges. Gradually the brightness softened, morphing into pastel shades until the sun popped up over the horizon to illuminate the blue cloudless sky.

Just watching the sky's transformation was breathtaking, but watching it while Joanne leaned against him to get a better look out the window was even better. Terry hoped this idyllic beginning was a precursor to a perfect day to follow, but the butterflies in his stomach fluttered more furiously than ever.

About an hour before they got to Lakeshore Drive, the bus driver made an announcement over the PA system, saying that due to tighter security restrictions they would not be allowed to take anything into the football stadium except for blankets. If they planned to eat what they brought with them, they should do it now, or wait until after the game.

Terry pulled the large grocery bag from the overhead shelf above the seats, took out the thermos, and opened it as Joanne handed out the sandwiches to Sharon and Chris. Sharon took small bags of chips from her bag and large homemade oatmeal raisin cookies.

The familiar smell of tomato soup made Terry smile. The Sunday tradition continued even today, and that made being with Joanne feel normal, like Sunday. More than anything else, that's how he wanted both of them to feel today. Normal, comfortable, and happy. He poured large steamy cups of soup and handed one to Chris, one to Sharon, another to Joanne and took the last one himself before sitting down to eat.

Before she ate, Joanne bowed her head and said a simple grace, and Terry followed along with her. He noticed that his sister was doing the same thing in the row behind them. Something about praying over tomato soup and grilled cheese sandwiches on a bus headed for a football game made Joanne even more attractive to Terry, and he wondered if Chris felt the same way about Sharon.

~*~

The leftover food, the empty cups, and the sandwich wrappers had barely been replaced above the seats when the bus turned onto Lakeshore and headed to Soldier's Field. The whitecaps on the bright blue Lake Michigan surface rolled in as always verifying that the Windy City was living up to its reputation. Terry noticed that Joanne couldn't take her eyes off the lake as the bus pulled up to let them off.

"It's even bigger and more beautiful than I imagined." Joanne pressed her face to the side window of the bus.

Terry could feel her excitement reflecting off the glass as he tried to calm his own frazzled nerves and convince himself that he had been to lots of Bears games in the past. This was just one more, but it was a very special one more and what made it that way had her face pressed to the window looking outside. He wanted everything to be perfect for her.

The bus driver stood up in front and keyed the microphone to the PA system to give final instructions. He told the group that he would be taking the bus to a designated parking area somewhere nearby and return again as close as he could to this same spot after the game to pick them up.

"Memorize 371," he said. "There will be lots of buses that look like this one in a line here after the game, but only this one has 371 on both the front and back of it. I'll have the heat on, and believe me it will feel good. Go Bears!"

Jumping off the bus, Terry tucked the blankets under one arm while Joanne pulled herself closer to him and shivered as the first major gust of wind from Lake Michigan welcomed them to Chicago. The erratic blasts of wind pushed them around together as they made their way toward the stadium laughing as they staggered, almost tripping each other.

"These the same blankets I wore the night you undressed me?" Terry squeezed Joanne playfully around her waist.

"Stop it right now, counselor." Joanne looked him squarely in the eyes and tried to keep a straight face. "It will be a long time before you get that opportunity again if you keep that up."

Her grin gave her away as she glanced behind her and noticed that Chris had offered his arm to Sharon, and she had taken it. Pulling herself closer to him, they laughed together as the wind pummeled them giving them all an excuse to cling to each other as they walked. And they did.

"Don't turn back now." Joanne nudged Terry. "But when you get a chance take a look at your little sister and Chris. She's holding on to him for all she's worth and trying to pretend she's just being polite. This gets curiouser and curiouser." Joanne giggled as she raised her eyebrows.

"Hey, it's windy out here." Terry glanced over his shoulder. "She just doesn't want to get blown away."

"Right," Joanne giggled again, "and no pun intended, I assume."

Laughing himself and shaking his head, Terry leaned into Joanne and pulled her closer to him as they approached the gate to the stadium. He unfolded the blankets and shook them for one attendant and handed their two tickets to a second attendant. Joanne opened her purse, and the first attendant looked at its contents. The second security attendant scanned the tickets with a hand held scanner and handed them back to Terry.

"Enjoy the game," the second attendant said, and just like that they were inside Soldier's Field.

~*~

No matter how many times Joanne had seen the field on television, it didn't compare to the way it looked when she and Terry walked through the portal to the stadium and saw the field stretched out in front of them. It was so much bigger and greener than she had expected. The goal posts looked enormous compared to how they looked on television, and the crowd noises, even before the game started, were electric.

"Wow!" Joanne said. "This is so awesome!"

"I get that same feeling every time I come here." Terry stood and looked at the field with Joanne. "I think I'm used to it before I get here, but then I walk in and get overwhelmed all over again. But, you ain't seen nothin' yet." He pulled Joanne closer to him. "The best is yet to come."

Terry and Chris took the outside seats of the four they had together, while Joanne and Sharon sat next to each other in between them. The seats were about two thirds of the way up the side of the stadium and about half way between the goal line and the end line of the field.

They had a good angle to see all the action on the field, and they had a great view of the giant scoreboard just above them and to their right. The scoreboard served multiple purposes besides the obvious one. It showed replays of crucial plays, local advertisements and an occasional personal message for a modest fee.

The blankets came in handy almost immediately. Soldier's Field had been completely opened to the elements before it was remodeled. However, even though it had been closed in significantly, Lake Michigan still managed to blow its icy breath into the oval from a few hundred yards away, and the stadium was frigid.

Joanne and Terry wrapped themselves together with the blankets almost as soon as they sat down, using the cold as an excuse to snuggle together under the blankets. At first, Sharon seemed uncomfortable with a similar arrangement especially when Chris took the blankets he was carrying and wrapped them around Sharon as she sat down in her seat.

Sharon kept looking at her brother wrapped together with Joanne and then looking at Chris, who insisted he didn't mind that she had the blankets. As Terry watched the apparent internal struggle his sister was having with the blanket dynamics, he looked at Joanne and shook his head, nodding at Chris and Sharon.

Joanne shrugged and whispered, "Why don't they just go for it?"

Finally, about midway through the first quarter, Sharon took a deep breath, closed her eyes, and did just that. She took one end of the blanket, wrapped it around Chris, and pulled the blanket so tightly around both of them that Chris was forced to put his arm around her.

"What was it you said…interesting?" Terry grinned as he talked out of the side of his mouth to Joanne.

"That's the word," Joanne said quietly, and for most of the rest of the quarter there were four smiles in a row sharing two sets of blankets.

Joanne cheered almost every play on the field, including two requests for time outs. She jumped up and down wildly when a Bears defensive back intercepted a Viking pass and ran it back into their end zone, spiking the ball into the ground right under them.

When the Bears left the field at half time ahead on the scoreboard 17 to 6, she stood up and cheered their departure like a long time season ticket holder.

"I can't believe this is your first game," Terry said. "You cheer like a veteran."

"This is so totally awesome." She turned to Terry. "Thank you so much for bringing me."

"You're welcome," Terry said. "I suppose the next thing you'll want is season tickets." Terry's last comment hadn't sounded like his heart was in it. He kept looking all around the stadium and glanced repeatedly at the scoreboard. Joanne had never seen him fidget like this before. It worried her.

"Is something wrong?" she finally asked. She felt the old

sickening feeling she got when her mother was about to yell at her and blame her for everything going wrong. *What did I do this time? Everything was going so great, and I was having so much fun. I knew it couldn't last. Lord, show me what to do. Don't let me ruin this.*

"I hope not," Terry finally answered not looking at her. He continued to look around and stare at the scoreboard. The answer and the fact that he wasn't looking at her when he gave it, didn't help Joanne feel any better. Suddenly his eyes brightened considerably. He took at least two deep breaths and put his hands on Joanne's shoulders, turning her toward the scoreboard.

"Look at that," he said with a shaky, but excited voice.

Joanne looked up at the scoreboard and saw a message in big orange capital letters. She read it quickly, but it didn't register at first. Then she read it again.

JOANNE LOWRY,

I LOVE YOU. WILL YOU MARRY ME?

TERRY.

Suddenly the message hit her. She turned back to Terry quickly, but he wasn't there. He was down on one knee with a mobile cameraman pointing a large lens at her. He held out two trembling hands with a burgundy, velvet-covered box that had a very, very large diamond ring sparkling in the center of it.

Although they were trembling, the hands in front of her weren't spotted, loose skinned or old. They didn't threaten harm but offered hope and love. They were Terry's hands, and they were all she saw at first.

"Please don't embarrass me in front of millions of people." Terry's face looked ashen and frozen with fear instead of with the cold around it. "Will you do me the great honor of becoming my wife? Will you marry me?"

"Are you totally out of your mind?" Joanne gasped. She felt like she was going to collapse. Her mind was spinning out of control, and here she was about to mess things up again by saying the wrong thing and giving the wrong answer. *What is wrong with me?*

Sharon grabbed her from behind and held both her shoulders firmly. She whispered. “Relax, Jo. Take a deep breath and for crying out loud, go for it! That rock has to be at least two carats!”

Perspiration now covered Terry’s face as he knelt in front of her, and the wind chill was well below 10 degrees. The camera pointed right at her, only inches from her face. The crowd started to buzz as it watched the proposal unfold on the giant scoreboard.

“Are you sure?” Joanne finally managed to ask. *Still not the right answer, but I’m getting closer.*

“Absolutely!” Terry finally looked like he had regained his composure, or was it her?

Joanne took two deep breaths as Sharon had suggested, and just before her knees refused to hold her up anymore, she held out her hand to Terry, and nodded. “Of course, I’ll marry you!”

The crowd erupted with a cheer like the Bears had just scored a touchdown as Terry slipped the ring gently onto Joanne’s trembling finger. Then there was loud, rolling applause as Sharon squealed with delight behind her and Chris hollered.

“You had me a little worried there for a minute, Miss, but congratulations.” The cameraman smiled and lowered the camera.

“Thank you.” Joanne’s heart was just catching up with what had happened in the last several minutes, minutes that almost seemed to last hours until they were over. Terry popped up in front of her and kissed her as he pulled her to him with both arms.

“You had me more than a little worried there for a minute too.”

“Do over.” Joanne put her hands on the sides of his face. “I wasn’t ready, and this is one time I definitely want to do better than that.”

“Gladly.”

Before he could do anything, Joanne held his face tenderly and kissed him, first gently and then about as deeply as anyone can kiss. The fullness of her heart mushroomed and translated itself to her lips.

“Whoa! I thought you said you never dated. Where did you learn how to kiss like that?”

“I read a lot,” Joanne responded almost casually. “I’m going to get you for this, you know.”

"I'm sure. I'm counting on it." He kissed her back softly. "Do you trust me now?"

"I guess so." Joanne batted her eyes and hugged him again, laughing and holding him at the same time.

"Does that mean we can at least start talking about those things I want to get you to do?" He winked at her.

"I already have a list. Two lists, actually. Do you want the short one, or the one with all the details?" Joanne brushed his lips lightly with hers. "Of course, until we're married it's for informational purposes only. How strong is your heart, by the way?"

"That depends," Terry brushed her lips with his in response. "How long are the lists?"

"You mean all ten pages…and the fine print? I know how you attorneys like fine print."

Terry smoothed her hair from her face as the wind whipped her red curls around. "I give up, you win."

"Get use to it," Joanne said, and she kissed him quickly on the lips.

"Could I break in here for a minute?" Sharon threw her arms around Joanne's neck and hugged her. They did the squeally girl thing for a few minutes, and Sharon finally said, "We're going to be sisters! Just think of all the shopping we can do."

"Uh oh," Terry said from behind her, but she chose to ignore him.

"Did you know?" Joanne asked, staring wide-eyed at her soon to be sister-in-law.

"I had no idea. I don't think anybody did. Way to go, big brother," She ducked in front of Joanne and poked Terry good-naturedly. "You don't deserve her, but I'm glad she said yes. I just love her!"

"Thanks, sis. I kind of like her too. Ah, I think this means you're next. Got any prospects?" He looked obviously at Chris who gave no indication that he heard Terry's reference.

"We'll see." Although Sharon smiled, it seemed to Joanne that she answered very tentatively, especially considering how willingly she had been sharing blankets with Chris during the first half.

~*~

Dave sat at home with Marie and cried openly as he watched Terry propose to his sister on national television. He was the only person who knew. Terry had asked him for permission to marry Joanne before he went to the game. Dave was honored, and his respect for Terry's old-fashioned gesture touched him deeply. He gave his blessing gladly, along with a totally uncharacteristic hug.

"Those two have something pretty special," he said and looked at his wife snuggled next to him. "Red did pretty good, I'd say."

"He is a hunk," Marie added. "There will be more than one woman choking on all those horrible things they used to call her after this. He's doing pretty well too, though. Jo has turned out to be quite a beautiful young woman."

"Comes from her beautiful heart," Dave said.

"And what she has in it," Marie added. "Maybe we should get a little of that ourselves. You can always learn, even at our age."

"Maybe," Dave responded. He had already been thinking the same thing. Now, all he had to do was figure out what it was she had there.

"Lots of morons in this area have always made fun of Jo, and I guess I may have been one of the biggest," Dave said. Marie didn't say a word, and Dave knew why. He also knew to quit while he was ahead.

~*~

Throughout the second half, total strangers waved at Joanne, smiled, and nodded in her direction. Several stopped and congratulated her as they walked by where they were sitting. As much as she loved the Bears, she hardly noticed that they scored two more touchdowns while limiting Minnesota to one. She just kept looking down at her left hand to make sure that the ring was really there. Sharon was right. The diamond was enormous. It was undoubtedly the largest stone Joanne had ever seen.

Joanne didn't remember much about the walk back to the bus after the game either. All she remembered was how tightly she squeezed Terry's hand as they walked together and how happy he looked when she did. He had told her before that he would never do anything in front of a group unless he intended to stick with it, and those words made Joanne shiver as she thought about them. She hardly noticed the wind off Lake Michigan even though the temperature dipped toward zero.

Everyone on the bus stood up and cheered as she climbed up the four short steps in the front of it. Even the gray-haired bus driver gave her a big hug and congratulated her. Joanne couldn't help think how good it felt to have a crowd of people sharing her happiness instead of causing her pain. She turned to Terry and hugged him as they walked to their seats. She couldn't help it. And the passengers in the bus cheered them on.

Somebody from the back shouted, "Speech, speech."

The thought of giving a speech petrified her, but Terry quickly stood up and told everyone that he was the happiest man in the world because the most beautiful woman in the world had agreed to marry him. He called her beautiful in front of a whole bus filled with people, and he said in letters two feet tall that he loved her so a television audience all over the country could see it.

She didn't think she would ever have questions about either her beauty or Terry's love for her again, and that made her feel strong and gave her the courage to stand up and address the group herself as the bus became completely silent.

"I'm not much at making speeches. That's one of the reasons I'm glad I'm marrying somebody who gets paid to make them."

The passengers laughed.

"First of all, thank You, Jesus. If any of you doubt what He can do in your life, talk to me. I am living proof of His grace because I don't deserve any of this. It's a gift from God.

"Second, thank you, Terry. Thanks to you and your fabulous sister, I've seen in the mirror how beautiful God's love can make even a plain woman like me. I don't think I'll ever see plain again, and I think you know what that means." She winked at Terry, and he nodded. "We have an awesome God. Everybody here should remember that when you remember what happened today. To God be the glory!"

~*~

Sharon shouted, "Amen," and several others, including Chris, said "Amen" too as Joanne sat down and leaned her head on Terry's shoulder. The bus started to buzz with excitement again, and Sharon looked at Chris as he looked back at her. She couldn't help it, she gave him a big hug and he repeated softly, "Amen, amen, amen," until Sharon let go of him and laughed almost uncontrollably.

"I've got plenty more." He grinned with that shy, infectious grin of his.

"Save them," she said as she continued to laugh. "We'll come back to those later."

"Hope so."

Sharon put her head on Chris' shoulder as she closed her eyes. He slipped his arm around her, and she patted his arm softly and murmured something that sounded contented.

"Amen," Chris whispered one more time.

Sharon smiled. So did Joanne as she heard Chris' Amen's.

CHAPTER 8

The week following the football game was barely ten minutes long for Terry and Joanne. They became instant local celebrities. Joanne was the beautiful Redheaded Princess and Terry was Prince Charming, a well-known attorney in the area.

And there was much weeping and gnashing of teeth among those who were used to calling Joanne plain, ugly, and all the various other names from the past. There may have even been a garment or two torn down the middle, but fortunately for a lot of people there hadn't been any sackcloth or ashes in the area for years.

Chicago residents had already moved forward. A small story appeared in one of the local Chicago papers about the Love Story at Soldier's Field along with a tightly cropped picture showing Joanne's stunned reaction. A couple of local television stations gave the story a full ten seconds at the end of the five-minute recap of a pretty noncompetitive football game.

But where Joanne and Terry lived in rural Iowa, they were big news. Not as big as the local girls' basketball team making it to the state tournament for the third year in a row, but big compared to almost everything else. All the local newspapers wanted the details of "The Romance of the Century." The local television and radio stations found new ways to provide the same facts night after night for nearly a week.

Terry and Joanne gave interviews individually and together over and over until they didn't think they could answer, "How did you feel when he asked you" and "How did you feel when she said yes," one more time. It was fun, but exhausting.

The attention was commonplace for Terry, even if it made him nervous. He was used to some degree of notoriety as an attorney. Joanne, on the other hand, wasn't, but she took it in stride, blossomed and then bloomed. People finally recognized her, accepted her, smiled at her, waved at her, and frequently went out of their way to give her a big hug.

Every smile, every wave, and every hug gave her confidence, and within a few days, she initiated the smiles, the waves, and the hugs. Each morning when she walked by the mirror in her hallway, she looked at her reflection and liked what she saw more and more. She had become slightly pretty and maybe even beautiful, but more importantly, she felt that way because she knew where it was coming from. *Thank You, Lord,* she said every time she looked.

The compliments and the congratulations continued to come her way from neighbors and friends even after the media frenzy slowed down. Now when people complimented her, Joanne responded simply, "Thank you so much. Praise the Lord." Her response frequently drew a smile and sometimes even a quizzical look, but it was her natural response. There was nothing forced about it.

Even Sandy and Jennifer went out of their way to come across the street the first time they saw Joanne. They hugged her like they were lifelong best friends and begged to see "The Ring," as it had been named locally by one of the weekly papers.

"It's even bigger than it looked on television," Jennifer said with sincere excitement in her voice. "That hunk of yours must really love you."

Joanne liked hearing that, especially from Jennifer. Sandy, on the other hand was reduced to a one-word vocabulary. "Wow!" she said as she looked at it, and she repeated it at least four or five more times.

"I'm glad we're friends now," Jennifer finally said. "Let's really start all over."

"Suits me." Joanne felt as warm inside as her smile looked on her face. "Life is too short and too beautiful to waste on things that aren't good." She was positive that both Jennifer and Sandy were trying so she would too even though it wasn't going to be easy for her. She forced herself to hug them both, and they walked away waving without the slightest hint of the old smirk. Joanne was amazed.

The faces in the church pews had bigger smiles on them when she walked in for morning services on Terry's arm. They seemed happier and more full of welcome than ever before. Sandy and Jennifer didn't flirt, smirk, or sneer at either Joanne or Terry.

They waved like friends wave to each other, like members of small churches do when they acknowledge one of their own. Joanne wondered if she had changed that much or whether she might be seeing for the first time what could have been all along if she had been more open to it.

Perhaps her isolation and feelings of worthlessness had been at least partially her fault. Maybe her mother had been right in a way. She did mess things up, but not because she was bad, but because she was afraid. Maybe it had always been easier for her to mess up and wallow in the self-pity that followed than to dare to succeed and expose herself to a chance at happiness and all its uneven possibilities.

It would always be a struggle for her, and she would never get things totally right, sometimes doing what she didn't want to do, and other times not doing what she wanted to do. It just didn't matter all that much anymore. She had people now, people who cared about her. And she had room for failure and success in her heart because the beauty that was already there was bigger and stronger than any failure or success that could come in from outside.

When it came time for sharing in the service, Terry stood up and asked for the microphone. He was shaking slightly, and Joanne couldn't understand why. They had talked to news reporters of every size, shape, and gender all week, and Terry had always remained calm. Certainly, telling their story one more time couldn't be that frightening.

"As most of you know, I have asked the most beautiful redhead in the world to marry me. She is one of your own, and I thank you for allowing me to share her with you," he began. "Thankfully, she didn't embarrass me in front of a few million of our new best friends on national television last week. She said yes!"

There was a spontaneous applause mixed with laughter at Terry's reference to new best friends.

"Now I have a promise to keep to her. A little more than a month ago Joanne pulled me out of a snowdrift just before I was about to freeze to death. She kept me warm all night, prayed by my side all night, and quite literally saved my life, and I can never thank her enough for that.

"There is nothing I can do to repay that. But she also took something from me that night, and at first I wasn't too happy about it. She stole my heart."

Joanne could feel herself blushing, but thankfully he hadn't mentioned anything about her undressing him. He had worried her for a second.

"She returned my heart, however, and when I got it back, it was different. It was crammed full of her love for me and her love for Jesus Christ. I wasn't sure I knew what to do with either of them. I've always gone to church, and I've always known Jesus casually. But when I got my heart back, I knew casual wasn't good enough. Joanne always thought she was a plain woman, even unattractive."

Thank you, Terry. That sounds so much better than ugly.

"Frankly, I always thought she was beautiful, but she said she couldn't see it, just like I said I couldn't see why casual wasn't good enough for Jesus. I told her when she could admit how beautiful she was, I would stand up here and give my life to Jesus, not just casually, but completely."

Joanne had forgotten about that conversation during the whirlwind of the week, but she remembered it well now. She also remembered how differently she felt when she looked at herself in the mirror. The two thoughts collided like a warm front and a cold front in her soul, and the rain that came from it were the tears from her heart.

"Well folks, do you see how beautiful our little redhead is? Do you?"

"Yes," a voice from the other side of the church said, "I sure do."

"Me too," a second voice said.

When all eyes turned to the source of the voices, Jennifer and Sandy were standing, looking at Joanne.

"She's the big red beautiful," they said almost in unison.

"Amen," came the responses from almost everywhere in a church where the word amen was usually only heard at the end of formal prayers and at the end of grace for church dinners.

"Do you see it?" Terry asked, looking down at Joanne, who had tears streaming down her face, "because all these people can't be wrong."

Reluctantly, Joanne nodded and said, "Yes."

"So do I, but then, I've always seen it." Terry took a long, deep breath and wiped his eyes with the back of his hand. "Then, since you see it, I don't want Jesus casually anymore. I want him to be my best friend, and I give my life and our lives together to him completely as I promised you I would." He looked up at the cross in the front of the church and held his arms open wide. "Here I am Lord. I'm Yours."

Joanne stood up next to Terry and hugged him furiously.

"This is even better than last week," she whispered to him. "Thank you Terry, and thank You, Jesus."

The chorus of Amen's that followed should have ended it, but they didn't. There was one more egg to drop out of the carton. Before Terry could hand the microphone back to the pastor, someone reached over his shoulder and pulled it from his hand. Terry turned and saw Dave holding the microphone.

"I can't top that. I won't even try," Dave said. "But if Jesus is that important to you two, I want Him too. Sis, if you'll show me how, I'll give my life to Him too, right here, right now. Looking at you two, even I can see He's real." He looked at Sharon, and she put her hand over her mouth as tears came to her eyes.

Joanne couldn't believe what she was seeing and hearing. Terry had been one thing. Jennifer and Sandy had been two more people who had touched her heart deeply, but Dave? Her brother Dave? Her heart nearly exploded as she put her arms around his neck and hugged him.

"You just did it, all by yourself, big brother. I don't need to show you anything. You told me once that Dad would be proud of me, and that meant a lot to me. I'm telling you that Dad is proud of you and your heavenly Dad is too. I love you, big brother."

Terry handed the microphone back to the pastor, who was standing a little misty eyed himself in the aisle. Terry gave Dave a hug, and Joanne, Dave, and he sat down in the pew.

"We're on a roll here, folks. Anybody else?" he asked, looking around. When nobody held up his or her hand, he said, smiling,

"Well, there's always next week. Let's pray."

The pastor prayed, the service continued, and afterward the fellowship area buzzed. People mingled and talked even more than usual.

Joanne went to Jennifer and Sandy first, and she didn't have to strain to hug them this time.

"That was one of the nicest things anyone has ever done for me. Thank you so much. I really mean it. This friendship thing is going to work out just fine. I wasn't sure at first, but I am now." Joanne could hardly hold back the tears.

"We owed you, big time," Sandy said. She was usually the quiet one, but she had been the first one to stand up in church.

"Consider whatever debt you think you owed paid in full," Joanne said. "Let's get together this week for lunch. You set the time, and I'll buy."

"We'd like that," Sandy said. "How about noon Tuesday at the café down the street?"

Joanne nodded. "I'll be there."

The small town congregation had never been a very demonstrative group before that Sunday, and perhaps it would never be quite that way again. But for that Sunday, it was, and there was an unspoken feeling among those who were there that a sweet spirit had been released that would be hard to hold back in the future.

CHAPTER 9

Fugue-Sharon's Song

Sharon watched quietly with Chris by her side. Tears streaked down her cheeks as waves of emotion rolled through her like the waves rolled in off Lake Michigan only a week ago. One wave would smooth out, and something someone said or the way someone looked would cause another wave to well up inside her and roll fresh wetness down her cheeks.

Controlling her tears was futile, and, in a way they needed to be released, understood and dealt with. They just couldn't remain pooled up inside her anymore.

Only a short time ago when she barely got to the truck stop during the blizzard, it hadn't occurred to her how hopeless her prayer was when she asked God to go get her brother. She just asked God for help, believing he would provide it.

And God sent the best he had: a small, insecure redheaded woman who locals called plain and ugly, a part time bookkeeper and an errand girl who had no emergency rescue training and no college degree. All she had was a snowmobile, a silver snowmobile suit and helmet, a coil of rope, several blankets, and a willing heart. She didn't believe in herself, but she trusted God, and when He called her to go out into the storm for Him, she went. Just like David went when God called him to meet Goliath.

"It was no big deal." That's what she told everyone. But so far, Sharon's prayer and Joanne's "no big deal" faithfulness had significantly affected the lives of Terry, Dave, Sandy, Jennifer, the entire congregation of the small rural Iowa church, not to mention Joanne herself. Terry's proclamation of love for her on national television went to millions of people, but she gave the glory to God on the bus afterward.

And Sharon might have been impacted most of all because she knew that God wasn't even close to being done with Joanne yet, and she also knew that God might be coming for her next. In fact, Sharon knew He was, as excitement mingled with fear in the pit of her stomach, along with the realization that she was the only one left between she and her brother. The only questions were how and when would God come?

After the service Sharon found her brother and told him how proud she was of him. Dave, on the other hand, found Sharon before she found him. The eyes that had looked so tired when she first met them at the truck stop were fresh and alive, flashing like lightning on a moonless night. He threw his big arms around her and almost crushed her. His embrace petrified her for a moment.

That kind of strength held her once before, and she would never forget it. Dave seemed to realize he had caught her by surprise and released her.

"Sorry," he said, sheepishly, "guess I got carried away."

Sharon took a deep breath and forced a smile. He meant no harm. "That's okay. I just wasn't ready for you. I'm really happy for you, and proud. I always knew you weren't an atheist."

His eyes flashed again, and they were younger eyes now. "Thanks. You deserve a lot of the credit here. You're the one who got me into this church thing to begin with."

"God got you into it. I was just the messenger," Sharon responded. "Give the credit to God, not me."

"Okay, I will." He nodded. "But I'm still glad I ran into you that night."

"Thanks. I'm glad you did too, but don't forget that you're the one that offered to help. You made the phone call. You're the only one that had a sister in the area. It was all part of God's plan, and you responded to it." Sharon touched him on the shoulder and smiled.

"I never thought of it that way." Dave rubbed his chin. "That is pretty amazing. Thanks."

"You're welcome."

"Take care of yourself. I have a feeling we will be seeing a lot more of each other in the future now that we're practically family." He turned and walked over to his wife who was still beaming as she looked at him.

Sharon looked at Chris, who was standing with a quiet patience next to her, and he smiled gently at her.

"You know, you don't ever give yourself credit for anything," Chris said, appraising her. "Every time someone tries to give you a compliment, you deflect it. When you should be happy, you almost seem sad."

"All the credit for everything belongs to God," Sharon responded, almost defensively.

"I know that, but don't you think God wants you to be happy? Don't you think a woman like you deserves to be happy?" His words were intense, but everything else about him was so gentle.

"What kind of woman do you think I am?" Sharon asked, almost softly. There was no coyness or flirtatiousness in her voice. She wasn't fishing for a compliment. Her question had the same ring of sadness that Chris had referred to moments before, and she didn't really mean for Chris to respond to it.

"I think you are an incredibly beautiful woman both inside and out who deserves to be happy," Chris said simply. He looked her in the eyes as he spoke. "I'm sure you know how beautiful you are on the outside, but I'm not so sure you know how beautiful you are inside, and that makes me sad."

The genuineness of his words soothed and hurt at the same time. All men liked the way she looked, and Chris was no different, but she almost shook from the inside out when she saw in his eyes how deeply he cared, and her concern that God might be coming to her next intensified.

Feelings similar to those she had for Chris had gotten her into trouble once before, but these feelings were even deeper, more confusing and downright terrifying. This time they felt so real, so right, but they had before too, and she had been so wrong. Giving into feelings like that again was going to be difficult, if not impossible.

Sharon remembered her promise to God when He gave her new

direction in the past. Her gifts, including her beauty would only be used for his honor and glory. Using them for anything else was selfish…and dangerous, not to mention petrifying.

Hesitant, unsteady words finally came out. "I'm not sure you see the real me, Chris, but that's an awfully sweet thing for you to say."

"You can't tell me that you don't notice how men look at you, and you can't tell me that you don't know how great you always look."

"Sure I notice," Sharon said, and then she stopped herself. "I'm sorry that sounds a little conceited." She lowered her gaze to the ground and couldn't look at him.

"No, it sounds honest." Chris wouldn't back down, and he dipped his head so he could look at her. "You are a beautiful woman, Sharon. It would be more conceited to try to convince others you don't know that. False modesty is never all that attractive. Your great looks are part of the real you. So is the beauty inside you that you don't want to accept. Somebody needs to help you come to grips with that if you can't do it yourself."

"Got anybody in mind?" Sharon raised her eyes and grinned almost losing her breath when she saw how close he was. She was flirting with Chris, and she hadn't let herself do that for a long time. Why did this genuinely complex, but self-described simple truck driver do that to her? Why was God allowing it? She had promised God she wouldn't do this again, but she couldn't seem to keep that promise when she was around Chris.

"What do you think?" Chris said, and then he turned slightly red, as he stopped himself. "I forget myself sometimes. I'm just…"

"A truck driver?"

"Yeah, I'm sorry."

"Well, don't be, and now who's being falsely modest?" Sharon looked at him with challenge in her eyes. "You asked me what I thought. I'll tell you what I think. I think I do need someone to help me, and I'm open…"

"Hey you two." Joanne bounced into the middle of their discussion, and they simultaneously took a half step back from each other. "Pretty awesome church service today, wasn't it? I hope I didn't interrupt anything." Her glance took them both in at once.

"No, you didn't." Chris gave Sharon a look that told her he

wanted to continue the discussion. "Sharon and I were just talking. Nothing we can't take up later."

"Terry and I have this Sunday tradition," Joanne continued, oblivious to the slightly exasperated stares she was getting from Sharon. "We go to my house and make grilled cheese sandwiches and tomato soup for lunch and watch the Bears game. Playoffs start today. You guys want to join us?"

"Okay with me," Sharon said, as she looked at Chris and shrugged. "Sounds like fun."

"I'm up for it." Chris couldn't help but show some of the excitement he felt inside at that moment. He put his hands together and rubbed them.

Sharon tried to focus her scrambled thoughts and calm the heart palpitations that threatened to give her away. "Should we bring anything? It would have to be something we could pick up on the way."

"Nope. I have a special Lowry family recipe for the soup. It's called a la can. See you in about half an hour or so."

"Sure." She and Chris had a discussion to complete. In spite of her inner turmoil, the thought of another simple, relaxed afternoon with Chris sounded good to Sharon. He was the kindest person she had ever known, the exact opposite of the high profile men she used to go out with in college. He was obviously interested in her, but he had always been a complete gentleman. He had held her hand and hugged her without expecting more. What a refreshing change!

~*~

Men fell all over Sharon, and she had dated some in the past who were totally gorgeous and some who were not quite as gorgeous. Getting a date had never been a problem. The problem came at the end of the evening when almost all of them expected more than they were entitled to expect.

She flirted with them, kissed a lot of them and even got more passionate with a few, but she had a line, and she never crossed it. Never. Until one night.

A smooth talking star football player at her medium sized college asked her out, and it wasn't long before they became an item. In spite of several bad habits he had, Sharon thought he might be "The One" and convinced herself she could smooth out his rough edges. They were a perfect couple in many people's eyes, an outstanding athlete destined for the Pros and one of the most attractive women on campus.

After a football party to celebrate winning the conference championship, and almost before she realized it, Sharon found herself on the wrong side of his bedroom door. When he shut the door and looked at her, she knew immediately where he was headed, and it was for her and the bed behind them. She tried to stop him, but he kept coming toward her.

"Come on, baby," he said. "You know you want to. We have something special going on." He grabbed her with his incredibly strong hands and refused to let her go. Truthfully, Sharon did have strong feelings for him, but the way he put it sounded so crude to her and suddenly, so did he. She knew better, and she knew this was wrong.

"No, I don't want to," she said firmly. "Not now. Not like this. Maybe not ever. Please let me go."

He laughed. She cried, begged, and tried to fight, but he easily overpowered her with those big, strong, ugly and totally frightening hands that held her down. She could still see them in the darkness, feel them tearing her clothes from her body just enough to see what he wanted to see and do what he wanted to do.

He didn't even care about taking them off and making love to her tenderly. He just took what he wanted and held her there against her will until morning when she finally managed to slip out of his room as he slept. She remembered wrapping her coat around herself to go back to her apartment.

The early morning sky that day had been far too beautiful, the air smelled too fresh, and the birds sang too cheerfully, but she somehow managed to stumble back with her clothes and her dignity hanging from her in shreds. Nothing was as ugly as it should have been, and nothing was as ugly as she felt. It should have been an ugly and vile day.

Her roommate took her to the student clinic immediately and insisted on filing a report with school officials. The hospital was required to do the same thing. She followed the required procedures, just as directed, and did everything she was supposed to do.

But even after the reports had been filed, her attacker bragged to his teammates about what he had done. When campus authorities questioned him, he said it was consensual. Maybe it had gotten a little rough, but that's what she wanted, he said. He told them he didn't do anything wrong.

Sharon told authorities that she had not consented, but she knew that she should have never been where she was to begin with, and her denials were full of insecurity and guilt as she told her story to the campus police, the school administrators, and the local town police officer that interviewed her.

He said it was consensual. She said it wasn't. He had more touchdowns than any other player in school history and was certain to be drafted by a professional team. She hadn't scored any touchdowns and had no pro prospects to ruin. Only her life.

He brought the school money, notoriety, and better athletes for future teams. She brought them a potential scandal. He was not allowed to start for his last home game as punishment, and she was allowed to transfer to another school where she could punish herself.

Looking into the mirror to brush her hair or put on makeup made her cry; her own reflection looked back at her with shame in its eyes and accused her. It was her fault. Even the police and college officials hinted at that. It was painful just to throw on clothes and drag herself to class and back to her apartment to study. Nothing else interested her. Nothing else mattered any more.

Her former roommate tried to keep in touch for a while, but the shame accumulated in her more and more each day, and the good intentions of her roommate were ignored, emails were deleted, letters returned, and phone calls avoided. School counselors were no help, nothing was.

Forgiveness wasn't hers to give to herself even though counselors said it was. Healing strength didn't lie deep down inside her, and taking charge of her own life, like the counselors told her to do, was impossible.

Sharon almost gave up.

Then one night a woman showed up at her apartment with a broad smile on her face and a Bible in her hand. Sharon hadn't been expecting anybody, so she was apprehensive when she opened her front door with the chain lock still in place and peered through the small opening between the door and the doorframe.

"Hi," the woman said. "My name's Sally Burns. I go to Riverview Church and am a licensed social worker at an agency it sponsors. Your name was referred to us by the university counseling center as someone we might be able to help. Judy is a friend of mine there, and she said they didn't seem to be helping you much. Would you care to talk?"

"Oh, I don't know. I've heard it all," Sharon remembered saying. "You're just wasting your time."

"How about letting me pray with you then? Just a prayer, then I'll leave you alone. We can pray right here if that's what you want."

"No need to do that." Sharon remembered the look on Sally's face and the words Holy Bible below it. "Come on in; just don't pay any attention to what a mess my apartment is right now."

"Don't worry about that," Sally said, smiling. Sharon opened the door and let Sally in. They sat down at the kitchen table, and Sally immediately bowed her head and reached over to put her hands on Sharon's.

"Lord, we don't always understand why things happen to us the way that they do, but help us to see that You love us and will help us no matter what has happened," Sally prayed. "Let Sharon know that You, and only You can heal her the way that she needs to be healed right now, but that all of us who have gone through what she has are here to listen and support her. Start the healing right here if that is Your will. Amen."

"Were you…?" Sharon began.

"Yes." Sally responded. "I was. I know what you are going through because I've been there, but with God's help, I'm getting better every day. He has been so faithful, and He can be the same way for you too if you'll trust Him." Her words were confident, but soft, soothing. "You can't fix all the things that hurt inside you, but He can, and He will."

"Would you like a cup of tea?" Sharon asked, and she began crying like she had never let herself cry before.

"Cry first," Sally said. "Get as much out as you can. Then I'd love a cup of tea."

The healing began that night. It was still not completed. Sally warned Sharon repeatedly that the process would take time and that it might never be over completely, but it would get better and become more manageable, if nothing else.

With Sally's help, Sharon recommitted her life to God, and her heart started to reopen almost immediately. Sometimes Sally talked, and Sharon listened. Sometimes they reversed roles.

Sally told Sharon that God had made her beautiful for a reason, and that she shouldn't hide her beauty or be ashamed of it. Chris had just told her the same thing, and he didn't know about her past. Sally suggested that Sharon use her beauty for God's glory and trust that He would show her what He wanted her to do with the gift of beauty He had given her.

At first, that was hard for Sharon to accept. It was her beauty that had caused all the problems. It hadn't been beauty that killed the beast; it was beauty that created him. She had enjoyed flirting, and she was good at it. She liked the way men looked at her because it made her feel good. How could something that worldly be used for God's glory?

But it was exactly that beauty that caught the eye of one of her brother's clients at lunch one day. When he learned that she had a marketing and public relations degree, he asked her if she wanted to interview for a job he had open.

Terry insisted that she give it a try. Josh Trammel was a good client of his, he told Sharon, and had a thriving business that was expanding rapidly. He was also a good man.

"Too bad Josh is happily married," Terry said, winking at his sister, "I'd fix you two up. Sorry to be the bearer of that bad news."

Actually, it was that news that convinced Sharon to interview for the job. If he was happily married, and a client of her brother's, he might not threaten her. He was safe or as safe as any man could be.

Sally also encouraged Sharon to interview so she did. She was offered the job on the spot even though there were two more interviews scheduled. Josh told his assistant to tell the people that he was sorry, but the position had been filled.

Taking the job meant she would be moving away from the immediate area and Sally, who had been her rock. Sharon felt queasy about that, but they agreed to get together at least once a month, by phone, and email if nothing else.

Josh was impressed with Sharon immediately, and everyone in his office noticed her the minute she started the job. Her confidence returned slowly, and meeting people again didn't frighten her nearly as much. She also allowed herself to become beautiful again, and people could see it, mostly men, but not exclusively. Business expanded even more rapidly at Trammel Inc. due to the addition of Sharon.

Josh and his wife were active members of their local church and committed Christians. In fact, Josh told her that she had impressed him at the interview because of her references to the grace and goodness of God and the support Jesus gave her in her life. Her references had convinced him to hire her on the spot, something he had never done before.

Her comments had just come naturally in the interview; she forgot she said them. Josh told her that's what impressed him the most; they weren't forced, and they came from her heart.

Only months after she started there, Josh offered her both a raise and a "new opportunity," as he put it.

"I can't afford to lose the work you're doing," he said, smiling in her office late one afternoon, "but I'd be willing to hire you an assistant to take on some of your duties under your supervision if you want to help me develop a project I've been thinking about for a long time."

"I'm interested," Sharon said simply. "What is it?"

"Part of your job would be to help me flesh *it* out," Josh said. "The Lord has blessed me more than I could ever have imagined at such a young age. To be blunt, I'm making bucket loads of money here. I want to give some back.

"I don't need nearly as much as I'm making. I've always had this half-baked idea to form some sort of Christian business organization. It's not a new idea, but I want to explore doing new, radical and totally Christian things by combining with other Christian businessmen."

"Sort of like a Christian Chamber of Commerce?" Sharon asked.

"Maybe," Josh mused. "But not so local and not focused on promoting business for business sake, but as a means to fund God's work. That's where you come in. I don't mean to be demeaning or crass here, but you are a very enthusiastic, intelligent woman who also looks very good."

Sharon felt the heat rising in her cheeks and a slight fear in the center of her stomach. "Thank you."

"You're welcome, and let me assure you, this isn't a come on," Josh said, smiling. "I think you are the perfect person to develop this concept for all the reasons I just stated."

"But I'm so new," Sharon protested.

"Exactly!" Josh said. "That's another reason you're perfect. You haven't been jaded and tainted yet. I want fresh. You can think fresh because you are fresh. No business baggage, no reluctance to try something because we've never done it that way before. What do you say? You want to give it a shot?"

"You're the boss. If that's what you want, that's what I'll do."

"I'm the overall boss, but you'd be the boss of this project. You'd report through normal channels on your other duties but only to me on this special project. Maybe it won't go anywhere, but maybe it will. Come back to me in a week and show me where you are on this, okay?"

"Okay," Sharon said. "And Josh, thanks. This is exciting."

He grinned and nodded. "I figured you'd see it that way."

~*~

That was nearly two years ago. The job and the special project had been an answer to prayer. Since then she had taken very little time off and kept herself fully occupied developing the new project and overseeing her regular duties. She now had two assistants to supervise as well. Sharon appeared to have it all, but she still had a lot of healing to do.

That's why Joanne had been such a blessing. Whether she knew it or not, Joanne had helped Sharon almost more than Sharon had helped her.

As Sharon helped Joanne look inside and come out of her shell, she had been forced to do the same thing. Sharon had full confidence in her natural attributes, but she had a total lack of inner confidence just like Joanne did. They had both been abused in different ways, and so they were both damaged and in need of repair.

Joanne broke out of her internal cocoon and fell in love with Terry. They gave their lives to the Lord as a couple and began planning a wedding. Sharon's example and words of encouragement gave Joanne the courage to believe that she could ask God for the nerve to do anything.

However, as much as the job with Josh had temporarily filled her life, Sharon's deepest desire was to have what Joanne had found, a lasting love and a normal life. She had helped Joanne; why couldn't she help herself?

Those strong, heavy hands still held her down in the darkness no matter how much she cried and begged them to let her go. The nauseating smell of stale beer on his breath still choked her, and the mirror still reminded her she shouldn't have allowed herself to get into that position in the first place. But he shouldn't have done what he did. Nobody has a right to do that. And he got away with it, which made it worse.

Chris sat next to her as they rode down the country road to Sharon's house, and even though he sat securely buckled in the passenger's seat, he was already too close. Until she could free herself from those heavy hands holding her down in the darkness, she couldn't allow Chris' gentle hands to hold her up, and she knew more and more every moment she was near him, that she really wanted them to.

It wasn't that she needed a man to be whole. Men had nothing to do with what she needed and wanted. Chris, on the other hand, was different, and she still wasn't exactly sure why.

CHAPTER 10

Joanne and Sharon chatted like they had been sisters all their lives as they buttered the bread for the grilled cheese sandwiches. They were different in so many ways, but they had connected with each other the first time they met. Something deep within both of them hurt the same way then. Sharon felt it. Now, something deep within both of them had started to heal in the same way, and this new connection was even stronger.

Terry and Chris finished stirring the soup and set it aside with the lid on the pan to keep it warm. They went into the living room and turned on the television as Joanne and Sharon purposefully took their time with the sandwiches so they could talk.

"So what's going on with you and Chris?" Joanne asked. "And don't tell me nothing because I have eyes, and I'm not buying it."

Sharon buttered a sandwich she had already buttered once and never took her eyes off it as she concentrated on spreading the butter more evenly thinking about her response.

"What do your eyes see?" Sharon finally asked, grinning slightly.

"My eyes see two people who would be awfully good for each other but seem to be afraid to do anything but nibble around the edges." Joanne looked directly at Sharon. "Chris is a great guy. I've known him forever."

"Did you ever go out with him?" Sharon asked.

Joanne couldn't help smiling. "Your brother asked me the same thing. No. I might have if he had ever asked, but it would have been almost like dating my brother. In some ways he was more of a brother to me than my own brothers were. At least he never made fun of me. Besides, he was always sure he was supposed to date

Cindy."

"Who was Cindy?"

"She was buddies with Jennifer and Sandy, and just like they were in high school most of the time."

Sharon tried to sound casual. "What happened to her?"

"Chris married her right after high school even though I begged him not to. They just weren't right for each other, but he couldn't see it. Chris wanted a family, even then. He came from a big family, but they are all dead or living somewhere else now. He was incredibly lonely, but he was never in love with her. It was more like he was in love with the idea of being in love."

Sharon tried to hide her disappointment. "So, he was married?"

"Only briefly. Cindy took off with some guy before they even celebrated their first wedding anniversary and never looked back. Chris used to pour his heart out to me about that. He sent her letters and tried to call her, but she never responded. One day the divorce papers came in the mail from Texas. She didn't even call him to tell him about them.

"He refused to sign them, but about six months later he got papers saying the divorce was final because he hadn't disputed it. Default judgment or something like that. I don't remember. Anyway, I think he was actually relieved when it was finally over."

"Why do you think he never loved her?"

"Because you and I both know that women just know stuff like that." Joanne looked at Sharon, smiling smugly.

"Maybe some women do." Sharon looked away. "I wasn't very good at it."

"Let's put it this way, then. I never saw Chris look at Cindy or anyone else, for that matter, the way he looks at you. But then I'm sure you're so used to having men fall all over you, you probably don't even notice the looks they give you," Joanne said, grinning.

"I notice." Sharon managed to force a faint smile, but her voice was weak. "I didn't always, but I do now. It isn't as great all the time as you might think."

"Well. I wouldn't know; I've never had that problem." Joanne took the sandwiches out of the skillet and piled them on a plate. "Do you know how you look when you gaze back at him?"

"I know how I feel when I do." Sharon looked back at Joanne. "I feel his gentleness, his kindness, and his warmth. I felt it the first time I talked to him. It was the night you rescued Terry. He got a whole group of his trucker buddies together to pray with me, and somehow, almost instantly, I knew that everything would be all right, and it was. I've known quite a few incredibly handsome men in my short life, but when I met him, I met a beautiful man."

"There's that look again." Joanne touched Sharon's arm. "You're giving me goose bumps. Does he know how you feel?"

"I don't know." Sharon covered Joanne's hand with her own. "I'm not blind. I can tell that he likes me, but lots of men like me for the way I look."

"Wrong! All men like you for the way you look!"

"Well, whatever." Sharon smiled at Joanne's teasing. "I have to have more than that, much more. I've been down that other road, and I'm not going again. It almost killed me the first time."

Sharon could see Joanne shudder when she said that, and she wanted to drop the entire discussion. Joanne didn't let her do that. "I can feel how much you've been hurt. I know what hurt is, and I'm so sorry. I'll pray for your hurt to go away."

"Thanks, Jo. You're probably the best thing that has happened to me in a long time. I'm convinced that God sent you to me as well as Terry. You have been such a blessing when I really needed one."

Joanne looked stunned. "I'm a blessing to you? I would never have bought the little blue dress if it weren't for you nor had the nerve to wear it. I would probably have backed out on that first date with your brother if you hadn't been there to encourage me. And, I almost said 'no' at the football game when Terry asked me to marry him. I was so flustered. But you whispered in my ear and helped me clear my head. You're the blessing. You will never know how much you've helped me. Can you believe I almost said 'no'?"

Sharon loved Joanne for her wide-eyed ramblings like this. Who wouldn't? "Then we've helped each other, and I still need lots more." Sharon felt a tear run down her cheek as Joanne watched. She felt so vulnerable, yet safe talking to Joanne. She flipped the final two sandwiches over in the skillet, and Joanne reached over and hugged her.

"We'll help each other," Joanne said softly. "It's what God wants his family members to do."

Sharon turned from the skillet holding the flipper in her hand and hugged Joanne back. “Thanks. All of a sudden I’m hungry. Let’s eat.”

“That’s how this tradition got started,” Joanne grinned. “I cried, Terry hugged me, and I got hungry.”

“For grilled cheese sandwiches?” Sharon winked.

“Sharon. You’re naughty, and I’m not going to answer that.”

Joanne grinned and turned toward the living room. “Hey you two, it’s time to eat.” Then she turned back to Sharon and winked. “Okay, soup and sandwiches were two of the things I got hungry for.”

Chris and Terry came out to the table quickly. Evidently they were hungry too.

“Why don’t we take our soup and sandwiches into the other room and eat them so we can watch the kick off?” Terry suggested. Everyone agreed, so they all moved into the other room just in time for the kick off.

The Bears dominated the Eagles in the first half and led by 17 points at half time. By that time, the tomato soup was gone, and only half a sandwich remained. Sharon nibbled on the last homemade brownie and looked at Chris for a moment.

“So, what’s it like driving a big truck all around the country?” she asked.

“I enjoy it. I meet a lot of interesting people. Some are nice; some are not so nice. Some smell like blankets even a horse wouldn’t wear, and others are pretty normal. Most of us have a full set of teeth, but there are some who bring the average down.”

Everybody laughed as Chris put his lips over his teeth to demonstrate. He was having a little fun at Sharon’s expense, but his descriptions were so clever that Sharon didn’t really mind.

“I get to drive around all day listening to music and watching the countryside. You can’t really appreciate how big and varied this country of ours is until you drive through it. Flying above it in a commercial jet doesn’t do it justice,” Chris said. “The main thing is I’m seldom bored. I’d never last in an office. I need more variety.”

“You ought to come to my office,” Terry said. “There’s all kinds of variety and never a dull moment.”

“Somehow I don’t think a simple truck driver like me would be much good to you unless you needed to ship something somewhere," Chris said, smiling at Terry.

"I'm not buying the simple routine anymore." Sharon looked at Chris with those same challenging eyes she had flashed at him earlier and smiled. "I think you've got a lot more going on than the good old boy 'aw shucks' act you try to play."

"Busted." Joanne teased. "You might as well give it up, Chris. Sharon sees right through you, just like all of us who know you do. You have lots of interests, are very well read, and are not nearly as simple as you try to make people think you are."

"Simple's okay." Sharon hadn't taken her gaze off of him. "As long as it's honest."

"Well, Joanne's right, I do like lots of different things." Chris looked back at Sharon holding his gaze on hers. "That includes some fairly nonstandard trucker things, but I also love to drive. It's just fun to me. Have you ever ridden in a big rig?"

"Never."

"Want to?"

"I'd love to." Their words bounced back and forth just like their gazes challenged each other, and before Sharon realized it, she let her words run away with her mouth even though she hadn't meant to.

"I'm going out to Omaha and back, Thursday." Chris responded quickly. "Full load out and deadhead back. If you want to ride along, I'd love to have your company. You could find out what it's like for yourself. It could be a pretty long day depending on how long it takes getting to the dock in Omaha, but like I said, the company would be great."

Sharon shuddered a little thinking about the trip. Even though he intrigued her and she blinked first in their contest of words, riding with Chris would mean she would be alone with him all day. She trusted Chris, but the thought of being alone with him all day scared her. And it excited her.

"Sounds interesting," Sharon managed to say. "I'll have to check on a few things at work and get back to you. What do I wear if I decide to go along?" Sharon hated to sound shallow, but she didn't have a lot of casual clothes. Plus she needed to stall and have more time to think.

"Most of the guys would probably like you to wear basic black, heels, and pearls," Chris said with a huge grin, "but don't, because my tux is at the cleaners. I'll probably be wearing my second best outfit that will involve some sort of exotic flannel and denim."

Sharon had to laugh. She realized how dumb her question must have sounded. It was a truck ride to a loading dock in Omaha and back. What difference did it make what she wore?

"Will you be wearing that cute green cap with the feed logo on the front?" she asked.

"I'll have to." He grinned. "My top hat doesn't go with any of my denim outfits. Seriously, you'll look good in anything casual. It's just a truck ride."

Sharon appreciated the compliment even though she was used to getting them. Chris had a way of saying things casually and gently, and his comments always made her feel relaxed.

"Thanks," she said. "Can I give you a call tomorrow?"

"You can do that," Chris said, "or, you can just drop by after five and tell me. I'll throw together a salad, fix some pasta and red sauce, and find something simple for dessert. I'm not a bad cook. Must be the Sicilian in me from way back. Joanne and Terry, why don't you come over too? I haven't made dinner for anybody but myself for a long time."

"I could be there by six or a little after, assuming you live around here," Terry said.

"On the edge of town, back about six miles. We drove right past it coming here."

"No problem for me, then. I could pick you girls up on my way."

Joanne looked over at Sharon and grinned.

"Did my fiancé just call someone girls?" Joanne asked with mock indignation. "You can pick this woman up, but I don't know what girls you are talking about."

"Actually, I'm going to be over this way on business. Sometimes my boss lets his girls drive around all by our self," Sharon said, piling on. "He thinks we're all grown up. I don't know where he ever got such a crazy idea. I'll just meet you two there, if my silly little blonde girl head can remember how to get there. If I get lost, I'll just ask some big, smart man for directions."

Terry frowned. "You going to help me out here, Chris?"

"Don't think so, Terry. I like you, but you're on your own here."

"Told you that you weren't all that simple," Sharon said, slapping Chris' arm playfully. "Good call." She realized almost immediately that this was the first time in two years that she had purposefully touched a man besides her brother in anything resembling an affectionate manner. Snuggling with Chris at the game and on the bus had been "incidental contact" by definition.

"What can we bring?" Joanne asked.

"Nothing," Chris said quickly. "I've got everything I need."

"I would really like to bring something," Sharon insisted, challenging him with her eyes again.

"Fine," Chris said. He wasn't about to lose at this point. "Bring an apron and your great sparkly eyes a little early, and you can help me get things ready."

Sharon gave Joanne a quick, panic-stricken glance. Joanne raised her eyebrow like she was saying, "What's the problem? You'll be fine," so after three imaginary deep breaths, she looked back at Chris. "I'll get there as soon as I can."

"Great! We're on, then."

The four of them settled back to watch the second half. The Bears, in Bear-like fashion, squandered their large halftime lead, and the Eagles pulled ahead by one point with less than a minute and a half to go. The Bears used a no huddle offense to bring the ball back down to the Eagles' 27-yard line where the quarterback grounded the ball intentionally to stop the clock with three seconds remaining.

With the wind swirling off of Lake Michigan as usual, the Bears' field goal kicker lined up the desperation field goal attempt, and the ball was snapped. The holder took the snap, placed the ball on the ground, and spun the laces, as the kicker drove the ball off the side of his foot.

The crowd went completely silent as the ball drifted, drifted, and drifted to the right. It grazed the right upright and bounced through the middle of the goal posts for three points. The Bears won by two points as the clock expired. It should never have come down to that final kick.

The crowd in the stadium went crazy, and so did the crowd in Joanne's little farmhouse. Joanne, Terry, Sharon and Chris jumped up and down screaming and dancing in circles. They gave each other high fives and low fives, hugging each other like it was New Year's Eve, first as a group and then as two couples. When Sharon realized she was hugging Chris and that he was hugging her back, fear surged through her.

Chris apparently sensed the fear and let go as he looked into Sharon's eyes with a gentle, almost apologetic smile. His smile calmed the panic inside her, and she realized that even though she had been afraid, and even though he had released her, she hadn't let go of him. More importantly, she didn't want to.

"Who told you to let go?" Her eyes returned his gentle smile. "I'm not done celebrating yet." He put his arms around her again and held her, pulling her even closer to him than he had before. "That's better." Her smile added a "thank you," and even though she was still scared, it felt right for Chris to hold her, and it felt good.

"That's nice," her words finally whispered, softly and simply.

"My pleasure," Chris responded just as softly, "and I mean that."

~*~

Sharon walked up to the front door of Chris' small house the next day a little before five o'clock. It could have been earlier, but she had been driving around aimlessly for a while trying to convince herself that she could do this. She imagined his arms still wrapped around her, and she couldn't get the mixture of warmth and gentle strength out of her mind, but she couldn't get the feeling of fear out of the pit of her stomach either.

She couldn't decide if she was afraid that Chris would hug her again especially when they were alone, or even more afraid that he wouldn't. The dark dreams that had haunted her almost every night for the last two years were becoming less and less frequent and significantly less vivid. New dreams replaced them, dreams with light in them, happy faces, and truck rides to Omaha. She wanted to take that trip with Chris.

It was time.

Sally confirmed that when Sharon talked to her about what was going on and promised to pray for her safety. Having lost herself somewhere between fear and recovery, Sally's assurance was exactly what Sharon needed to find herself again. Having dinner with Chris, her brother and Joanne tonight wouldn't hurt either.

Beautiful classical violin music floated from inside the house as Sharon raised her hand to knock on the front door. It froze her there for a few moments with a sweet melody that filled her ears and threatened to spill over into her soul. She closed her eyes and imagined the master violinist stroke the bow smoothly over the strings. Softly, gently, and full of love—as if it were just for her. That's one of the things Sharon loved about classical music. It was personal if you let it be that way.

Sharon knocked on the door, and after a few minutes and some scurrying inside the house, Chris opened the door, but the music was gone.

"Hey, good to see you again. Are you ready to cook?"

There was a time in her life when Sharon would have never let a straight line like that get away, but she let it pass this time. Things were different now, but around Chris they were only slightly different and in a good way.

"That's why I'm here," she said simply. "I heard the most wonderful music when I came up to your door. What happened to it?"

"You liked it?"

"I adored it."

Chris hesitated for a minute and then asked, "What did you like about it?"

Sharon didn't have to think about her answer. "It was almost as if it were written especially for me. It spoke to my heart if that isn't too corny." Unconsciously, she touched her heart with her hand, spreading her fingers so that the crimson red blouse shown between them. "But it was so personal, so incredibly beautiful, and maybe even a little sad."

"You're saying it reminded you of yourself a little then?" There was no shyness in his eyes like in the past, no challenge, only an ageless, almost loving gaze. "I didn't even realize you could hear the music clear out here. I guess I must have had things cranked up a little too high."

"It didn't really seem loud to me." Sharon's gaze connected with his, and for a moment, she knew they were both somewhere else, but she couldn't tell where. It didn't matter because wherever it was, it was beautiful, safe, and she wasn't afraid there. She drifted back to the front porch. "It was just haunting and special. What was it?"

"I didn't catch the name," Chris said quickly. His eyes appeared to jump back from somewhere else too. "It was some obscure composer nobody has ever heard of. Undoubtedly Italian."

"Can we listen to more?"

"Sure," Chris said. "You felt like it was written just for you, huh? That's pretty amazing." He invited her in. "Let me take your coat."

Sharon noticed that Chris' hands were shaking as he helped her out of her coat and hung it in the hall closet. She had never seen his hands shaky like that before.

Chris guided Sharon to the kitchen and went into the adjoining dining area to turn on the satellite radio. It was classical music, but not the music she heard when she came to the door. They had missed the rest of it, evidently.

The kitchen was so full of the smells of tomato, basil, oregano, and garlic that Sharon wasn't sure there would be room for both the smells and the two of them there. He uncovered a large pot of slowly bubbling tomato sauce, and the aromas intensified. Large hunks of precooked sweet Italian sausage filled a plate next to the sauce.

"The sauce needs to be stirred almost constantly from this point on and reseasoned." Chris handed Sharon a large wooden spoon. "I'm glad you're here. I can take care of the bread. Just before we serve things, we'll add the sausage back in just long enough to heat it up again. Taste the sauce and tell me if it needs anything." He handed Sharon a teaspoon and a tablespoon just to use for tasting.

She took the spoons but stopped wide-eyed for a moment when she saw the homemade loaves of bread Chris put into the oven. "You have homemade bread? I don't know when I had homemade bread last. I can't wait."

"Not just anybody's homemade bread," Chris said proudly. "The best homemade bread you'll ever have. My grandmother's recipe. Her mother gave it to her before she came to this country. Please, taste the sauce." He gestured with his hands and seemed very Italian at that instant with broad shoulders and strong arms, matched perfectly with dark, gentle Mediterranean eyes. And now those gestures. How had she missed those before? She could watch his hands talk all night.

Her gaze returned to the pot in front of her. "Okay." She dipped the smaller spoon into the sauce and put it into the larger spoon so she could blow on it slightly. She slipped the sauce off the spoon with her lips. "Wow! This is great," she said.

"Too spicy?"

Sharon shook her head. "Not for me."

Chris smiled. "Does it need more?"

"Well, I'm not the expert here, but I could stand more. I love spicy sauces." Another spoonful slipped over her lips.

"You from Sicily?" Chris asked with a grin. "I love spicy sauces too, but I always cut them back because a lot of people out here in the middle of Iowa don't like things spicy. I put garlic butter and red pepper flakes on the bread and toast it too, like my mother and grandmother used to."

"Sounds great to me."

The glow in Chris' eyes as he spoke about his grandmother and mother made her warm like the sauce did. "I'm basically middle European something, not nearly as romantic as Sicily, but if it's up to me, I say we jack this incredible sauce up a little."

"The red pepper is out." He pointed to a jar with what looked like homemade red pepper flakes. "Jack it up as much as you want. I've never met a red sauce that was too spicy for me, but remember, Joanne and Terry have to be able to eat it too."

"Done." Sharon reached for the red pepper flakes, shook a generous amount into the sauce, and tasted it again. Even though it made her lips tingle slightly, she shook a little more into the bubbling sauce for good measure, and tasted it again. *There we go. Perfect.*

"So, are you from Sicily?" Sharon asked as she continued to stir the sauce.

"Never been there, but my grandmother used to tell me about it all the time…about the hills over the blue sea below and the food and good times they had when they lived there. Someday maybe I'll get there to see if she told me right. I'll be right back. I want to change the station and get a little softer music." He left the kitchen, and for a moment Sharon thought about calling Joanne and telling her that the dinner was cancelled so she could enjoy the evening with Chris alone. Alone? What was she thinking?

The music started again, and she recognized the opening piece as Mozart. It was gorgeous, but it wasn't the piece she heard from outside the front door. Chris had brushed that piece off. *Curious.*

Sharon tasted the sauce again now that she had given the additional pepper time to season the sauce, and it was much hotter than before. "Oh, oh." She waved her hand in front of her mouth. "This is really spicy. I hope I didn't ruin it."

Chris tasted the sauce from the same spoon Sharon had used and didn't even think twice about it. "Wow. That's what I'm talking about. You sure you're not just a little Sicilian? That would do my grandmother proud. She'd be hugging you and kissing both your cheeks if she tasted that."

The thought of a jolly old Sicilian woman hugging her gave her a contented, comfortable feeling. "It's your sauce. All I did was add some more red pepper."

"No, actually it's grandma's sauce, and you seasoned it just exactly like she did. That's why she'd be hugging you. Even my mother never got it quite right for Grandma. You nailed it. If you aren't just a little Sicilian, you should be."

His dark Sicilian eyes danced in their Iowa body, and Sharon wanted to dance with both. "Do all Sicilians exaggerate as much as you do?" She took the spoon back, poured some more on it and offered it to him for another taste.

"More, according to what I remember. I'm just part Sicilian, and I've lived in Iowa most of my life. Sicilians love to exaggerate though. It's part of their joy. I was afraid I was losing my touch." He took the sauce from the spoon she offered without lowering her gaze from his incredible eyes and he locked his gaze on hers.

Without thinking, she continued to watch his eyes and filled the spoon again, tasting it herself. "You should go to Sicily, for your grandmother, if for no other reason. She sounds like she was an incredibly beautiful person."

"And that's an incredibly beautiful comment." He touched her cheek, and to her surprise, she turned her cheek into his light touch gladly. "It's very Sicilian. It shows respect. You want to go see Sicily with me?" He stopped and dropped his hand. "I'm sorry. I'm forgetting my manners. I didn't mean to offend you by that."

"I'm not offended at all." Sharon took his hand, lifted it slowly back to her face, and laid her cheek into it again. He smiled softly and caressed it again just as she hoped he would.

"In fact, I'm flattered you would want to take me there. I know you didn't mean anything wrong, and if things were different, I'd be honored to go with you and let you show me your beautiful country, especially if the food there is anywhere near as good as this."

"Thanks." Chris stroked her cheek with the other side of his hand and smiled. "I would love it if things were different. Maybe they can be." He held her cheek in his hand and brought his lips to hers. "Sharon, when I'm with you…"

"Hey guys, anybody home?" Joanne hollered from the front door. Her timing was impeccable as always. Chris looked a little frustrated, and Sharon felt a little cheated by Joanne's interruption. This was getting to be an unwelcome habit. Chris patted her check, sighed and turned toward the hallway to welcome Joanne and Terry.

She grabbed his arm and he turned back to her, looking at her hand on his arm and then raising his eyes to meet hers as they both smiled at each other.

"Before we get too tied up, what time are we leaving Thursday?" There was no point in putting this off. After looking into those eyes and feeling the gentleness of his hand on her cheek, she was going, and that was all there was to it. She was still afraid but wanted to hear him finish his sentence.

How did he feel when he was around her? She had to know. And she wanted even more to know how much closer his lips would come to hers. Unconsciously, she felt her lips with the tips of her fingers and then reached over and touched his.

"I know," he said softly. "I felt it too." He took her fingers in his hand and smiled, kissing them silently as he held them.

"Can you be here by six?"

"Uh huh," she heard herself say as he kissed her fingers again. "It sounds like fun." Sharon would have said those same words as flirtatiously as possible in the past, but she learned that lesson.

Her words to Chris were simple, cheery, and as sincere as her words had ever been. They felt so much better that way. They felt like his touch…and his lips on her fingers.

Chris smiled, nodded, and squeezed Sharon's hand gently.

"I'd better get their coats; keep stirring the sauce."

Reluctantly, Sharon lifted her fingers from his lips but not before she looked deeply into his eyes and felt them, offering her soft gaze in return. Chris didn't miss the message and brushed her cheek gently once more with his hand before heading for the hallway.

As soon as he turned away, Sharon put her fingers to her own lips kissing them where he had just kissed them and then returned her attention to the pot of bubbling sauce in front of her and stirred.

With her lips still tingling from the heat of Sicilian red sauce and the warmth of Sicilian lips, she wrapped herself in the fragrances of garlic, tomato, sweet basil and parsley, seasoned with just the right amount of red pepper flakes and warm touches. Fragrances and touches of the past flavored with the present, becoming better and stronger, the longer they simmered.

"So?" Joanne interrupted, and Sharon jumped back to reality.

Smiling, she said as calmly as she could, "So, I'm going to Omaha Thursday in a big truck."

"That's so great!" Joanne almost squealed as she gave Sharon a big hug.

"I hope so." Sharon took a deep breath and let it out slowly, because I have to do it."

"Do you want to do it?" Joanne asked hesitantly.

Smiling, Sharon nodded. "More than anything I've done in a long time." She shuddered. "He felt it too. He said so."

Joanne shook her head. "I'm not even going to ask. I'm making up my own story."

Abruptly, Sharon's mood changed. "I have to be here by six, and I really have no idea what to wear. You got any suggestions?"

"Simple." A wide, almost devious grin curled the corners of Joanne's mouth. "I'll take off Wednesday and come get you. We'll go shopping in Iowa City at Farm and Fleet or a couple of tire and feed stores I know about. You'll be fun to shop for. You'll look good in anything, even trucker babe clothes."

Both Sharon and Joanne laughed.

"I guess I kind of have that coming, don't I?" Sharon nodded.

"Why Sharon, I don't know what you're talking about," Joanne said, and they both laughed again. "I'll guarantee you there will be no little blue, spaghetti strapped numbers. And undergarments will be a breeze. T-shirts and boxers will definitely work!"

"Great." Sharon just shook her head.

"You can spend the night at my place Wednesday night, and I'll bring you here by six and go to work early. Chris can bring you to my house when you get back, or you can just call me and I'll come get you."

"Are you sure?"

"Of course," Joanne answered. "No problem."

"Chris said it could be kind of late when we get back. I don't want to wake you."

Joanne shook her head and frowned. "You kidding me? No way am I going to bed until I get to hear all about the trip, and I want details, lots of details."

"What's going on in here?" Terry asked as he and Chris came around the corner and into the kitchen.

"Not much," Joanne said casually as she winked at Sharon, "just girl talk, that's all."

"Seems to me, I got in trouble for using that word," Terry said.

Sharon put her hand on her brother's shoulder. "That was different, big brother. It's okay when we use it." She and Joanne giggled like two eighth graders sharing a secret. "We'll set the table. I hope the food's ready pretty quickly. I don't think I can stand to just smell it much longer."

"All I have to do is take the bread out and finish cooking the pasta," Chris said. "Ten minutes, tops."

Joanne took a deep breath taking in the kitchen smells. "That sauce does smell good."

"Actually, Italians call it gravy," Chris said, "but that confuses people here in Iowa. Would you like to taste it, Jo, no matter what we call it here?"

"Sure."

Chris took a clean spoon and dipped out a spoonful for Joanne to taste. She blew on it and tasted it. "Wow! That is wonderful. Has a great bite to it too."

"Thank Sharon," Chris said. "She's part Sicilian."

"I didn't know that." Terry raised his eyebrows and tilted his head as he smiled at his sister.

Sharon threw up her hands like she had seen Chris do. "All I did was add the red pepper."

"You can add the sausage any time," Chris said, giving Sharon's hand a playful squeeze "and all you did was add just the right amount of red pepper. Only a Sicilian can do that."

CHAPTER 11

Thursday couldn't come soon enough for Sharon. Even with the diversion of shopping and foamy hazelnut lattes, she couldn't relax. Frequent nervous checks of her watch and counting off the hours one by one didn't make the time move any faster. And for what?

The smell of diesel fuel in the morning? The sweet perfume of body odor, dirty truck stop restrooms, grease stained and well used cloth towels hanging by one end of the towel dispenser, with the loose, wrinkled end dangling uninvitingly? Not to mention globs of brown gelatin masquerading as gravy on instant mashed potatoes?

And Chris. Oh yeah, Chris. He was the reason Sharon ignored her fear and said she would go, and for some reason that made all those other things perfectly acceptable. She wanted to see what he did all day, go where he went, and do what he did. She wanted to know everything about him.

Most of all, she just wanted to be with him, and wanted him to be with her…alone…just the two of them…so they could share their favorite things, how they felt about them, and maybe even how they felt about each other…without being interrupted.

Why was this simple truck driver with Sicilian ancestry and Iowa roots so fascinating? He wasn't as polished as a lot of men she knew, although in his own way, he was certainly every bit as handsome. He didn't have multiple college degrees, and he certainly wasn't as wealthy as many she had turned down. Why didn't any of that seem to matter? Why did "I felt it too" echo inside her?

Joanne chattered almost nonstop about Chris even when they got back to Joanne's farmhouse and took their packages inside. She tried to fill in the details of his family background, his high school activities, and every other small detail she could remember.

Sharon barely listened but imagined scenes Chris had described to her from his grandmother's past instead. The scenes and the stories that went with them were almost like a song, and its melody started in the present and moved quickly to the future.

She and Chris skipped through the streets of Taormina, holding hands, exploring the ruins of the ancient Greek theater, and stopping to look down at the surreal blues of the Mediterranean Sea. Mt. Etna watched happily in the background, and the shops along the Corso Umberto provided friendly shopping and even friendlier people. Windows invited them to press their noses against the glass and look inside at happy well lit scenes of family and friends.

It was always sunny in Taormina; pasta and the best tuna dishes known to any culture were fresher than fresh. Flowers and the smells of flowers were everywhere as color hung from balconies, grew up in planters along the streets, and surrounded even the most mundane objects. Old men walked with peaceful, knowledgeable steps, and old women watched them walk by, smiling and flirting with them in their hearts.

Chris was always kind and gentle while she was always clever and witty, spinning dizzily in circles from one place to another, while her brightly colored skirts twirled around her in just the right way, always coming to rest perfectly around her legs that felt only warm breezes. And at the end of the day they were exhausted from happiness with each other and filled with the excitement that tomorrow would be better yet.

And even though rumors and whispered stories of the Mafioso coated the old stone fountains and narrow streets like dust from the countryside, she was never afraid. She never smelled stale beer on anybody's breath or dreamed of heavy, rough hands in the darkness.

Was that what this was all about? Finding safety? Escape? Or was it about finding love so forgiving, so accepting and so strong, that it was everything? Nothing else mattered, nothing else even came close?

"Sharon, are you okay?" Joanne's voice brought her back to Iowa.

Sharon nodded. "Yeah, I'm okay, why?"

"Because I've been talking to you and it seems like you're someplace else." Joanne seemed almost panicky. "I've been telling you all about Chris, but you have a faraway look on your face. I've never seen you like this before. What's going on?"

"It's nothing." Sharon forced her usual smile to come back to her face. "I'm just worried about whether I have the right clothes for tomorrow. I want to look right. I know how to dress for public relations work, but I don't know how to dress like a trucker's girl."

"Is that what you are?" Joanne grinned and poked her in the arm softly. "Are you a trucker's girl?"

"I don't know," Sharon said, shaking her head almost as if she were still dreaming. "I'm not sure I can be."

"Why not? I've seen the way Chris looks at you, and I've also seen the way you look at him…the way you're looking now. What's holding you back?"

"The past," Sharon said, not guarding her words.

Joanne looked closely at Sharon. "Do you want to talk about it? You've always been there for me; maybe I can help you now."

The hands grabbed Sharon and held her. "No!" Sharon said, more forcefully and angrily than she had meant to be. She took a deep breath. "I'm sorry, Jo. I would like to talk, but not now. I'm too confused. I guess I'm just nervous about this truck ride thing. Maybe I'm making a mistake."

"Now you are scaring me, Sharon. I've seen you in action. The more men the merrier. You're never confused or afraid. That's one of the things I have always admired about you."

"All show." Sharon tried to sound unconcerned. "I'm always confused and always afraid."

Moving closer, Joanne attempted to make eye contact with her friend. "Are you afraid of Chris? He'd be devastated if he thought you were afraid of him. He's one of the kindest, gentlest…"

"I'm not afraid of Chris," Sharon interrupted, putting her hand in the air to stop Joanne. "I know he's kind and gentle. I'm afraid of being with Chris…alone, but at the same time, I'm looking forward to it. Does that make any sense at all?"

"Not really. Are you afraid you won't like him if you're alone?"

"No. I'm afraid I will like him. What do I do then?"

Joanne sat up straight. "Are you serious?"

Sharon nodded slowly. "Yeah, very serious."

"You can trust him. He's a gentleman."

Sharon narrowed her eyes and looked at Joanne. "But, can I trust myself? Am I still a lady?"

"Where's that coming from? That sounds like something I would say." She leaned over to Sharon and put her arms around her. Sharon started to cry, then sob.

"Talk," Joanne said simply and gently. "We've got all night."

Joanne listened to everything, including some things even the counselors didn't know. The dam burst inside Sharon, and the pain couldn't be held back anymore. The flirting, the door slamming behind him, his eyes, his laugh and his hands, they all gushed and grabbed from dark places.

There were the nightmares, the fear, the guilt, and the feeling she should have known better. Even then she was a Christian. What was she doing even jokingly letting him chase her into the bedroom? What had she expected would happen?

"So you blame yourself, then?" Joanne asked gently when Sharon had finished.

"I don't know," Sharon sobbed. "If I hadn't let him chase me into the bedroom, it wouldn't have happened. I shouldn't have been there."

"You don't know that it wouldn't have happened," Joanne said, holding Sharon by the shoulders and looking her straight in the eyes. "Okay, so you shouldn't have been there. All you did was make it easier for him. You don't know that he wouldn't have done the same thing at a party, after a date, on a picnic, or just about anywhere else.

"The point is, you told him 'no' and he didn't listen. He didn't respect you. He had no right to do what he did. You may have shown some bad judgment, you may have trusted someone you shouldn't have, but he was wrong. Not you."

Rubbing her forehead with both hands, Sharon began sobbing even harder. "That's what I've tried to tell myself, but I can't stop thinking I shouldn't have been there, and I can't stop being afraid."

"Did you report what happened?"

Sharon nodded. "I reported it to just about everybody, just like we're always told to."

Shrugging, Joanne asked calmly, "What happened?"

"School officials ran an internal investigation. They worked with both the campus and the local police. It's a small town, you know."

"And?"

"The Head Coach kept him out of the starting lineup for the final home game, and the local police said it was an unfortunate case of my word against his word. They kept asking me, 'You were in his bedroom, weren't you? You did go in there of you own free will?' I got the meaning of their questions." She looked down at her feet.

Joanne slapped the table. "That's outrageous. All they did was bench him for the final game?"

Still looking down, Sharon shook her head sadly. "No. All they did was keep him out of the game until the middle of the first quarter. After he went back in, he scored three touchdowns, including the winning one. He signed a nine million dollar contract to play professionally," Sharon added through clenched teeth. Her anger about that still soured in her stomach.

"They told me it would be better for me if I made a fresh start at another school and finished up there. I had 12 credits to go, and I had to take 30 at the new school because it had a two semesters on campus requirement."

Joanne couldn't hide her outrage as she slapped the tabletop again. "You have got to be kidding!"

"I wish." Sharon finally raised her pain-filled gaze to Joanne. "He was the best athlete in school history. He took them to a conference championship and a bowl game. He helped them get some of the best recruits from all over the country. He'll probably make the school millions of dollars in the future. Who knows, they may name a scholarship after him."

Sharon's tears were bitter, but they were still flowing freely as the mounting anger in her staccato words got louder. "All I had was a perfect four point average and a shot at being Valedictorian. I guess that isn't worth all that much compared to football and money when it comes right down to it."

Sharon reached to her friend and grabbed her hand. "I'm sorry, Jo. I shouldn't be putting all this on you. I've never told anyone as much as I've told you. I guess I didn't realize how angry I still was about this."

Joanne nodded once at Sharon. "Do you think he should have been punished?"

Sharon turned her eyes to the ceiling and said in a voice full of pain, "Of course I do! But…"

"Nobody punished him, and somebody needs to pay for what he did, so you're punishing yourself. It must have been your fault, or they would have punished him. Right?" Joanne spoke gently, but firmly.

"I don't know," Sharon said. "I shouldn't have been there."

Joanne squeezed her friend's hand to bring Sharon's gaze back.

"We've established that. The fact is, you were. It still wasn't your fault! But, if it were even partially your fault, God forgives you, Sharon. Do you believe that?"

"Yes, I guess so," Sharon said weakly.

Joanne asked Sharon softly, "Have you ever asked him to forgive you?"

"Come to think of it, no." Sharon shook her head.

"Have you ever asked him to forgive your attacker?"

"No!" Sharon's eyes lashed out almost as furiously as her voice did. "And I've tried, but I can't and I know I should."

Joanne put her arm around Sharon's shoulders. "Do you think it might help if you did? All that counseling and nobody ever suggested the obvious? You need to give this to God and let it go."

Sharon thought about Joanne's questions and comments. She was angry; she did want someone to pay. She knew better than to be angry, but she was anyway, and who had it helped? Nobody. It had only hurt her and kept her from being happy.

People in the local business world knew her as a success. Her reputation had spread in the short time she had been working, but that only helped so long, and it wasn't really what she wanted forever anyway.

No matter what she did or how well she did it, it wasn't enough. Some little sound or smell or word triggered a memory, and it would all come back again. She should have been able to stop him, she shouldn't have been there, she was unworthy, and she had to pay. Nobody else had.

Sharon's meticulously constructed protective shell of blonde hair, stylish clothes, a great shape, and a bouncy perkiness attracted men, but ever since that night in the apartment, Sharon had used that shell to attract them and keep them away at the same time.

But it hadn't worked with Chris. It hadn't kept him at arms' length like it had everyone else because she wanted something else from his arms…she wanted to be held in them, loved by them, and be safe in them, so she could never be hurt again.

How could they do that unless she let them get close enough to hold her, unless she took off the shell and exposed herself? She wasn't sure she could, at least not yet, and maybe not ever, but tomorrow she would take the first step and find out.

She was certain now that she had feelings for Chris, and they started when he offered to pray with her during the blizzard and when he spontaneously gathered others to join them. Something about a truck driver praying in a green baseball cap and a dirty vest in an Iowa truck stop validated prayer itself.

At first, she thought her feelings were based on her curiosity for his gentle simplicity. But, when he shyly took her hand to walk across the parking lot to Soldier's Field, she was more than just curious.

When he wrapped the blanket around her at the game, she not only felt warmer, but she also felt protected and she hadn't allowed herself to feel protected since the horrible night in the bedroom. It was part of her self-flagellation. She told herself she deserved to feel the fear and the lack of protection.

When Chris wrapped the blanket around her and refused to take any for himself, she wrapped it around him too. She was the one who leaned against him, took his arm and put it around her waist and pulled the blanket snuggly around both of them, maybe even more snuggly than it really needed to be.

"I don't deserve someone like Chris," Sharon finally said. Joanne waited quietly and patiently for Sharon to continue. "I'm damaged goods. He doesn't deserve to get mixed up with somebody like me."

"Why don't you let Chris decide that?" Joanne asked softly as she took her arm from around Sharon's shoulder and laid her hand gently on Sharon's arm. "It seems to me like you both care for each other, and you're both adults, I might add."

"That's what makes it so hard," Sharon looked at Joanne. "I used to go out with some of the hottest guys on campus. I meet lots of men on my job almost every day. Some looked like rock stars, I mean truly gorgeous. They are always asking me to have dinner, coffee, or whatever."

"And that's a shock, why?" Joanne asked. "You are an incredibly beautiful woman and very intimidating to us mere mortals."

"Don't start that again," Sharon said. "You are very beautiful yourself."

"Well, whatever," Joanne said. "I'm happy with who I am now, but I'll never be in your league. Let's just leave it at that."

"You don't want to be," Sharon said. "It's not always a good league to be in. Anyway, as I was saying, I've always had these incredible looking guys drooling all around me, and, I admit it, I liked it."

"Who wouldn't?" Joanne asked, smiling.

Sharon smiled and continued. "Having all those adoring fans gave me a sense of power. I was totally in charge. Great for the ego! But…then…I found out what it was like to be powerless." Sharon wiped a tear from her eye but forced a smile and went on. "Sorry. Being powerless really messed me up, in case you couldn't tell." She managed a weak laugh.

"I'm so sorry, Sharon," Joanne said. "I wish there was something I could do to take the hurt away."

"You are. You're listening," Sharon wiped more tears from her eyes. "That helps. I've had lots of counselors listen to me babble, but it's a lot better to have a great friend listen, and care."

"I'm really flattered that you think of me as a friend because I want to be one," Joanne said. "You helped me when I needed somebody desperately, now I want to return the favor." Joanne stopped for a moment and then continued tentatively. "Do you think…maybe I shouldn't go there? It sounds a little strange."

"Go ahead," Sharon said. "Please, I want to know what you were going to say."

"I hope this comes out right," Joanne said, biting her lip. "Do you think you would have even given a guy like Chris a second look if that terrible night hadn't happened first? I'm not trying to say that being raped is good because that's a dumb thing to say. But maybe, and I'm just saying maybe…God took that evil and is showing you that He can use the vilest evil for His good and holy purposes. Do you think that's possible? "

Joanne looked closely at Sharon as she digested Joanne's suggestion, hoping she wasn't making things worse.

"That's one strange way for God to get my attention especially since I already knew Him at the time," Sharon responded. Joanne could see that Sharon was still processing the concept as she spoke.

"Maybe it wasn't God trying to get your attention, but Satan trying to destroy you. Maybe the hands you still see in your dreams are Satan's hands, not the guy who attacked you. Maybe the stale beer is on Satan's breath. Maybe both of us have been allowing the Enemy to keep us from moving on and doing what God wants.

"Maybe God is trying to tell us both that He is holding the Enemy down now. He's telling us to get out of here and go live our lives for Him while He holds Satan until He's ready to deal with him. Maybe He sent both Terry and Chris to be part of our lives. I know He sent Terry to me."

"Or you to him," Sharon said. "You found him, remember?"

"Maybe he wouldn't have given me a second look either if God hadn't half frozen him first and made him stand still in that snowdrift. Of course, that little blue dress didn't hurt either," Joanne said, smiling.

Sharon thought another moment. "Do you really think that we need men to do God's will?"

"Probably not, but maybe God just sent them because a man is nice to have around now and then." Joanne winked. "Maybe God sent them because they need us! Did you ever think of it that way?"

"Lots of times." Sharon gave Joanne a playful nudge. "Why do you really think God sent Terry to you?"

"Simple. I asked Him to," Joanne said. "I wanted somebody special to share my life with, to pray with, to worship with, to raise a family with, and to grow old with. Sometimes I think God sent me Terry so I would quit bugging Him." Joanne chuckled to herself. "I was quite a pest." She shook her head. "I know God gives us what we need, and He doesn't always give us what we ask for, but sometimes He does. Sometimes He sends us a Terry. We can't give up. We can't quit asking. How about you? Why do you think Chris is in your life now?"

"I asked too, and so did Terry," Sharon said simply.

"See?" Joanne nodded. "We are both a little strong willed, in our own unique ways."

"Do you think?" Sharon laughed.

So did Joanne. "Maybe God had to show both of us what love isn't first, so we would recognize what love is and accept it when He gave it to us."

"You are beautiful, Joanne," Sharon said, "I mean really, really beautiful. I know why my brother is so crazy about you."

"I like hearing that." Joanne giggled. "You wouldn't mind elaborating a little would you? Just how crazy is he? I'll take details if you've got them."

"He is totally nutso, mindlessly, stupidly, can't live without you crazy. I haven't heard him say another woman's name since he met you. He even calls me sis or hey you. Of course, this is just between us girls."

"Of course," Joanne said. "And also just between us girls, I feel the same way about him."

"I know. You're both a little nauseating," Sharon whispered back, laughing again. Sharon turned serious for a moment. "Something you said is sticking in my head."

"What's that?" Joanne asked.

Sharon's voice wavered. "I haven't asked God to forgive either me or Jess. I don't know if I can do it alone, but I need to do it. I feel it very strongly all of a sudden. Would you pray with me?"

"I'd be glad to." Joanne reached for her friend's hand and held it.

Sharon squeezed it tightly and swallowed several times. "Lord, I'm sorry. I shouldn't have been anywhere near that bedroom that night. I shouldn't have been such a tease. Forgive me; I won't do it again. Please heal me and let me go on." There was a pause, but Joanne knew Sharon was not done. "I don't know if I can forgive Jess, so You're going to have to keep helping me with that, but I ask You to…forgive him for what he did. Just show me the way to move on, Lord. Thanks for sending Jo to all of us. Amen."

"Thank you," Joanne said when she opened her eyes. "I will pray for you all day long tomorrow. I promise. It's only a truck ride. Have fun. Enjoy being with Chris. Eat a good deep fried pork tenderloin at a truck stop. Relax. If it's supposed to work out, it will. If not, God will take care of you anyway. Just take it one ride at a time."

"So, you think I should go, then?"

"Duh! Besides, I bought you a little present for tomorrow. You have to go."

"You didn't have to do that, but as long as you did, what is it?"

"Stay here. I'll be right back." Joanne got up and went into her bedroom. She came out with a plastic shopping bag that had a big red ribbon tying it shut. "Here," Joanne said, handing the bag to Sharon. "You need this to complete your outfit. I know how fashion conscious you are."

Sharon pulled the bow so the ribbon came off, and she opened the plastic bag and looked into it, laughing immediately. Inside was a green baseball cap with a feed logo on the front just like the one Chris wore. She reached into the bag and pulled the hat out, putting it on her head.

"This is perfect." Sharon wasn't sure whether to laugh or cry when she looked in the mirror. "Thanks, Jo. I usually accessorize with shoes and jewelry, maybe a purse, but this will work better with my outfit."

"Trucker babes like baseball caps and flannel shirts better," Joanne said, laughing at the way Sharon kept rearranging the hat on her head and making faces at herself in the mirror. "You are going to look great!"

"Trucker babe," Sharon repeated. "I like that. I am going to take this one day at a time, like you said, Jo, and tomorrow I'm going to be a trucker babe."

"Look out truckers!" Joanne shook her head and pulled Sharon's hat down over her eyes.

CHAPTER 12

Joanne knew it was painful for Sharon to relive that horrible night from the past one more time, but she hoped talking with her about it helped. Joanne knew what it was like to hurt, to feel worthless, and to be afraid. Their knowledge came from different sources, but the feelings were similar. The guilt and hollow loneliness were the same.

There were still moments of panic and irrational thoughts about who she was and if she was really attractive, but she didn't wonder or care nearly as much anymore. Whether she was plain or attractive had never been the real issue anyway. What haunted Joanne more than anything was a trap door left open in the hayloft years ago. It should have been her that fell through it, not her father.

She was supposed to go after the bags, but her father had offered to go for her, and he had taken the fall instead. And died. It should have been her. She could still see her father's crumpled body lying on the ground, clutching those burlap bags her mother sent her to get.

Her mother never once asked who had left the trap door open. Joanne always wondered why. All her mother ever said was that she should have gone after the bags, like she was supposed to and her father would still be alive. After that she was the plain looking girl who would never amount to anything. It was almost like a code word.

In spite of that, Joanne had become comfortable with who she was, and Sharon was a large reason why. When Joanne told Sharon she would pray for her, she meant it. She planned to lift her up all day long.

~*~

The green, sleeveless down jacket matched her baseball cap. No wonder Joanne had insisted that she get the green jacket. Sharon completed her trucker babe outfit with her favorite blue jeans, a new dark olive T-shirt and an orange and green plaid flannel shirt left open about three buttons worth. If she'd worn a flannel shirt before, let alone one this bright, it was a memory she couldn't pull up.

She pulled her hair into a ponytail, held it with a green scrunchie, and pulled the short blonde ponytail through the opening in the back of the baseball cap. Then Sharon yanked it about halfway down on her forehead before checking herself in the mirror one last time. Shrugging, she pushed it back up a little and nodded.

"It's definitely a new you," Joanne laughed. "I knew there was a real person under all those fancy clothes. Still, you'll be the hottest trucker babe to hit Interstate 80 in an awfully long time."

"But I'm still a trucker babe, right?" Sharon asked, grinning, "because that's what I want to be today, a trucker babe. Actually, I like the look and the feel of it. I could get used to this."

Joanne raised her eyebrows and her hands at the same time. "I've created a monster. We've got about ten minutes to get you there."

Fidgeting with her hat, Sharon spoke to Joanne's reflection in the mirror. "Do I need to take snacks or anything?"

Joanne shook her head decisively. "Nope. Trucker babes don't do snacks. They slurp bad coffee from a thermos and eat donuts, cold pizza, or truck stop food. Every now and then they even eat something that's almost good for them." Joanne put both hands on her stomach. "Kiss your diet good-bye today. It's just not happening."

"How do you know so much about trucker babes?"

"Been around them all my life." Joanne's eyes twinkled. "And...I'm making most of this up."

"I wondered about that." Sharon tugged on her baseball cap one last time. "Let's go."

"We're off then." Joanne slapped both knees and got up, heading for the door. "You want me to teach you some country songs on the way?"

"Chris likes classical music." Sharon turned her nose up into the air. "He's a high brow trucker."

"He'll still pretend to like country when he's around the other truckers."

Sharon looked at her suspiciously. "You're making stuff up again, aren't you?"

"Maybe just a little." Joanne grinned and closed the door behind her.

~*~

Chris had his truck idling in the street in front of the house when Joanne pulled up. Sharon took one last deep breath as she reached for the handle to Joanne's pickup truck. She looked over at Joanne and forced a smile, pushing the door open.

"Here goes," she said, trying to sound convincing. "Make sure you pray for me."

"I will. Have a good time. You'll be fine." Joanne tried to look and sound encouraging. "If you're a good girl, maybe he'll let you honk the horn."

Sharon looked confused. "Where is the horn on one of those things?"

Joanne sighed. "Oh boy. Don't worry, Chris will show you."

Sharon smiled at Joanne and got out of the pickup truck. She had stalled as long as she could. Chris came over to meet her immediately. Joanne waved, and pulled away.

His eyes widened as he looked her over from head to toe. "Nobody is supposed to look that good in flannel. It's supposed to be comfortable, not a fashion statement."

It broke the ice, and Sharon relaxed. "Thanks. It's a Joanne original."

"I like it!" Chris helped Sharon get into the cab and pushed the truck door shut behind her. He walked to the other side of the truck, and Sharon leaned out the window to watch him give everything one last inspection. He checked the hitch one more time before he climbed into the cab and pulled his door shut behind him.

"It's not as easy to get into one of these things as it looks,"

Sharon said as Chris started the truck rolling and made his way methodically through the gearbox.

"You'll get used to it. You'll be hopping in and out of this thing like a pro before we get back."

The casual way he said that and his straight ahead grin made her feel as if they had done this for a long time together, and Sharon couldn't help but wish that were true. Where had he been all these years? "So, we're going to be getting in and out a lot?"

His eyes brightened. "You bet! I may never get a pretty little thing like you in this rig again. I'm showing you off as much as I can. The guys will be talking about you for years." He winked. "Maybe a few of the gals will too."

"So is that why you asked me to come along?" Sharon frowned and crossed her arms in front of her, uncertain how to take that comment. "You wanted to show off and build up your reputation?"

Chris turned to her sharply as he continued shifting gears. "Course not. A man would have to be a total jerk to abuse a wonderful woman like you that way. I was just kidding."

I could give you a name. "Why did you ask me to come along then?" The question popped out of her mouth before she could stop it.

"Because I like you." Chris dropped the trucker talk. "I wanted to spend a little more time with you, if you want to know the truth, just you and me, even if it's just for today."

"I like you too, and I'm fixin' to be your trucker babe all day long." She tried to capture the right intonation and rhythm as she grinned at Chris, and she uncrossed her arms.

"Well, don't call yourself that in front of the others." Chris tried to stifle a smile. "They'll think you're my girl if you call yourself my trucker babe. That's what some of the guys call their girlfriends. Didn't Jo tell you that when she taught you that phrase?"

Sharon smiled. "What makes you think Jo taught me that?"

"Because I know our sweet little Jo pretty well, and she's not as quiet and innocent as most people think. There's a lot of mischief behind those blue eyes. Most people don't take the time to get to know her so they miss all that."

The fascination of the truck ride had already captured her attention as Sharon gazed out her side window. Without looking back she mused, "Mischief indeed. To answer your question, no, the little scamp didn't tell me that trucker babe meant girlfriend. I'll have to get her back for that one. She made it sound so sweet the way she said it."

Shrugging, Chris kept his eyes straight ahead. "Well, that's what it means, at least to some of the guys."

Sharon smiled as she thought about the way Joanne slipped the phrase into their conversation. There was definitely a lot more to Joanne than met the eye. She should have been annoyed with Joanne, but instead, she liked her even more now. That was the kind of prank good friends play on each other fully expecting to be paid back in the future. Besides, Sharon could use this to her advantage.

"So, Bubba, you got a problem with this 'pretty little thing,' as you so delicately put it, being your girl for the day?" Sharon put her head in her hand and leaned casually on the side of the truck on her elbow as she looked at him.

"Well no," Chris stammered, "I just thought you…"

"Neither do I." Sharon tugged on the bill of her cap. "I like the sound of trucker babe, and I may use it a lot today. I've been counting on it, so get used to it. And while we're at it, I expect to be treated like your best trucker babe all day long."

Chris took a deep breath, puffed his cheeks, and blew a long, slow stream of air out. "Okay, then, trucker babe, my one and only for the day."

"And that makes you Bubba." Sharon laughed and reached over to Chris tugging the bill on his hat. "Got any tunes in this rig, Bubba?"

A grin covered his face as he pulled into a long line of trucks already moving down the interstate at a mile or two above the speed limit. "Sure." He reached over and punched the button turning on the CD player. Sharon recognized the CD from the night they had pasta. Mozart. Still no hint of the haunting music she heard when she waited at the front door.

"Do you have that song that was on when I came to the door the other night? It was one of the most beautiful melodies I think I have ever heard. I'm pretty sure it was a violin piece."

Chris turned his head toward Sharon quickly with a startled look on his face. "You really liked that? I thought you were just making conversation when you said that."

"I loved it. I told you that. It was beautiful, and it felt...never mind. Do you have it?"

"It felt what?"

Sharon waved her hand and blushed slightly. "I'm embarrassed. I was being stupid. Forget it."

"No, I really want to know. Please," Chris almost pleaded with something in his voice that tugged at Sharon in a way she couldn't quite understand, though she felt it all the way through her.

"Like I told you, I felt like it was just for me." Softness coated both her words and her face, softness that made her shiver as she looked at him. "Beautiful music has that affect on me sometimes." She looked down at her hands. "I know it's silly, but that song spoke to me and really moved me. I'm sorry. You probably think I'm really stuck on myself now."

"No. I don't. If anything, I think you're trying to hide your sadness. Music is supposed to move you... especially a piece like that one. It can be just for you if you want it to be. I didn't know you really meant that."

Sharon felt him at that moment without actually touching him; she felt so much about him: the happiness behind the grin, the softness of his eyes, and the gentleness of his soul, a soul that reached out to hold hers, and join it. And had he asked, she would have handed it to him willingly right there in the truck because she knew he would take care of it.

"Well, I did mean it." Her tone was bold. "Are you going to tell me what it was called?"

She watched the hesitation in his eyes before he answered. "I would if I could, but I don't know what it's called."

"Who was the composer then?"

Chris shrugged. "Just some obscure guy I'm sure you've never heard of. It wouldn't mean anything to you."

"Will I ever get to hear it again?" A pounding inside her convinced her that the song could fill the hole left by the night and bring back the daylight beauty that was stolen from her in the darkness of that apartment. Now, especially when she was around Chris, she wanted what was taken from her back. She wanted to fill that hole and become whole again.

"I'll see what I can do about that," Chris said. "I'll have to find it again, and then I'll let you know."

Gently putting her hand on his arm, she looked at him intensely, feeling the desperation inside her. "Please try really hard."

Almost as if he felt her desperation, Chris nodded. "I will."

She let the subject drop for now, but she intended to bring it up again. She had to hear that song again. She just had to.

Sharon pointed to the CD player as Mozart came softly from its speakers. "Won't music like this ruin your reputation with the other truckers?"

"Not if I put Johnny Cash on before we stop anywhere." Chris grinned again now that the subject had changed. "Actually, there are probably lots of other drivers who play stuff like this. We just keep it secret. I like Country music too; in fact, I like all kinds of music."

"This is okay. Us trucker babes have to listen to the tunes our Bubbas play, I reckon." Sharon smiled like she got it right.

"You know, somebody once asked Mark Twain if his wife swore as much as he did. He answered saying something like, she knows the lyrics, but I'm not sure she'll ever get the melody."

"Teach me the melody, then" Sharon slid over and barely whispered the words inches from his ear. "I want to learn all the melodies." She hadn't forgotten how to flirt. Flirting was like riding a bicycle to her; she never forgot how, but as she flirted it hit her. This wasn't an act, or a tease with him. It was real.

"It'll take more than one ride to Omaha to teach someone like you all the melodies."

A sideways glance from him confirmed what she felt, and even though he appeared to be teasing her back, Sharon caught herself and was barely able to whisper, "I'm willing to take as many trips as we need to, but let's just take it one ride at a time, okay."

Chris turned his head to her. "Are you serious?"

Sharon looked out the side window, then down, before blinking and turning her gaze to his. His eyes were so hopeful, so gentle and so sincere she felt them holding her…all of her, and softly she answered, "Why wouldn't I be?"

"Because I'm not in your league. That's why."

"And just what league is that anyway?"

Chris thought for a minute. "Let me describe it this way. I love classical music. You *are* classical music. There's a big difference."

Sharon shook her head and looked straight into his eyes. "Sorry. I don't see the big difference between us, but if you don't want to play in my league…I'll play in yours." Glancing away only momentarily she looked back again. "Do we have a deal or not? Are you going to teach me all the melodies?"

Her hand trembled as she reached slowly to his face and touched him. "Please. No strings, just teach them to me."

Chris turned his head toward her sharply when she touched him and exhaled. "Of course I'll teach you." He grinned. "But it could take a lot of trips."

"One at a time. That's all I ask."

"One at a time," he nodded. "But about the no strings part…"

Sharon touched his lips lightly with her fingers like she had when they made red sauce. "One trip at a time," she said.

He nodded.

"Thanks, Bubba."

"No problem, Babe," he responded, grinning as he kept his eyes on the road ahead and his lips on the still trembling tips of her fingers.

~*~

Mozart, orange and green flannel, a baseball cap and work boots: how comfortably ordinary. Especially when sheltered in the cab of an eighteen-wheeler chugging purposefully down Interstate 80 as the Iowa countryside rolled by. High above the mere mortals or the traveling salesmen in nondescript four-wheelers, Sharon felt like she did the first time she had black licorice as a little girl. Nothing should be this good.

Chris' hand shifted up and down through the gearbox like he was practicing scales on a musical instrument, and he steered the rig's big wheel effortlessly like he was playing a solo. His hands were every bit as strong and powerful as the hands that had hurt her, but Sharon knew already that these hands were hands that could be trusted. All she had to do was believe in their touch, accept their love, and allow them to get close enough to hold her.

She started out small. When they stopped to get coffee at a large truck stop, she willingly put herself into Chris' hands when he offered to help her down from the cab. His firm but respectful grip on her waist as he lifted her down to the ground helped erase the much less respectful feel of the hands in the darkness. Her trust in these new hands was well placed, and so was she.

With his hand gently in the small of her back, he led her around the vehicle, showed her how the trailer was connected to the cab and double-checked all the cables. They inspected the lug nuts on the truck's huge wheels, and they pulled the long handles on the doors at the back of the trailer to make certain that the doors were still fastened securely. Chris patiently explained everything he did.

"Time for some coffee," he said, smiling. He held out his hand to Sharon, and she took it, but she didn't hold on to it. She put it around her waist instead and then put her arm around his waist and pulled him closer to her as they walked toward the coffee shop.

"We want to look authentic." Sharon grinned and leaned her head against his shoulder as she walked. "Okay with you, Bubba?"

"Sure," Chris said. "I was trying to be a gentleman, but I'm not stupid, and I'm just a man. If a beautiful woman like you wants my arm around her waist, that's where I'm going to put it."

"That's where I want it." There wasn't even a hint of hesitation in her voice, but it was hard for her to hide the flutter she was feeling as they walked across the parking lot brushing against each other.

"Okay, then." He pulled her closer. She nodded, and the flutter almost took flight.

Walking arm in arm felt natural, and even though she hadn't planned to do it and she hadn't planned to be so insistent about being his trucker babe, both things just happened like so many other things lately. And they were okay…no…they were better than that…they were slightly great!

The quilted vest, the flannel shirt, the T-shirt under it, the jeans and most of all, the green baseball cap were all part of a ticket to normalcy. There was no competition out here to see whose bun was tighter, whose skirt was shorter, whose body was the thinnest, or whose smile was the most genuinely disingenuous. There were only grins, some almost toothless, little whistles, nods, and the arm of someone she trusted securely around her waist, where she hoped it would stay...one trip at a time…for lots and lots of trips.

Of course Sharon was noticed. The clothes helped her blend in, but they didn't make her invisible. She still looked good, and many of the men said so, but they didn't undress her with their eyes like some of the so-called professional men did. They looked at her, enjoyed what they saw and often told her so. But it was as simple as that.

She was part of the group. She was just the prettiest part, like Chris was the quietest, a guy named Harry was the biggest, and wild man Willie was the loudest. For once, she wasn't the center of the group, just a part of it. And the day flew by.

When they got to Omaha, they had to wait an hour and a half to get into the dock to unload. The slot he finally got was narrower than usual, so Chris told her that he needed a ground guide just to be safe. Sharon begged to do it until he agreed. She didn't even wait for him to help her down when he stopped his truck. Instead, she jumped down from the cab eagerly and climbed up on the dock.

With a series of waves and a few whistles she didn't even know she had, she guided Chris into the spot with a minimum of effort.

"Prettiest ground guide I've ever seen," another trucker said, leaning out of his cab. "Nice job, little lady. You want to give me a hand?"

"Sure," Sharon said, and she ran down to the opening two trucks over from Chris' truck and waved in the second truck just as efficiently.

The driver jumped out of the cab when he got the trailer in place and hopped up next to Sharon. "Thanks," he said, grinning and extending his hand. "Name's Bill. I'm sure somebody as pretty as you are isn't running around by herself, but I'd be glad to buy you a coffee if you want to ditch whoever brought you here."

Bill's hand felt friendly, not frightening, and it didn't bother her at all that he put his hand out before she did. "That's very nice of you, but I came in with Chris over there. I'm his trucker babe, so I'd better decline. I appreciate the offer though."

"Lucky dog!" Bill said. "If you get sick of him, let me know."

"I'll do that." She shook his hand again. "My name's Sharon, by the way. Nice to meet you."

"Thanks again for the hand. Hey. Chris." He waved. "Lucky dog," he said again as he turned and walked back to unload.

Several dockworkers had already started to unload Chris' truck when Sharon got there. The two guys helping Chris stopped what they were doing and gave Sharon an admiring look as she walked up to Chris and asked if she could help.

"You back in one more truck, and they'll make you get a union card, you know." Chris grinned. "They pay people to do that here sometimes."

"How much?" Sharon responded. "I think it's kind of fun."

"Not enough, although you'd probably never have to pay for your own dinner again." Chris' grin grew wider. "Just try not to draw too much attention while we finish. I see you met Bill."

She nodded. "Seemed like a nice guy."

"One of the nicest," Chris said. "I'm surprised he didn't try to steal you. He's a real hit with a lot of the women because he has tons of money and pretty decent manners for a trucker."

"What makes you think he didn't try to steal me?" Sharon gave him a slightly sultry smile. "In fact, he did. I told him I was your trucker babe."

"How'd he take that?" Chris continued to work.

"Called you a lucky dog," Sharon said. "Told me to look him up if I ever get tired of you."

Chris kept looking at his load and laughed. "Give me about an hour here, and we'll go get lunch. You can listen to music in the cab or crawl up on the bunk and take a nap if you want."

"Is it okay if I just stand here and watch? I don't want to miss anything." Sharon was hypnotized by the strength in Chris' arms as he loaded pallets and moved the boxes in the back of the truck around with hardly any effort. She wondered how someone so strong could be so gentle.

"Do what you want." He pulled an empty wood pallet from the back of the truck and set it on its side. "You'll be more comfortable sitting though." He motioned for Sharon to sit down.

"Thanks, Bubba," Sharon said playfully. The two men helping Chris grinned when she called him Bubba, and Chris turned around and looked at them.

"You guys better quit grinning and forget you heard that, or I might forget to pay you."

"Forget what, Bubba? We didn't hear a thing, did we, George?"

"No, Mr. Bubba. We didn't hear anything, honest." The second worker looked at Chris and grinned.

"Oops." Sharon put her hand over her mouth and sat down.

"Yeah, oops." Chris nodded and tried not to grin. The two workers couldn't help laughing even louder than before.

The truck got unloaded, and they had lunch. Sharon tried one of the deep fried pork tenderloins Joanne recommended. She hadn't had one since she was a girl and her family used to go to the local drive in restaurant. Tenderloins were still good especially with a few pickles and lots of ketchup. The onion rings weren't bad either.

On the way back from Omaha, Sharon looked at Chris very seriously. He looked back, not knowing what to think.

"Would it be possible for me to toot the horn?" she asked.

"Time for a melody lesson," Chris said, laughing. "This is a semi, also known as many other things like rig, or eighteen-wheeler, but no matter what you call it, you don't 'toot' the horn. You can blow it, blast it, or maybe even honk it, but you can't toot it."

"Okay." Sharon wasn't intimidated even slightly. "Can I blast it, or whatever?"

Chris looked around and saw there wasn't too much traffic around them. "Sure, blast away. Just be careful."

"Great!" Sharon reached over toward the steering wheel and tried to press it in the middle.

"What are you doing?" Chris asked.

"I thought you said I could blast the horn."

"You can," Chris said, reaching up his left hand to a cord running along the window and pulling it. A loud blast came out of the horns on the front fenders of the truck cab, and Sharon jumped at the bone-jarring sound. "This is how you blast the horn on one of these things. That's why I said to be careful. I'll need to be able to see."

"Sorry. I didn't know that." She crossed over in front of Chris without thinking and pulled the cord hard twice with her right hand. Even though she was ready for the loud noise this time, it still made her jump when she pulled the cord and the loud blasts came out of the horns.

"Oh my, that's even loud in here."

"Why mess around?" Chris asked. "Big trucks need big horns. You wouldn't respect a big truck like this that sounded like one of those little four-wheeler compacts would you?"

"I guess not," she said, giggling.

"Ah, this is a great view," Chris said, smiling, "but I really need to see the highway any minute here."

Looking down, her body was only inches from Chris and directly in his line of vision. Sharon froze for a moment, but her old flirtatious skills kicked in, and she turned a little sideways so Chris could duck down and look below her. The Old Navy logo on her T-shirt was still only inches away from his face, maybe only a fraction of an inch.

"Can you see now?" she asked in a purposefully smoky tone.

"Old Navy's never looked better, or clearer. Good thing I'm not far sighted." The expression on his face didn't change.

"They're big enough, it shouldn't matter... I mean the letters of course." Sharon slid slowly back to her seat with a grin on her face. "That was fun. Thanks." She just couldn't help herself with him.

"Anytime." Chris shook his head and kept looking forward, but his grin gave him away.

The rest of the trip back was small talk, a full moon lighting the roll of the hills in the empty fields, classical music and the comforting rumble of the diesel engine as the truck gobbled up the miles. Sharon didn't remember when she had felt this good.

"So what'd you think?" Chris asked, as they pulled into a parking lot near his house to drop off the empty trailer. "Was it what you expected?"

"I think it might have been the best day of my life," Sharon said before she had a chance to measure her words. "When can we go again?"

"You really liked it?" Chris took off his cap and shook his head. "What did you like most about it?"

"It was just so basic, so open, and so pure. I loved just riding down the highway listening to classical music. I thought the tenderloin was great. I liked being a grounded guide..."

"Ground guide," Chris corrected, smiling.

"Whatever." She brushed away her mistake with a wave of her hand. "I loved blasting the horn..."

"And I loved the view." Chris smiled. "They definitely are big enough.... I mean the letters of course."

Sharon looked away so he wouldn't see her grin. "I don't know what you're talking about."

"Uh huh." He grinned.

"I don't know how to explain it really. It was almost like I was doing what I should have been doing all my life."

"You mean you think you should have been a trucker?" Chris asked.

Sharon's gaze drifted off and fixed on something bright and beautiful that she couldn't define even though it made her smile.

"No. I mean I think I should have been a trucker babe. I loved playing the part today, and I loved all those people we met."

"There are some that are a little undesirable and some that aren't so nice, but for the most part they're just good honest folks," Chris said as they climbed out of the cab and stood beside it. "So…" he looked at his feet, turned to the truck, kicked a tire, then turned back to her, "is that all it was, playing a part? It's okay, really. I can't complain. It was great…you were great." He shoved his hands into his pockets.

Sharon was certain he was asking more than that. When he looked back at her again, he kept looking at her lips as she talked, and when he did that, it made her stop talking and look back at his. A kiss was definitely on her mind, and her lips trembled. She could almost feel his kiss as he looked at her.

They narrowed the distance between them a half step each. He took his shaky hands out of his pockets and reached toward her face to caress it as she closed her eyes and moved to him.

"Hey, you two. It's about time you got back." A familiar voice from the shadows startled her.

Not again! Joanne, what did I ever do to you?

The old pickup truck pulled up next to Sharon and Chris. "I was starting to get worried about you. Have a good time?" she asked. She was too cheery and quite oblivious to the moment she had just crushed.

"Great time," Sharon said. She forced a smile as she scowled at Joanne and backed away from Chris.

"I'm going to Chicago next Tuesday and back to Omaha in two weeks." Chris looked at his feet and then at Sharon with a look that told her he was as disappointed as she was. He winked. "It's okay; I felt it too."

She knew what he was saying. He'd told her the same thing in his kitchen when they were making the red gravy for the pasta.

"You want a trucker babe on them?" Sharon forced her voice to come out stronger than it felt.

"Don't have one on either trip. That's why I mentioned them," he said, fidgeting before he stuck his hands into his pockets again.

"Count me in, then." Sharon nodded confidently. "I've got lots of vacation time built up."

"Great," Chris looked awkwardly at Sharon and then over her shoulder at Joanne, who sat in her truck smiling innocently at them, and remaining oblivious as she leaned her chin on her arms watching..

"Well, thanks again for going along. I had a great time today." He looked at Joanne again, and she smiled back at him.

"Well, goodnight then," Sharon said, putting out her hand to shake Chris' hand. "I had a great time too." She shook his hand after he hurriedly pulled it from his pocket. After holding it for a minute, biting her lip and taking a deep breath, she let it go and turned to walk toward Joanne's truck. Chris turned and walked back to his.

Sharon took two steps and hesitated. *This is stupid. We're both adults. Sorry, Joanne. You're going to have to wait a minute here. Close your eyes.*

"Chris." She turned and ran back to him, keeping her eyes on him as he turned around and waited for her.

"I can do better than that. I did feel it, and if you don't mind, I'd like to really feel it." She threw her arms around his neck and kissed him. His lips were even softer than she had imagined, and she could have melted into his arms as he lifted her off the ground and held her there for a long time…a very long time.

"There. That's how a trucker babe should thank her Bubba for one of the best days of her life. Did I tell you, I like being your trucker babe? I liked it a lot." She clung to him, and he didn't seem to be in any hurry to put her down. That was fine with her.

"Yes, I think you did." He pressed his lips to hers again before setting her back on the ground. "I'm sorry. I…I didn't…" He grinned. "We both know better. Of course I did, and I'm going to do it again." His lips consumed her as he held her, warm, soft, and oh so welcome. Never had she been kissed so well or enjoyed it more.

Sharon touched her finger to his lips. Then she kissed him one last time, wishing she didn't have to stop. "See you at church Sunday." She had little breath left as she slowly backed away.

"I'll be there," he said. "For the record, you're the prettiest trucker babe Interstate 80 ever saw. Probably the prettiest it will ever see."

"Thanks." Sharon turned, skipped to Joanne's truck, opened the door, and hopped into the seat with a huge sigh and a big grin on her face. "You didn't tell me that being a trucker babe meant I was his girlfriend." Sharon grinned and looked at Joanne.

"Looks like you figured it out," Joanne said, grinning back. "I take it everything went okay?"

"Duh." Sharon could still feel herself being held in the air securely in his arms as she leaned toward Joanne and frowned.

"Details. I want details," Joanne said, almost squealing.

"You just saw the best one," Sharon said. "Next time, he'll bring me out to your place. Don't come looking for me again, okay, mother?"

"You are something else," Joanne said, laughing and shaking her head.

"I'm working on it." Sharon sucked in a big gulp of air. "I liked being Chris' trucker babe. It's one of the best things I've ever been. Oh man, that was so great!"

"Good for you, Sharon." Joanne pounded the steering wheel. "I'm so happy."

Yeah. Good for me. Thank You, Lord. Sharon sat back into her seat and closed her eyes, trying to find a way for her heart to slow down, but it just wasn't happening.

~*~

It took a quart of milk and a half a pan of brownies for Sharon to tell Joanne about the shortest 16-hour day she had ever spent. Joanne made Sharon tell the story twice to make certain she hadn't missed anything, and Joanne assured her that she had prayed for her almost constantly all day long.

"It worked." Sharon reached for her third brownie. "I had a

spectacular day. Pretty good brownies." Sharon examined the huge chocolate square in her hand. "Nothing like milk and chocolate after a hard day on the road." She bit off another corner and wiped the crumbs from the sides of her mouth.

"You ought to have Chris fix his hazelnut, chocolate mousse cake for you sometime if you think those are good." Joanne winked. "He brings it to church potlucks, and even the older women beg him for the recipe. It's Italian, I think."

"Really? I know he makes good pasta and red sauce, excuse me, gravy, but he cooks other things too? There's a lot about that guy that I still don't know. Anything else you'd care to mention?"

"He's a fantastic cook. He plays the violin too, you know. He's very shy about it though. I've only heard him play a couple of times. I'm no expert, but if you ask me, he's incredibly good."

Freezing with a brownie half in her mouth, Sharon vaguely remembered a prayer Terry made after the blizzard. He had thanked God for her and compared her to a violin. The prayer had made her uncomfortable then, and it made her even more uncomfortable now.

"I didn't know he played a musical instrument at all, let alone a violin," Sharon said very slowly so she could swallow the brownie that suddenly stuck in her throat.

"Yeah," Joanne said. "Like I said, he's really shy about it. He's only played for a few people. He has to feel totally comfortable with you. From what I saw in the parking lot, I'd say you have a very good shot at hearing him play. He looked pretty comfortable with you. So…how was it, anyway?"

"Joanne!" Sharon pretended to be shocked by her question.

"Ah come on, Sharon. This is me you're talking to. Just between us girls, how was it?"

"Well, frankly, if you hadn't made your untimely entrance when you did, I might have a little more to tell. I know he was about to kiss me when you hollered at us. I already had my eyes closed waiting for him."

"Sorry." Joanne winced. "I was worried, and it never dawned on me that I might interrupt something."

"It never dawned on me either, but looking back on things, it had been building all day, and it finally just sort of happened." Sharon smiled as she remembered. "But to answer your question, it was good. Very good. Very, very good. Curl your toes good…"

"All right, all right. I get the picture." Joanne pretended to stick her finger down her throat.

"I was just getting started." Sharon laughed, as she looked off into the distance, her eyes glazed over.

"So, is it serious good?" Joanne asked.

"One trip at a time, Jo, one trip at a time. Remember? I'll tell you this much, though, I'm really looking forward to the next one! Looking forward to the trip too." She couldn't help but giggle.

CHAPTER 13

When Chris saw Sharon at the truck stop during the blizzard, he didn't think he had ever seen blonde hair as soft and beautiful as hers. He watched it flip outward and barely graze her shoulders and couldn't stop looking at it as it bounced lightly around her soft face. If anyone was ever meant to be a blonde, she was.

Even if her hair wasn't naturally blonde, as one of the truckers suggested, it should have been. It brought out the green in her eyes. He had walked by her table, just like all the men did, to get a better look at the gorgeous blonde everybody was talking about.

The talk had been right. She was gorgeous. Normally, he would have flirted a little with her and gone about his business, just like most of others did. But then she asked him if he prayed. He hadn't expected that question from someone who looked like she did. It caught him totally off guard, and maybe that's why it got to him so quickly. He didn't have time to put up his defenses, and he answered honestly. He didn't pray much anymore, and he didn't know why. His mother and his grandmother had taught him differently.

She asked him to pray with her, and he couldn't refuse. Her prayer was so simple, so direct, so heartfelt, and so trusting. When he opened his eyes after she prayed, he just couldn't help himself. She had him, and it was that quick…in the blink of an eye.

Why did it have to be someone like Sharon? He was stumbling along quite nicely, keeping his thoughts and feelings safely tucked away where they didn't show. He planned to go back to church…some day. He hoped to meet a decent woman and raise a family this time…some day.

He just hadn't planned on it happening that day, that instantly. Not with somebody like Sharon. And yet, the answer to his unasked question sat right there in front of him with blonde hair and hazel eyes, and she seemed so out of reach for him it wasn't fair. He couldn't ever hope to interest someone like her.

He tried to get her out of his mind, but she wouldn't leave quietly. Sharon made him pray again. He asked God to help him get over her and ended up with her sitting next to him in church. He tried to avoid her, but she ended up sitting next to him at a Bears game, sharing a blanket, hugging him when the Bears scored and again when his good friend Joanne agreed to marry Sharon's brother.

Today she spent the entire day with him and called herself his trucker babe, flirted with him when she "honked" the truck's horn, and came back to him just when he thought it was all over, and kissed him...more than once...touching him in so many ways...and asked for more. She went to church, prayed, knew what was and wasn't important, and brought him back to where he needed to be, to where he wanted to be.

It was almost as if God wasn't listening to him. He kept getting the opposite of what he asked for, but Chris knew that the prayers on his lips and the prayers in his heart were very different, so maybe God was listening to the prayers Chris couldn't hear with his ears. Or, maybe it was Chris who wasn't listening to the answer even though she was right there in front of him.

He was sure that some demon haunted Sharon, and fairly certain he knew the demon's name. As an avid sports fan, he followed college sports closely, and he remembered a few short news stories about a first round draft pick from an area college who was accused of sexual assault.

Joanne let it slip that Sharon had attended that college and transferred with less than a semester left to earn her degree. The stories referred to an attractive blonde coed, and then the stories stopped suddenly, shortly before Sharon transferred.

Joanne told him indirectly something she couldn't tell him directly and gave him enough details so he could fill in the rest. Another trucker who knew more about the story asked him if he knew who the woman he sat with was and then filled him in, "just to let him know." It had taken all the restraint Chris had to keep from decking the guy right there on the spot.

None of that mattered, but how did he tell her that? He knew her heart. He had seen it from afar for weeks and close up all day today. Sharon's past was her past. He had one too with Cindy.

All he was interested in was her present and her future, and he was very interested in both of those, but he still wondered how an ordinary guy like him could have a chance with a beautiful woman like Sharon. As a couple, they weren't exactly Beauty and the Beast even though the role of Beauty fit her perfectly. He wasn't exactly the Beast, but he would never be mistaken for the dashing Prince Charming either.

It was easy to understand why he was drawn to her; she was gorgeous but fun; beautiful, but ordinary. He had the ordinary part covered, but that's where it ended, so why did she like calling herself his trucker babe…why did she kiss him…more than once…and way more than an ordinary guy like him could expect?

What if she liked him, but didn't feel as strongly as he did and he told her how he felt only to be humiliated? That would almost hurt more than anything, and it would ruin the fantasy. The fantasy stayed alive as long as he didn't know for sure, but once he knew for sure…either way…the fantasy became real and he had to do more than just dream about it. He had to act.

Chris took his great grandfather's old violin out of its case and set the meticulously preserved, chestnut brown instrument carefully on his lap, laying the violin bow next to it. He placed a very old piece of music on the stand in front of him and picked up the bow to tighten the white horse hairs to just the right tension, sliding the rosin bar over the bow lightly several times before laying the bar back into the case.

Holding the violin under his chin, he tuned the strings one at a time, using a small pitch pipe to get the right tone for each string. Lowest to highest, G, D, A, and finally E to get the perfect fifth intervals required. Chris always prepared to play the same way.

Sitting forward on the edge of his chair, he warmed up his fingers with a few scales and several short practice pieces. Turning his focus to the old score on the music stand in front of him, he played it from memory as he had since he was a young boy. The piece of music on the stand in front of him served as a reminder of who he was and where the violin and the music had come from.

The notes on the sheet had never been changed since the day the composer wrote them there by hand. They were still the same notes today as they were when they were created, and they would always stay the way they were, as far as Chris was concerned. The only thing that ever changed was the person who played the piece and the passion the musician brought to the notes that made it up.

In the past, Chris had played the notes fast when he was happy and slower when he was sad, reflecting all the different allegros and adagios in his young life. The notes always provided him with a place to go, no matter how he felt, and he needed somewhere to go right now because what he felt filled him up and overwhelmed him.

Playing with quiet precision tonight, he squeezed passion from the notes to make them as beautiful as he possibly could, just as he had since he met Sharon. He had been playing the piece just this way when Sharon came to his door that first night and startled him.

He hadn't been ready for her, and even after she told him the piece was beautiful, his feelings confused him, like the ride to Omaha had today, and like Sharon's kisses had; still, when the time was right, if it ever was, he would play the piece for her, but not now, not yet. He needed more courage first and lots more practice.

~*~

Chris, Terry, Joanne and Sharon sat in their usual pew in church on Sunday. Dave, Marie and the other Lowry brothers sat in the pew behind them as they always did since that first Sunday.

The entire family still came to church even though the one-month trial period had passed, and the church had started to grow faster now. Joanne was getting married to her brother. Sharon's job was going better than she could ever have hoped for, and, in short, her life hadn't been this good for a long, long time.

So, why didn't she feel better? Why did she still feel uncomfortable and unworthy? The answer to her questions was sitting on her left, and his name was Chris. It had been easier for Sharon to deal with her feelings when she had none. It was easy to do good as long as it didn't require her to feel good.

Then Chris showed up in that goofy green baseball cap. She didn't think anything about it at first. He was a truck driver. She had handled much more stylish and aggressive men. He was sweet, innocent in his own way, and a little cute, but she wasn't looking for a man. She had turned away lots of gorgeous guys because she had been ready for them, but she hadn't been ready for one beautiful guy, and now she couldn't and wouldn't turn him away.

She cared about Chris, and she cared a lot. With caring came feeling, and with feeling came her past. It was impossible to keep it buried now that she felt this way. The bad came out with the good, the ugly with the beautiful, and it would soon be there, all of it, in plain view. Then what?

How would she ever be able to face Chris once he knew? How could she still be his innocent, happy-go-lucky trucker babe then? She loved that role. It was so uncomplicated, so stupidly exciting, so real, and so liberating. It had been an honor to be offered the role, and she embraced it totally, bad coffee, fried tenderloins, smelly rest rooms, and all.

It hadn't been forced on her by a pair of oppressive hands in the darkness or equally oppressive cover-ups and whispers in the daylight. It had been offered in gentle humility, lovingly, full of genuine compassion, and she wanted it more than anything she had ever wanted.

It was her decision, and it was the right one. She was positive. God had led her to it and to Chris, and surely God wasn't just teasing her. He would follow through now that He had her where He wanted her to be, next to someone gentle and kind like Chris, but would both of them make a place for her to stay there?

~*~

After church, Chris, Sharon, Terry and Joanne went to Joanne's house as they always did. Football season was over, but now there was NASCAR. It was a good excuse to keep the Sunday afternoon get together going.

They ate the traditional grilled cheese sandwiches and tomato soup, always talking about changing the menu next week, but never actually doing it. Usually they finished with brownies that Joanne and Sharon took turns making.

Today, however, Chris brought his notorious Gianduia Mousse

cake for dessert. He copied the recipe from one of the gourmet food magazines that he read secretly. He figured being a part Sicilian, violin playing truck driver from Iowa, who also loved classical music, was anomalous enough. He didn't need to add gourmet cook to the list for others to tease him about.

Joanne called it that killer, Italian brownie, chocolate thing. It was more words, but she said it was a lot easier to pronounce correctly. Sharon asked Chris to bring it because Joanne bragged about it constantly, and she loved chocolate almost as much as Joanne did.

"What is in this?" Sharon made sure she scraped every single crumb on her plate. "This is incredible."

"Let's just call it a light mixture of a stick of butter, a cup of whipping cream, slightly more than a pound of chocolate, a container of Nutella, a cup of hazelnut butter, made from scratch, lots of sugar and a half dozen eggs." Chris took a breath. "The whipped cream is extra. It's very close to something my grandmother used to make."

"Low calorie, then," Joanne said with a straight face.

"Not much cholesterol either," Sharon chimed in. "I think I'm in love. Will you marry me, Chris?" Sharon shifted forward on the sofa; she hadn't meant to go that far in her teasing.

"You bet." His wry smile let her know that he was both teasing and serious at the same time. "Does that make it a binding contract, counselor?" He glanced at Terry.

"I'll need to see a retainer before I answer that," Terry said, smiling. "The bigger it is, the better you'll like my answer."

Everyone laughed, and Sharon sucked in a deep breath, knowing she was off the hook, at least for the moment.

It wasn't as if the idea hadn't crossed her mind on several occasions, it was just that she hadn't planned to say it quite so flippantly, and she certainly hadn't wanted to put Chris on the spot like she did.

On the other hand, as she looked at him gazing back at her, Sharon thought maybe she hadn't put him on such a big spot after all. Was it possible that he might not be joking?

~*~

Sharon spent the night at Joanne's again Monday.

"I might as well rent a room here," she said as the two of them sat and chattered about Joanne's upcoming wedding and almost everything else, with one obvious exception. Even though Chris was constantly in her thoughts, Sharon didn't say much about him.

"It's okay with me," Joanne responded. "I love having you here. You're the sister I always wanted."

"Same here," Sharon replied. "Terry's a great brother, but he's still a guy. Sometimes you want to just talk to another woman. You know what I mean?"

"Sure, although Terry and I can talk about pretty much anything. How about you and Chris?"

"We're working on it." Sharon didn't elaborate and was glad when Joanne didn't pursue her question and the lack of a response.

~*~

The next morning Sharon put on an abbreviated version of her trucker babe outfit, which eliminated the flannel shirt and vest and replaced them with a pink Tommy Hilfiger stretch top. Substantially backless, it tied around her neck. She told herself that the flannel shirt and vest would be too heavy for the warmer temperatures expected for today.

"Good look for you." Joanne held her chin in her right hand and gave Sharon the once over. "If you've got it, you might as well feature it, and honey, you've definitely got it."

"What? You think I dressed this way to show off?" Sharon tried to keep the grin on her face from being too wide. "It's going to be warm today."

"Especially for Chris," Joanne fanned herself. "Whew!"

She turned her head down coyly. "Why, Joanne!"

"Hey, this is your adopted sister, remember? I'm not criticizing. I'm just saying. I don't blame you. You are in marketing, aren't you? You're obviously very good at your job."

Sharon just grinned but didn't comment as she put her right foot on a kitchen chair to tie the lace on her work boot and then did the same thing with her left foot. She took her baseball cap, put it on her head and pulled her ponytail through the back of it as she had done the last time.

"Really, am I dressed okay?" Sharon asked. "I know the hat doesn't really match with this, but it's Chris' hat, so I have to wear it."

"When did you start taking fashion advice from me?" Joanne shook her head. "Of course you look all right, even with the hat. You know you look good. What's the problem?"

"I just want to do it right, you know? I…I don't want to send the wrong message…I want to look good for him, but I don't want to embarrass him. I don't want him to think I'm a tease, but I don't want him to think I'm not interested…Man, I don't know what I want!"

"I think you do, and I think you're getting there, but we can talk about that tonight," Joanne said casually. "Right now, just be satisfied that you look just about perfect for a truck ride with a hunky guy you're more than a little sweet on."

"Who said I'm sweet on him?" Sharon asked, trying not to smile.

"You didn't wear the form fitting pink tank top for an ordinary grease ball did you? And I noticed you didn't deny he was hunky." Joanne looked at Sharon again and snapped her fingers. "Wait a minute. I'll be right back."

Joanne disappeared and returned with a pair of cut off jean shorts. "I think these might work for you. Do you think you could wear them? I'm thinking trade these for the jeans, lose the boots, and wear sandals. You might as well show those great legs off too."

Sharon held the shorts up and looked at them. "You're a genius, you know that?"

Joanne winked. "Had a good teacher."

The boots and jeans were quickly replaced with the shorts and the sandals. "What do ya think?" She turned around so Jo could look at her. "A little short and tight, but…"

"Do you have anything white and lacy to go with that?" Joanne asked. "I could show you how to let it drop over your shoulder."

"That good?"

Joanne nodded. "Oh yeah. They cling just right."

A pillow from the couch came flying at Joanne, and Sharon chased her to the truck. They hopped into the truck, and Joanne peeled out of the gravel driveway. It was like being in junior high school again.

"Sharon likes Chris…Sharon likes Chris…"

When they got to Chris' house, the truck was warming up just like it was the last time. Chris leaned into the open window to say hello to Joanne, but his eyes immediately fixed on Sharon. She tried to pretend she didn't notice how he looked at her.

"Whew." He blew a long slow stream of air out of his mouth. "My babe's going to break quite a few hearts out there today. Lookin' good, babe. Lookin' real good!" He put both thumbs up into the air.

"Just make sure one of those hearts isn't yours." Joanne winked at Chris.

"Too late for that." He shook his head. "She broke mine a long time ago, the first time I saw her."

Sharon waved both her hands to get their attention. "Ah, hello, I'm sitting right here, you know. Don't we have somewhere to go?" Getting out of the truck, she looked at Joanne and wagged her finger. "Remember, mother, you don't have to come get me tonight. Chris will bring me back home by curfew."

"What's that all about?" Chris asked.

Joanne tried to smile innocently. "It means that she wants to kiss you goodnight without me watching this time."

"That's it! I'm waiting in the truck." Sharon stomped off toward the truck.

"If you miss curfew, you'll be grounded," Joanne shouted as Sharon walked away. Sharon didn't respond or look back. She just waved her hand in the air and accentuated the stomp in her stride.

"Got to go." Chris patted the side of the pickup. "This is my favorite part, helping her in and out of the cab."

Joanne just shook her head and smiled. "Kids!" She rolled up her window and pulled away.

~*~

"I hope you enjoyed that," Sharon tried to sound mad, as Chris climbed into his side of the truck and put the gearshift into the lowest gear. She tugged on the bill of her green baseball cap as the truck started to roll away from the curb.

"Actually, I kind of did." He reached over and pulled the bill of her cap up so he could look at her when he told her that. "So did you and you know it?"

Without responding, Sharon opened the thermos sitting on the seat and poured incredibly strong black coffee into one of the two mugs sitting next to the thermos. She handed it to Chris. After filling the second mug for herself, she sat back in the seat, keeping her head down to hide the smile on her face.

Chris pulled her cap up again and looked down at her. "Thanks. You mad?"

"No." She drew out the one syllable word for two complete counts. "You really think I look okay?" She knew she looked good, but she wanted to hear him say she looked good. Something about the way he looked when he complimented her just did something to her.

"Yep." He answered without any further explanation, but the look she was so shamelessly fishing for was there, and that was good enough.

That was another thing about being a trucker babe. You didn't always need a lot of words. Simple gestures and simple words like "thanks" and "yep" worked just fine. There wasn't a lot of pretense in that, but there was a lot of warmth that made her tingle.

Sharon held the steaming coffee mug in one hand and reached over to the CD player with the other, punching the button to turn it on. Beethoven this time. Still not the music she heard the other night when they had pasta.

"Did you ever hear that piece again that was playing the other night?" Sharon asked.

"Actually, I did," Chris responded.

Sharon's eyes brightened. "What was it?"

"I missed the name again, but it was written by some obscure guy with an Italian sounding name like Mario or Antonio. It was the only piece the guy ever wrote. I did get that much."

"Could his name have been Christopher?" Sharon asked, grinning. "That is your full name, isn't it?"

"My full name is actually Cristafo, so technically Chris shouldn't have the 'h' in it, but I got tired of correcting everybody, so I just agreed to spell it Chris for short. When you live in Iowa, you have to adapt. I did not write the piece, if that's what you're suggesting. Wish I would have."

"Joanne said something about you playing the violin. Just checking. Was it your mother or your father who was Sicilian?"

"My father's name was Hans Schmidt, so obviously it was my mother who was Sicilian although she wanted to be an American, so she didn't dwell on being Sicilian like my grandmother did. My grandmother was intensely proud of being Sicilian, and she told me stories all the time about Sicily. She described it so beautifully.

"My mother was attractive, but Grandma was a very beautiful woman even when she got older. That's why I teased you about being Sicilian. You two have a lot in common, including making pasta gravy."

"How many times do I have to tell you, all I did was add the red pepper?" Sharon squirmed a little.

"And you're incredibly beautiful."

"And you're definitely Sicilian, laying it on like that, but thank you."

His compliments always felt so different than other men's had and in a really great sort of way. She didn't feel like she had to protect herself as soon as they were made, only open her arms and accept them, like you would for someone you wanted to hug.

"Maybe I'm laying it on a little about the gravy." He grinned with his eyes at her. "But my grandmother always said the two most important things about authentic Sicilian gravy were quality tomatoes and just the right amount of red pepper. I could never get it right. You got it right the first time. Grandma would have loved you for that."

"It was an accident," Sharon almost whispered. "You really thought a lot of her, didn't you?"

"I loved her to death, my mother too, of course, but my grandma was truly special. Women like her only come along once in a great while. I can still see her face and hear her stories. She's been gone a long time, but she's never left here." Chris touched his heart lightly with his fist.

"I'm flattered that you compared me to her, then." Sharon could barely speak. "I don't deserve it."

"Yes, you do." Chris looked over at her softly. "Family is very important to me. You show respect for my family. That alone makes you beautiful, and I'm not laying it on at all about how beautiful I think you are. Grandma would put a curse on me from heaven if you didn't deserve it. Sicilians are big on curses, you know."

Even though the sincerity of the word "beautiful" was clear in his voice and his eyes, it froze her and warmed her at the same time.

"You don't really believe in curses, do you?"

"Of course not," Chris said, and then he looked up and added quickly, "Forgive me, Grandma." They both laughed at the way he did that. "But there are a lot of things in this world we just can't explain."

"Like?"

Chris hesitated. "Like love. How do you explain why people fall in love with the person that they do? How do you explain why it feels like it does, getting stronger when that person sits next to you, but never going away even when they're not there?"

"Good point." Sharon found herself wondering if that was a question or a statement, and hoping it might be a little of both.

"Religion's another one. My mother never forgot her Catholic upbringing. Catholics have a lot of mysteries. It's what they call things they can't explain. Mom went to Mass and also to services at my father's Protestant church. She enjoyed them both, so I got a mixture of both growing up. She used to tell me that it didn't really matter what the church said on the outside, it was what the people believed about the man on the cross inside that mattered."

"Sounds to me like you had a very wise mother." Sharon smiled softly. "Why did you tell me that you didn't pray that much the night we met at the truck stop?"

"Because it was true. I hadn't prayed for quite a while, besides the other guys were saying you were some kind of evangelist or something, so I was hoping you'd ask me to sit down and give me a little personal attention. Worked to. You asked me to sit down and pray with you."

Sharon touched his arm, softening her frown. "Chris, without an 'h', is that true?"

"Not really," he said through a grin that brought light to his eyes. "The truth is I was shocked when you even noticed me. I was even more shocked when you talked to me. I just walked by your table to check you out like all the other guys were doing."

"Well, you're honest, I'll give you that." Sharon turned sideways and tucked one leg under her so she could look directly at him while they talked. "Why were you so shocked I talked to you?"

"Because you are the most beautiful woman I have ever seen," he blurted before he could stop himself, "and…I'm…not…all that much, especially compared to what you're probably used to."

"You have no idea what I'm used to," Sharon said almost as much to herself as she did to Chris, "no idea."

"I guess not. I'm just a truck driver with a strange taste in music and a few other quirky interests." He nodded once.

"And I'm your trucker babe." Sharon looked at Chris as earnestly as she knew how and brushed her hand lightly over his forearm as he shifted gears. "And believe me, that's a lot better than what I'm used to. I like it…a lot!"

Taking a deep breath, he turned his head so he could look at her and keep an eye on the road at the same time. His voice had a hoarse edge. "It's something Joanne mostly made up as a joke. Guys know what it means, but it's really a Joanne creation."

"I guessed that." Sharon rubbed his forearm again, knowing she probably shouldn't, but not caring about should and shouldn't at that moment. "I went with it anyway because I like the way it sounds, the way it feels, and… I like what it means."

"Really?" Chris turned his eyes back to the road, but a grin spread across his face as he looked straight ahead.

"Really," Sharon responded.

The broad grin on his face alone made the trip worth it, even if they didn't drive another mile, but she wasn't ready to stop or turn away at this point. Even though Chris had stopped working through the gear box, he left his arm on the shifter and Sharon left her hand on his arm. She said nothing. Words just didn't seem necessary to communicate at that moment.

~*~

Chris was right; Sharon got a lot of appreciative looks when she walked in and out of truck stop coffee shops with him. And he got a lot of "you lucky dog" looks too, but the men noticed all the women, whether they were short, tall, thin, or not so thin. For that matter, the women did their share of noticing the men too.

It was just part of the deal. Returning glances was also part of the deal, so she did. Out here she wasn't a freak or a goddess, just a woman like all the rest, and she enjoyed that. Some of the men were cute, and some were not so cute…some were maybe even a little repulsive, but it didn't matter. They exchanged winks, laughed and moved on.

The trip to Chicago was even better than the first trip had been. Sharon saw part of the near north side she had never seen before, learned it's the grease from the pepperoni that makes Italian-style pizza so good, and that goodnight kisses are even better when there isn't an audience and Chris initiated them. Way better!

The only problem was that the trip to Chicago was too short, and the day went too fast. Sharon wished she could just erase the days on the calendar between now and next week's trip to Omaha. She wanted to get right back into the truck with Chris so they could talk some more and have another adventure, and another, and another. Just the two of them.

But Sharon was even more afraid now in some ways, not of the past anymore, but of the future. Becoming a trucker babe for a day confirmed that she had fallen in love with a simple trucker, and now she wanted a full time job, but she wasn't certain she was qualified for the position.

Would Chris still think she was like his grandmother when he found out who she was? Would he speak passionately about her like he had about his grandmother and ask her to be part of the family he loved so much? She wanted that, just like she wanted to see that same, soft stare as he touched his heart and talked about her. Would she? Did she really have to tell him? Couldn't she just pretend nothing ever happened?

Sharon listened to the beautiful sound of a diesel engine rumbling into the darkness along a rural gravel road in Iowa. It was almost better than Beethoven. When she opened the door to the small farmhouse, Jo was standing there smiling, ready to listen. And, she had brownies!

CHAPTER 14

"I just want to know one thing. Do you love him?" Joanne held Sharon's hand as they sat at the kitchen table, and she spoke like a best friend speaks at a time like this.

"Shamelessly, totally, completely, head over heels, I could never love anybody else, I can't breathe, love him. How's that?"

Joanne took a deep breath. "Wow! That's a pretty good list."

The excitement inside Sharon wouldn't stop. "Jo, I love the flannel shirts, the work boots, the baseball caps, and the smell of diesel everywhere you turn. It reminds me of how good I feel when he's around. Every time I see a big truck anymore, I imagine that we're sitting in the cab talking and drinking awful coffee, and we're headed somewhere new."

Her gaze drifted off to that far away place it went to a lot these days. "I still wake up sometimes at night and think I'm in that room again, and I still see hands, but then I see they're Chris' hands. They're soft, and they aren't holding me down; they're holding me gently and loving me, and I want them to do that. I never thought I would want to be held again, but now I do, as long as it's Chris holding me." Shaking her head, she sighed. "A little crazy, I know."

Joanne smiled and put her hand on Sharon's arm. "Maybe, maybe not." Her words were almost a whisper.

Sharon acknowledged the touch by putting her hand on Jo's. "I think I'm through the worst of it. I'll never forget it entirely, but God has shown me that there is somebody out there that wants to love me the right way, and I want to love him back the same way, but…"

"But?" Joanne leaned closer to Sharon frowning. "How can there be a but here?"

"I'm afraid he won't want me once he finds out. I'm afraid he'll be ashamed. He's so big on family and honor. Do I have to tell him? Can't I just hope he never finds out?" Her eyes begged Joanne to answer "yes."

"I think you know the answer to that, or you wouldn't ask the question," Joanne said. "You're right, he might never find out, but you would always know, and you would always be worried that he might find out. You have to tell him. You can't build the kind of relationship you both want unless you do."

Sharon looked down at the floor and then up at Joanne again. "Chris is so kind, so gentle, so trusting. What if I hurt him? What if I…lose him? I don't think I could stand that. It would almost be worse than the hurt from that night, and it would bring it all back again. I know I couldn't stand that."

Joanne shook her head and sighed. "I don't think you're giving him enough credit here. You said you were sure God led Chris to you that night during the blizzard. You said you love Chris totally. I think I know him well enough to know he feels the same way about you. Do you really think your past will matter?"

"I don't know." Tears started running down Sharon's cheeks. "No matter how much better I feel, no matter how much I love Chris, and no matter how much I pray, there's still a part of me that feels so ugly and repulsive. I just can't help it."

Joanne held Sharon's beauty in her arms and hugged it, willing to share its pain until the internal ugliness marring it, convulsed and died under the weight of its own vileness.

"Cry." Joanne held her tightly and closed her eyes, rocking slowly together with her. "Cry until you can't cry anymore. Get it all out this time, once and for all. I'll hold you until you're done, and then we'll pray. The rest will be up to you.

"We're a lot alike in some ways," Joanne said when Sharon finally stopped many long moments later, "but we're totally different in other ways."

"What does that riddle mean?" Sharon asked, wiping her eyes.

Joanne laughed. "It is a bit of a riddle isn't it? I mean I used to look into the mirror and see an ugly girl. That's what people always told me I was. So what I saw was a reflection of what I heard. To be honest, some days I still look a little plain to myself, but your brother challenged me one day. He told me to look inside and asked me how I could be so sure I knew Jesus was there when I couldn't even see what I looked like inside."

Sharon looked up at Joanne and smiled. "Are you sure you're talking about my brother?"

"Yes, I am. Then he confessed that one of the reasons he went to law school was to get over his fear of talking in front of large crowds. He said when I saw how beautiful I was, he would stand up in front of the church and tell everybody he accepted Jesus. He said the thought petrified him, but he would do it anyway. Then the stinker proposed to me on national television.

"He was shaking like a leaf, but he did it anyway. It sounds dumb, but it made me feel beautiful inside, and I could actually see it. I could have frozen up. That's what I do most of the time…or did. I could have said no, but I didn't. Terry kept his bargain about giving his testimony in front of the church, and that made me love him even more.

"I've been afraid all my life, but your brother took a chance on me and God did the rest. You've been afraid for several years, and for good reason, maybe even a better reason than I had, but now it's time for you to take a chance like your brother did.

"You have a gift. You are beautiful outside and inside, Sharon. Chris has seen that. Take a chance on him, and trust God to do the rest. No matter what you do, you can't do it alone." Joanne tilted her head, raising her eyebrows as she waited for a response.

"Could we pray now?" Sharon's voice was hoarse but lined with hope and fear at the same time. "Chris is probably still up, and I need to talk to him and get past this while I still have the courage to do it. Will you pray with me?"

"I said I would." They bowed their heads and held hands as Joanne prayed.

"Lord, You brought them together. We trust that You will take control and finish it because You have promised in Your word that he who began a good work in You will carry it on to completion."

"And Lord," Sharon added, "I believe You will, but please help my unbelief. Put the right words in my heart and let me say them the right way. Amen."

Joanne smiled and winked. "You know, Sharon, I used that same verse before I went out with Terry that first night. You saw where that went. Be careful what you ask God for."

"I know exactly what I'm asking for, and so does God. Don't wait up." She patted Joanne's arm lovingly. "I could be there a while."

"Are you kidding me? There's no way I could sleep. Remember, I want details, lots of details...and...I'll be praying for you."

"Thanks." Sharon walked out the door, got into her car, and drove to Chris' house.

~*~

A warm spring breeze carried Sharon to the open door of his small house. Lilacs perfumed the air, and Sharon took one last, deep breath of their fragrance as the haunting melody she had heard the first night welcomed her at the doorway and invited her inside.

Helpless to resist, she accepted the invitation and let the siren song draw her down the hallway to the back of the house where Chris sat, eyes closed, playing a violin lovingly tucked under his chin. Even if she had been tied to the mast of a ship with bee's wax stuffed into her ears so she couldn't hear the temptation of the music, she would have felt it vibrating in her heart and been willing to risk it all to draw closer.

It had been him all along, and somehow, now that she knew him, that didn't surprise her. In fact, it made her smile. His music made love to the air and seduced her shamelessly as it gently led her to the overstuffed blue chair across from him. Chris smiled softly when he saw her sit down, and he gently laid the old violin into his lap and held the bow in his right hand down to his side.

"I've been expecting you," he said even more lovingly than usual, and his words sent chills down Sharon's exposed back even as they seemed to reassure her that somehow everything would be all right now that she was there. The memories of that horrible night in the college apartment dissolved completely when he smiled at her, and she had no fear of crashing on the rocks with Chris there to protect her.

All she could do was shake her head. "Why? Did Joanne call and tell you?" How else could he have known she was coming unless the feelings that filled her had somehow shouted to him all the way from Joanne's house? Or perhaps her gaze alone betrayed those feelings in a whisper only he heard.

He smiled again and shrugged. "No, she didn't call. I just felt you stirring. I knew you would hear the song if I played it because you've always heard it, and here you are. Just you. You're the only one who has heard the melody so clearly. A mystery, I guess."

For some reason, his strange, almost disjointed words made sense to her and filled her with knowledge that she didn't understand but didn't care to. She didn't have to understand them, just believe them. "Why didn't you tell me it was you all along?"

He shrugged again, and that was so like him. The mysteriousness of the shrug mingled with his strange words and so many other things that she felt for him made him much more than the "ordinary trucker" he always claimed to be.

How could she ever let him go? She made up her mind as she looked at him that she wouldn't, whatever it took from her, because she wanted to see that shrug for the rest of her life, starting now.

"Since you were playing it for me, are you going to tell me about the song then?" She could feel the coy boldness in her words as she had neither the desire nor the ability to hold back and be afraid any more.

He nodded. "I guess I have to now, for a lot of reasons."

Sharon relaxed back into the softness of the chair and exposed her heart as she laid a hand to either side on the overstuffed arms of the chair and closed her eyes. "I want to know the reasons, and I'm tired of only one at a time; I want to know all of them…tonight."

Chris leaned forward, careful not to drop his instrument, and touched Sharon lightly on her knee. "Are you sure? I may make up some just to get you to stay."

The warmth of his hand on the bareness of her knee was almost more than she could take. She bit her lip and kept her eyes closed as she tipped her head back even farther. "I'm positive, and I may stay just so you'll make more up."

He traced slow, light circles on her knee and then pressed his warm, soft lips to the middle of the circles. "As you wish," he whispered softly, and he kissed her knee again.

Letting out a deep sigh, Sharon murmured, "I hope you have no idea what I wish right now. I shouldn't be wishing it."

Chris chuckled quietly. "And I hope I do because I'm wishing for the same thing."

He was driving her delightfully crazy, and she opened her eyes and smiled at him. "So what are the reasons?" She tucked her feet under herself and smiled as she sat forward to listen like a hopeful child waiting for her favorite bedtime story.

Chris sat back in his chair and picked up the violin and bow he had been holding. "This violin has been in my family for three hundred years. It's one of less than 600 like it left in the world. My Grandpa taught himself how to play it and won Grandma's heart because of it. So he decided to write her a special song, from here." He tapped the middle of his chest. "He had no formal training, but he had so much love for her."

Sharon raised her head. "Ah, so that's where you get all your talent."

"Or passion," he countered with a half smile that made her cringe.

"Or both." She smiled flirtatiously, meaning every bit of it. "You are one of the most eclectic people I have ever met, and to use the vernacular, that kind of turns me on."

Chris grinned and shook his head, looking down at the floor. "Somehow eclectic, turned on and vernacular don't seem like they belong in the same sentence, but it works for you, just like wearing that incredible top, cut off jeans and a green baseball cap with a feed logo on it."

The warmth of her body told her she was blushing readily, but she liked the way it felt on her. It made her feel alive again, and it made her bold. "I was trying to make a fashion statement, now quit stalling and tell me about the song."

He nodded again. "My grandfather played the song over and over for Grandma trying to find the perfect ending for it, but he just couldn't find one. My grandmother said she didn't care because if the song had no ending then their love for each other would never end, and she loved listening to the song just the way it was."

He smiled almost to himself, but when he looked at her, she felt as if the heat building behind the smile also included her. "Grandma said she would sit by his side and cry as he played because every time he played the song, it became more and more beautiful.

"Then one night as Grandpa played for her, an intruder broke into their house to rob them. They had nothing for him to steal except for the violin, and he didn't want that, so he said he'd take Grandma instead because she was so beautiful."

Chris stopped and took a deep breath. Sharon leaned over to him and touched his arm, and he nodded to her as if he appreciated the gesture. He looked up at the ceiling and took another deep breath, then another and wiped the tear running down his cheek with the back of his hand before lowering his water filled gaze back to hers.

Finally, he started again in a shaky voice that Sharon had never heard from him before. "The intruder had a knife, and he stabbed my grandfather repeatedly as he protected the woman he loved. Even though Grandpa killed the intruder with his bare hands, he... ah....died... in Grandma's arms."

Chris reached up to wipe a tear from his cheek again and took several more deep breaths in and out.

"Grandma said she begged God not to take Grandpa. She squeezed her hands together praying so hard, they hurt. She begged God..."

With tears running down her own face, Sharon got up and went over to Chris, putting her hand gently on his trembling lips. "I'm sorry, Chris, you don't have to tell me this. Just stop, okay? Stop. I didn't mean to be so selfish. I...can't stand to see you like this." Sharon leaned over and kissed the top of his head and then stroked his hair lovingly.

For a few seconds Chris sobbed, almost uncontrollably, but then he looked up at Sharon and smiled through his tears. "I have to tell you the rest. It's meant to be because I've found the ending for the song, and...it's a happy one."

Nodding, Sharon kissed him on the forehead. "Okay. I'd like to hear it then." She caressed his face with her hand and then went back to the overstuffed chair and sat down again slowly, waiting for Chris to continue.

Swallowing the knot in his throat, he smiled at her, took a deep breath, and closed his eyes. "With his final breath, Grandpa looked up at Grandma, took her hand and told her to remember how much he loved her every time she heard the song he had written... and he begged her to find someone… to play the song… for her."

His gaze reached into Sharon's heart as he looked at her, and suddenly she knew what he was saying.

"You?"

He turned his eyes to the floor and nodded. "Me."

"Oh, Chris. Now I know why you loved your grandmother so much. That is so sad, but so beautiful."

He looked back up at her with moistness still glistening in his eyes. "I played that song for her almost every day, and she always cried. I played it at her funeral, and I cried. I loved that woman so much, and I love that song. I never played it for anyone but her, and I never knew for sure why it made both of us cry…until…"

He looked deeply into her eyes, and she felt chills on her back again. She tried to control the swirling feelings inside her, but his eyes wouldn't let her and she realized she didn't want to control those feelings anymore; she wanted to surrender completely to them.

She let her arms drop to her sides as her heart beat wildly beneath the low cut top, and she hoped Chris could see every single pulsation. Closing her eyes, she leaned her head back and took a deep breath. "Until what?"

Chris reached over to her and touched her cheek softly with the hand holding the violin bow, and she opened her eyes to see his smile. "Until I found someone I loved even more than Grandma, someone who knew how much red pepper to put in the pasta gravy, someone who is so full of life, so beautiful…someone…I would die for, just like Grandpa died for her. I would die for you, Sharon, and I feel all of the song now, even an ending. Grandma told me to pass this song along to the woman I loved with all my heart."

Sharon couldn't breathe all of a sudden, and she couldn't move. She could only sit, feel his touch, and stare at the most incredible person she had ever met.

"Grandma told me not to worry about writing the ending because love like they had goes on forever. She said…love should be the ending because it's the beginning too." He sucked in a deep sigh never taking his eyes from hers. "I never really understood that until you came along, and now I not only understand it, I feel it, here, in my heart."

He took his hand from her cheek and touched his chest lightly as another tear rolled down his face. "And I know the feeling I feel is so much more than just being in love; the love is in me. It hurts… and I want it to because you're part of it…and you're in here. You are the love." He pressed her hand to his chest. "It's where you belong. Sharon. In here, and I want you to be the ending and a new beginning for me."

Sharon couldn't take her hand from his chest. "Chris…don't." Her heart had more than enough tears to fill her eyes again…and again… and again, and she had to tell him, even though all she really wanted was to touch him like this and have him touch her, hold her and let her hold him so their hearts could beat together.

He didn't listen and shook his head. "I have to. The way I feel about you won't let me stop, and it helps me understand why Grandpa was willing to die for my grandmother…and why I ache the way I do whenever I even think about you, and why I ache even more when you're here with me."

The sobs coming from Sharon's heart made it even harder for her to breathe than before. She reached out to him with her free hand and begged, "Chris stop…please…I'm not what you think…I'm not. That's why I came here, because I…wish…I ...was…"

Chris laid the violin bow across his lap and reached his hand to touch hers. "I love you, Sharon…with all my heart. Don't you get it? I know about the football player in college. Another trucker told me the story the day after I met you in the truck stop. I know it must be a nightmare you can't get out of your mind…and, I'm so sorry. I would gladly take that pain for you if I could, but I can't. All I can do is offer to love you so much, so hard, and so completely that the pain dissolves and goes away."

Sharon sobbed uncontrollably, but Chris grabbed her outstretched hand and held it to his chest with her other one.

"It's never mattered to me. You're all that matters. And you can't let some creep who should be rotting in jail tell you who or what you are.

"God doesn't think there's anything wrong with you and neither do I." He let go of her hands, picked up the violin bow, and put the violin under his chin. "Let me show you what we think you are. You are the woman Grandma told me to play this for, and now I will. You and Grandma are the only women I have ever played this for."

"CHRIS…"

Before she could say anything more, he laid the bow decisively on the violin and stroked it firmly. Every note was clear, every note was pure, and every note was more beautiful than the one before it. She watched as his magnificent hands moved precisely over the strings with his left hand moving up and down setting the fingerings and his right hand rocking the bow smoothly back and forth over the rosin-covered strings.

She couldn't help herself. Unconsciously she went to his side and stood there like his grandmother had done watching him play. Just as his grandma had, she cried for the song. The more she cried, the more passionately Chris played as the notes resonated deeper and deeper into her soul until she couldn't take any more and held her heart with both hands to keep it from exploding. Finally he finished… exhausted… having played until he couldn't play anymore, and he lowered the violin to his lap.

But there was more. He turned to her and said, "That's how you sound on a Stradivarius, and that's what I see and hear when I look at you." He stood up beside her and brushed the side of her face with his lips, kissing her tenderly on the cheek and then again on the tip of her nose. "And that's why I gave this old piece of music Grandpa wrote a name, and when I named it, I realized it was what Grandpa was always looking for."

He handed her the yellowed, dog-eared piece of music with light and dark stains on it.

At the top of the sheet of music were the words, *Sharon's Song*.

When she read the words, her knees buckled and she dropped to the floor clutching the music in her hand. "Oh my," she said as she put her hand over her mouth. Tears from her eyes splattered on the old piece of music joining the stains of three generations.

Chris sat down next to her, put his hand softly on her cheek, and turned her face gently to his. "Are you okay?" He brushed his lips over her forehead and then kissed it.

"I'm not sure," she heard herself say. "It's just that my brother once called me a Stradivarius when he prayed for me, and he asked God to send me someone who could play a Stradivarius." Sharon closed her eyes and sighed deeply. "I…I told him I wasn't a Stradivarius." She opened her eyes again, and Chris was barely inches from her.

Laying his instrument to the side, he put his hands on either side of her neck. "You were wrong, Sharon." He kissed her on the forehead and ran his hand lightly down the side of her neck sending more chills through her body. "I just played you on a Stradivarius just like your brother asked." Chris moved his hand slowly to her shoulder and rubbed it lightly.

Sharon sucked in her words as she tried to breathe. "I know." She kissed his hand as he held it on her shoulder. "And just for emphasis, you put my name on a love song written one hundred years ago for a woman you keep comparing me to, a woman you love with all your heart." She kissed his hand again and took a deep breath. "It's a bit overwhelming!"

Chris held her chin so he could look at her and smiled all the way to her lips, and she smiled back the same way. "So, what do you think that means? I'm Sicilian." He kissed her chin and then her cheek. "Things like that always mean something to a Sicilian." He kissed her cheek again and then the side of her neck. "Tell me what it means; I have to know."

She turned her head exposing more of her neck, enjoying how she shivered under his lips as they kissed her. Then she put her arms around his neck. "It means I want to be your trucker babe, Chris with an h; it means that I love you forever, and I'm not afraid anymore."

He traced the side of her arm with his fingertips. "Does it also mean you will marry me?" He rose to his knees. "Sharon, I want you forever too; will you marry me?"

She took another deep breath. "You aren't going to cut an emotionally exhausted girl a break, are you?"

He shook his head and traced his fingers up and down her arm again. "The way I see it, you love me, and I love you. Grandma will certainly put a curse on us if we don't get married and make a family."

Sharon rose to her knees and put her forehead on his, and then looked deeply into his eyes as he ran his soft hands over her bare shoulders. "Of course, I'll marry you, Chris with an h." She grinned as broadly as she ever had. "We wouldn't dare disappoint Grandma."

FINALE

The dark stains on the old piece of music were from the blood of a man who gave his life to protect the woman he loved. The lighter stains were from her tears and the tears of the generations who have been loved as she was loved. The hand written notes have never changed, but *Sharon's Song* has been added at the top of the old yellow, dog-eared sheets of music because a half Sicilian Iowa truck driver loved a woman no matter what she had done in the past, and she loved him back. The title, the notes on the pages below it, and the love of generations, are like the music. They will never end, even though after a hundred years they finally have an ending.

ENCORE

Ten months later, a few days after they were married, Chris and Sharon looked out over the beach below Taormina, Sicily, to the blazing blue of the Mediterranean Sea below them and held each other, savoring a land that was just as his grandmother had described it. And more.

Sharon breathed in the sweet Sicilian air smiling at the irony that the warmth of today began in the cold of last year's blizzard with a simple prayer in an Iowa truck stop. She prayed for her brother as he lay freezing to death in the blizzard, and God called an insignificant, insecure, small redheaded girl with nothing but a coil of rope and a snowmobile, to risk her life to save Terry's. She didn't hesitate; she went, and Terry lived, fell in love with her and married her.

But the love they caught that night in the cold infected not only Joanne and Terry, but also Sharon, Chris, Dave, Jennifer, Sandy, the small church in Iowa, truckers, their wives, their children and countless others. And Sharon was certain that Terry was right when he said, "You ain't seen nothin' yet."

Chris brought his violin and his music with him on their honeymoon and played for the Sicilian people whenever he could. That night he sat in front of a small hotel on the outside of town and played as a curious crowd gathered. Sharon sat beside him and wept as she always did when he played.

A strikingly beautiful older woman came up to Sharon with a younger woman at her side and put her hand on Sharon's face, wiped her tears with her soft, gentle hands, and said something in the local dialect. Then she put her hand over her own heart as she pointed at the yellow piece of music Chris was playing and said something else. Finally, she put her hand on Sharon's stomach and patted it as she smiled and said a few more words Sharon couldn't understand.

The look on the woman's face warmed Sharon even more than the Mediterranean sun had in the afternoon, and the older woman tilted her head as if she expected Sharon to reply, but Sharon didn't understand what the old woman had said.

The younger woman noticed the perplexed look on Sharon's face, so she stepped forward. "Mother and I both speak English," she said proudly.

"Thank you." Sharon nodded and turned to the older woman. "I feel like I should know you, but I can't place you, and I didn't understand you. Could you please tell me what you said in English?"

"Gladly," the older woman said. "I said you are a very beautiful woman and that your nice young husband was meant to find you even though you probably think you found him. I also said his music and your tears touch my heart and that your first child will come soon and will be the first of many beautiful children for you."

"That's very sweet of you. Thank you." Sharon stopped and took a breath. "Soon? How soon?"

"Who knows exactly about these things?" The older woman shrugged and held up her hands. "But he will be conceived here in Sicily, so he will have to return to see us and become part of us as you have."

"Really?" Sharon said as she blew some air through her lips in a wistful sigh. "That means I might beat Joanne."

"Is Joanne your friend back in America?" the old woman asked.

"Yes, she is. She's married to my brother," Sharon looked at the older woman curiously. "How did you know that?"

"A mystery." The old woman smiled. "Your babies will play together and grow up to be best friends too."

"Did you say babies? How…how…many babies?" Sharon felt her stomach nervously with both hands.

"Again, who knows for sure?" The old woman shrugged as she had before. "But I feel there will be many, and they will all be beautiful like their mother."

Sharon leaned to the old woman and kissed her on the forehead. "Thank you; you are very beautiful yourself. I want a large family because family is very important to my husband…just not so soon."

"Why put off the blessings my beautiful one? You have made my daughter and me very happy, and your children will do the same thing for you. You'll see." The old woman hugged Sharon like a close relative would hug someone and turned to walk away. Then she turned back and winked. "We know each other better than you think. Don't forget to add enough red pepper to the pasta gravy."

"I won't." Chills ran up Sharon's spine. She tugged on Chris' arm as he finished playing. "Do you see that old woman with the younger one?"

Chris studied them as they turned and waved.

"Do you know her?"

Chris squinted as he stared at the two women in the distance and shook his head. "It couldn't be…it's not possible…"

"What's not possible?" Sharon stepped in front of Chris to look him in the eyes. "What?"

Chris tipped his head to the side so he could look at the women again as he put his hand over his eyes to shield the sun. "I'm sure it's just the light, but…that older woman looks an awfully lot like my grandmother's pictures when she was younger, and, the younger one is a ringer for my mother when she was that age."

Sharon moved in front of Chris again. "They called each other mother and daughter; does that mean anything?"

"Oh?" Chris got a faraway look in his eyes.

"And the older one said I would conceive a son here. She also said we would have lots of beautiful children." Sharon rubbed her hands together nervously, touching her stomach again. "And that our children would be best friends with Joanne's children, and I never mentioned anything about Joanne."

"Really?" A nervous grin spread across Chris' face, and he put his arms around Sharon's waist pulling her closer to him.

"Yes, really. She also said we knew each other better than I thought, and to make sure I didn't forget to add the right amount of red pepper to the pasta gravy. Then…she hugged me. Didn't you say your grandmother would hug me if she tasted my pasta gravy? Don't you think that's all…a little…strange?"

"Did she hug you like this?" Chris pulled Sharon even closer to himself and kissed her lightly on her lips…a strange kiss…tingly, romantic, sensual, but almost ageless… in a way Sharon had never felt before but was powerless to resist.

Even though the violin lay on the chair next to the bow behind Chris, she could hear it playing and feel the music almost caressing her lips with each note of *Sharon's Song* through the touch of her husband's lips to hers. "Kiss me like that again," she whispered.

Chris obliged with even more fervor, and the music grew louder as her lips tingled even more.

"And again," she said, rubbing the back of his head and pressing her body as close to him as she could. "And again."

His kisses went beyond tingling and consumed her, surrounding her with a symphony of sounds, feelings and emotions all playing *Sharon's Song*, all taking her back to yesterday and into tomorrow through the place they stood now as they held each other. If Chris hadn't been there, she would have dropped to the Sicilian dust helplessly, but he held her firmly.

Chris picked up his violin and bow with one hand and handed them to the hotel owner who watched them with tears in his eyes and nodded, taking the instrument inside. Then Chris picked up Sharon who still clung to him with her arms around his neck, and he kissed her again.

"I think we better not disappoint an old Sicilian woman and her daughter, especially if they're..."

"That's what I was thinking," Sharon brushed his cheek lightly with her hand. "Kiss me like that forever starting right now. This moment is one of those mysteries you were telling me about, and I want it forever."

"I'll do my best, love," Chris whispered as he carried her to their room in the hotel, "but remember, I'm only half Sicilian."

~*~

A tear rolled down the old woman's cheek, and she smiled and put her hand on her heart as she and her daughter watched from the distance. The sun set over Taormina, throwing off oranges, reds and yellows like streamers from a departing ocean liner leaving port. She looked down at her daughter, who nodded and smiled at her mother.

"Don't cry, Mama. They're beautiful, just like I knew they'd be."

About the Author

"Getting older but feeling younger by the minute." That's how Dennis Bates describes himself since he retired from his job as a government attorney. And this father of two daughters and husband of 39 years, credits following his dream to write with a good part of that. *Sharon's Song* is his second publication following *Under the Burr Oak Tree* which was released earlier this year by Spirit Light Publishing.

All of Dennis's stories involve three things: a Christian world view, although admittedly from the edges sometimes, where he feels real people live; one or more love stories at least partially from a male perspective, and some tie to his home state of Iowa, where he and his wife live.

With an undergraduate degree in journalism from the University of Iowa, Dennis frequently uses Iowa City as a setting and a source of inspiration and almost always has something to say about the small Iowa towns that he both loves and can't resist poking fun at on a regular basis. "Iowans are special people to me," he says, "but we have our quirks, and I'm thankful for all of them because they give me an endless supply of things to write about."

His ***Second Calling Author*** website can be found at dennisbates.com, which features a page about his latest books and a link to the blog at www.spirtlightbooks, where he writes about whatever happens to come into his mind every Tuesday and Wednesday. He invites you to visit his website and the blog site often.

Also Available from Spirit Light Books

Déjà Vu Bride

Furious with God, Olivia Roseman vows to never trust Him again. Why should she? Once again her prayers have gone unanswered, and once again another loved one has been ripped from her. With no job and only a few dollars, Olivia makes a choice to start over again. Without God and without love. However, her handsome new boss isn't going to make forgetting God or keeping her vow to never love again very easy.

Reunion

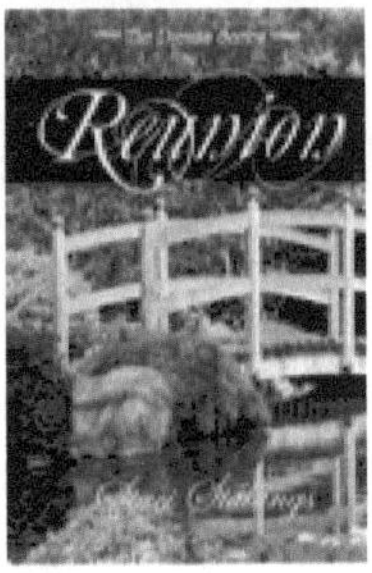

The sequel to "Dreams by Starlight"

Camille Wright and Jaylon Quinn met in high school and fell in love, but their dreams under the stars took them in two different directions. Now an aerospace engineer, Camille is successful in her career but struggling in life. Jaylon's life took him where he never expected to be, and now he's building a life that looks perfect—from the outside. Both remember the love they shared but understand that love once lost hardly ever comes back around…

Under The Burr Oak Tree

Just when Lindsey Miller has overcome the shattered dreams of her past, the man who shattered those dreams shows up again. Just when Lindsey's sister has erased the sordid life she used to lead, a young man with high ideals asks her to become part of his life. Forgetting and moving on requires all of them to learn how to forgive family, friends, each other, and themselves before they can be happy. Forgiveness must be offered and accepted, but once it is, it consumes everything in its path and lets new life begin again.

Dreams By Starlight

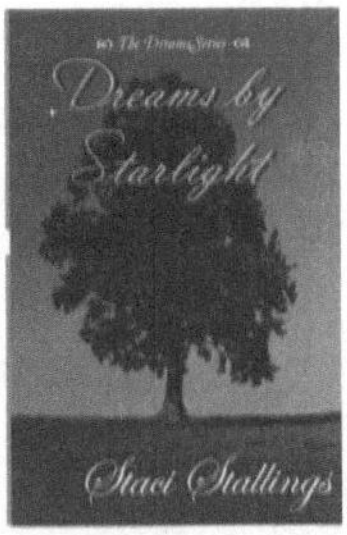

If all the world's a stage and each of us plays a part, then Camille Wright is the high school wallflower nobody remembers and only the bullies ever knew was there. But sometimes where you want to be isn't where you are destined to be at all…

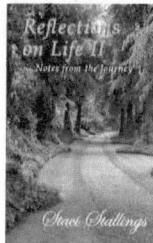

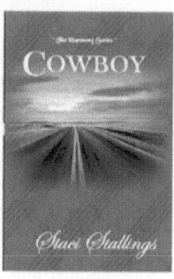

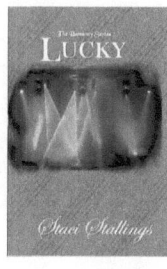

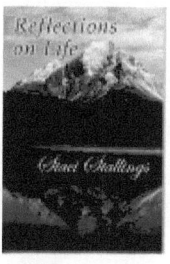

www.ingramcontent.com/pod-product-compliance
Lightning Source LLC
Chambersburg PA
CBHW020948180626
46814CB00003B/990
* 9 7 8 0 6 1 5 2 6 0 7 5 4 *